defying DEATH

in HAGERSTOWN

defying DEATH in HAGERSTOWN

JOHN PAUL CARINCI

New York

defying DEATH *in* HAGERSTOWN

Published in New York, New York, by Morgan James Publishing. Morgan James and The Entrepreneurial Publisher are trademarks of Morgan James, LLC. www.MorganJamesPublishing.com

The Morgan James Speakers Group can bring authors to your live event. For more information or to book an event visit The Morgan James Speakers Group at www.TheMorganJamesSpeakersGroup.com.

A **free** eBook edition is available with the purchase of this print book.

CLEARLY PRINT YOUR NAME ABOVE IN UPPER CASE

Instructions to claim your free eBook edition:
1. Download the BitLit app for Android or iOS
2. Write your name in **UPPER CASE** on the line
3. Use the BitLit app to submit a photo
4. Download your eBook to any device

ISBN 978-1-63047-351-8 paperback
ISBN 978-1-63047-352-5 eBook
ISBN 978-1-63047-353-2 hardcover
Library of Congress Control Number:
2014944783

Cover Design by:
Rachel Lopez
www.r2cdesign.com

Interior Design by:
Bonnie Bushman
bonnie@caboodlegraphics.com

In an effort to support local communities, raise awareness and funds, Morgan James Publishing donates a percentage of all book sales for the life of each book to Habitat for Humanity Peninsula and Greater Williamsburg.

Get involved today, visit
www.MorganJamesBuilds.com

Habitat for Humanity
Peninsula and
Greater Williamsburg
Building Partner

DEDICATION

To all the great storytellers of the past, who have
inspired us to dream big, fantasize much, press on,
and share our stories with the world.

To my wife, Vera, my ongoing inspiration.

And to my mother, who first instilled the
confidence in me that I can be great.

CHAPTER ONE

I t was pouring outside, harder than I could remember it doing for some time. I was drenched to the bone. My hair looked like a slick, matted crop, and I had just gotten into a car accident.

"Just another lousy day in paradise," I mumbled as I made my way through the huge glass doors of Number One, Terminal Place, headquarters of the *Washington Gazette* newspaper. I walked gingerly through the atrium and past the guards, Carlos and Russell, acknowledging their cheery "good mornings" as I headed for the elevator.

I was feeling very conspicuous as I passed the morning crowd of my co-workers on my way to the sixth floor reporters' desk.

The woman who had rear-ended me had no control over stopping her large Lincoln Navigator on the slick, cool roadway. The slamming of her huge SUV startled me as I sat waiting at a red light. I had seen her SUV coming in the rearview mirror, approaching too rapidly. Then the bang from the rear, and the jolt that caused my shoulder to slam against the rigid seat belt, and suddenly I was wearing half a cup of hot coffee on my lap.

The coffee made me jump. "Son of a bitch!" I screamed, now fully awake on that Monday morning, a morning I was already running late for, a morning I really didn't want to get out of bed—a dark, gloomy morning I was convinced was my worst in many months.

As I surveyed the damage along with the very shaken young woman who had been driving the SUV, I noted that my 2010 Chevy Malibu had a badly scratched, cracked bumper, while her vehicle had virtually no damage. She was clearly shaken up, while I felt pain setting in. Ten minutes later, after we had exchanged information, I continued on my way to work. I had told her I would call the insurance company from work because I was already a half hour late.

Now as I made my way from the sixth-floor elevator, I could feel my underpants sticking to me, just as Russell's greeting of "Have a good one!" resonated in my head. I sat down softly in the chair at my desk and tried to comb my matted hair into something remotely presentable. It didn't help. So I sat staring at my desk clock showing 9:42 and my gold nameplate, which reads "Louis Gerhani, Junior, Reporter," distinguishing my personal workspace. Just as I was calming my nerves, a flunky named Jamie Lynch, a redheaded, freckle-faced kid, rushed by screaming, "The boss wants to see you pronto! Holy crap! What happened to you? Fall into a puddle?" He laughed as he rushed away.

I felt like I looked—like crap. I was in no mood to talk to anyone, much less my boss, the editor of the *Washington Gazette,* Mr. Harold Glavin. My boss is a real hard-ass. He thinks he is a king and the employees are peasants in his kingdom. He has been all over me for the past few months. I knew I had been off my game, just going through the motions, but he won't cut me any slack. My heart just isn't into reporting as of late. Sure, I was still doing my job, writing insightful stories for the paper, but it is never good enough for Glavin, never "cutting-edge," as he calls it.

There are times when a writer produces copy to the best of his ability but without a lot of heart. There is no way to feel passionate about every story you write, every day, all the time. I know my writing has been off, and I know why, but an astute editor is like an art connoisseur who can spot a counterfeit painting that from twenty yards away.

Harold Glavin is just such a connoisseur of reporting and writing. I've seen him kick back a story upwards of ten times to a junior reporter. It is a frustrating job, this reporting. There are many months when you just know you are writing in the zone, when the words flow as quickly and precisely as a waterfall, when you are right on and there is little editing needed. There've been times when my pen has had a life of its own, flowing easily. I can't remember the last time I felt like that and what story inspired me so powerfully.

I used to love to write short stories. There was a time awhile back when I planned to publish a book of my best short stories. That, now, was a distant memory; I hadn't written a decent short story in many months, and none at all in the past three months.

My shoulder ached as I stared at my phone as if it were going to speak to me and make me feel better. I felt so alone as of late, but at that moment, I felt as if I were on an abandoned island. I waited a few more minutes, hoping for my hair and clothing to dry a bit before I visited the King and Master of Himself, Harold Glavin. I combed my hair again. It was still a soaking mop of glop. I wondered what Harold Glavin would yell about today. I knew he was pissed about something. Maybe it was the story about the use of cell phones while driving. That story was due to print on Sunday of next week, but I had turned it in last Friday— early. I was sure he would can the story and make me rewrite it.

I thought about what my life had become and how I had arrived at such a mental state. "Crap!" I said to my trusty black phone. "My life is real crap lately!" The phone was at least pleasant. It never tried to convince me that I was wrong. I thought about my father, Lawrence.

It had hit me hard that morning while I was exchanging personal information with the woman who rear-ended me: Today was the tenth anniversary of my father's passing. As I wrote the date of the accident, 6-10-2013, I felt a sudden skip of my heart. I suddenly realized that exactly ten years ago my father was killed in a tragic accident. It was the worst day of my life, and nothing else has ever come close. That day, I had thought that I would not make it through. To lose a parent is a traumatic experience for anyone, but to lose a parent suddenly due to an accident is so heart wrenching that you almost don't want to take another breath as you wonder, *Why did this happen? What's the use?*

How ironic it was that ten years later to the day, I, too, should have an accident. Does it really matter whose fault causes an accident? I realized that I, too, could have been killed. I thought of all the what-if scenarios that could have happened: What if the huge SUV had hit me on the driver's side while running a red light? What if someone had run me down on the sidewalk while I was walking the last block to work that morning? It made me miss my father that much more—all the inner pain attacking the brain cells that never let us forget, the cells that vividly recall sights, smells, tastes, and heartaches in an instant with only one slight thought.

All the memories of that day flooded my brain. *If my brain were a computer, it would surely crash,* I thought.

All the details I had tried to forget for a decade were suddenly crystal-clear, as if they had just happened yesterday.

It had happened on a Thursday afternoon. The weather was much the same as this morning—cool and rainy, making the road surface slick. My father was returning from an errand, traveling home on the highway. He had hit a huge pothole that I later learned had destroyed the tires and rims of numerous previous victims' cars. And like them, he ended up stuck on the side of the road in the pouring rain, fixing a flat. It was sometime after he had jacked the car up and was changing the front driver's-side tire that a commercial van, trying to avoid the huge pothole, swerved out of control and into my father and his car. My father was pinned against his Buick 88. By the time the ambulance arrived, he was unconscious and bleeding heavily. We were notified by the hospital at around 2:30 that afternoon.

Dad was in the intensive care unit, and the doctors didn't hold out much hope for him because he had lost so much blood and had slipped into a coma. Over the next twenty-four hours, we prayed and kept vigil by his side. There was a four-hour period during which his condition improved. Then, as if he was stabbed in the back by a ruthless villain just when he was almost free and clear, his condition turned suddenly dire again.

As we gathered around his bedside, my mother, my sister Alice, and my sister's best friend, Karen, we witnessed my father's gradual demise as his organs slowly and brutally shut down. The torture was excruciating to our hearts and brains. We were helpless as we watched this once-powerful man slip away far too early.

Life is not fair. We are never promised that it will be fair. When we least expect it, something tragic happens, just to remind us that we are like ants in the great wilderness of the world, and anything can easily destroy us.

By just before midnight, it became clear that only the machines were forcing my father's body to react with false signs of life. As hospital staff turned off the machines, we watched him leave us forever.

Ten years later, sitting at my desk, still wet, I remembered how I regretted never having taken my father to a baseball game; how I didn't pay enough attention to the man I had most admired for years before he died; how I never got to tell him how much I respected and loved him.

Just memories left. Just regrets of "what if?" Just pain that comes rushing back, reminding me of the regrets I must live with forever.

I smelled like a damp basement as I waited, to no avail, hoping to dry off before having to show up for my command performance. I wondered if I smelled more to myself than to others, as hot air rises and the smell of my wet pants and shirt rose naturally to my nose. My eyes felt very heavy as I fought the urge to nod off for a few minutes. I knew I could fall asleep on the spot, sitting there in my chair, and sleep easily for an hour. I was exhausted from thinking and from the adrenalin rush of the morning accident.

The need to close my eyes was so strong that I gave in to the urge, knowing I wouldn't be able to stay awake if I tried. I knew that I would feel refreshed after perhaps ten minutes of quiet time. Boy, was I wrong!

I was startled by a loud voice and a hand on my arm.

"Lou! Lou! Hey, Lou Gerhani, wake up!" I felt myself jump as if I'd been stuck with a needle. After a second, I realized that my great theory about a short rest had been wrong. My eyes focused on the redheaded Lynch kid. What a sight!

"Lou! The boss sent me back. He's been waiting for you for almost an hour. He's pissed! Are you all right?"

I looked at my watch; it showed 10:35. I had been in a dead sleep for almost forty minutes.

"Holy crap!" I snapped. "I just, I just . . . ."

"You just better get your ass into Mr. Glavin's office. I think you're finally gonna get fired this time," Jamie said, and he shook his head from side to side as he slowly walked away.

"Listen, Red," I screamed, "I've been thrown out of better places than this dive!" The Lynch kid turned and just shook his head; he knew I was dead meat.

I knew I was in big trouble, too, but something inside kept telling me, "Screw it!" There are always two personalities, I feel, occupying our minds—the good-guy angel personality and the devil personality. I knew the devil personality must have drugged my inner angel awhile back, because I hadn't felt the angel's presence for quite some time.

I think Harold Glavin was clearly burnt out. After nearly fifty years of newspaper madness, of deadlines and declining sales, he clearly hated the job but couldn't walk away from his mega-bucks paycheck and bonuses. So he took his grief out on poor writer slobs like me. Sure, he was nice to the premium senior writers who hogged the hot page one stories. But he had been riding me for many months now. I couldn't remember the last juicy story I had written. The crap assignments I had received didn't belong on the obituary page. But what the heck, it was a paycheck. I wondered how much unemployment was paying these days, and how long I could collect it. I had never collected unemployment before, and I knew nothing about applying. Facing the boss, now, freaked me out.

As I stood up on slightly wobbly legs, I took in one big sniff. "This'll have to do."

CHAPTER TWO

It was eleven o'clock when I knocked on Glavin's office door. His office was like his own kingdom: elaborate, show-offy, and full of over-the-top memorabilia. Every time I sat in one of the guest chairs in front of his desk, I felt so out of place. And I suspect that is exactly what the boss wanted. He wanted everyone to know that they were inferior to his level of education, finances, and knowledge about the newspaper industry. After all, he was the king of his empire.

"Yes! Enter!" he screamed in his booming voice that reminded me of a foghorn warning of oncoming danger.

"Glavin, you wanted to see me?" I asked with a smile.

"I told you before to address me as *Mr.* Glavin. And what the hell happened to you?"

"I had a nasty car accident this morning on my way to work."

"No wonder! I'm not surprised. You probably were half loaded."

"Boss, no, I didn't even really get hurt, but thanks for asking. I'm just real sore."

"The only thing that could help you at this point is a good hard bump to the head! You look like crap! And I have a few choice questions to ask you other than 'Did you scratch a knee or a forehead in a minor crap car . . . .'"

"It was more than minor."

"Listen, butthead. That fits well because your hair and you look like crap. So listen here, what the hell do you think this place is?" His ears were as red as tomatoes.

"This is my place of employment, sir."

"Gerhani, don't you get snide with me. I'll fire your ass right now on the spot. I'm this close to boiling over with you. We don't need wise-asses at this newspaper."

He took a brief pause for breath before launching into his rant. "Do you know anything about this newspaper, son? Do you know the great history of printing newsprint, set by hands of men sweating over hot ink and presses since day one of 1898? You have no clue. The forefathers broke their asses so you little turds can work in luxury today, sitting behind fancy desks and computers, enjoying heat in the winter and air conditioning in the summer . . ."

I heard his voice and saw his mouth moving but I didn't understand any more of what he was saying. I felt myself fixating in a zombie-like trance on his tomato-red ears before almost passing out. I fought the urge, but the dizziness persisted. I hadn't eaten anything that day; then the car accident, the bump to my head, being abruptly awakened from my nap—it would all lead to passing out if I let my guard down slightly. I tried to tell him, but to no avail. He kept clamoring for ten more minutes. I did respond to his last command quite readily.

"Get the hell out of here! Now! Get out! And don't come back until you complete that assignment. This is your last shot. If it's not perfect, I'll fire your worthless ass. Now get the hell out!" he shouted, loud enough to wake the dead.

My mind said "Go" but my body stood frozen in a weakened, dizzy state, which was quickly helped with some added encouragement. "Are you deaf? You're fired! I'll fire your ass right now! Get out! Are you stoned, or still drunk from this morning? Now get the hell out of my office. Now!"

My legs were wobbly but finally managed to carry me through the walnut doorframe of Mr. Glavin's office.

As soon as I exited, I held onto the wall for guidance and slowly and carefully made my way back to my desk where I slumped down into an uncontrolled sleep.

It was 12:30 when I awoke to the sound of my name. Graham Griffiths was calling me. "Lou, Louis Gerhani! Lou, you okay, man?"

"Oh, Graham . . . ."

"Geez, what happened to you, man?"

"It's a long story, bro."

"Well, it's twelve-thirty. Let's get some lunch and you can fill me in."

The Au Bon Pain is a great place to eat either breakfast or lunch, and the coffee is the freshest. They bake everything right in the store, so you can have anything from bagels to muffins to sandwiches—whatever you fancy. I opted for the super-chug Colombian coffee to help me out of my near-comatose state. Graham was right there with me, and we each had ham and cheese on the tire-sized bagels they sell. After five minutes of some of the strongest coffee around, I was perked up and almost ready to run a block or two. So I filled Graham in on my eventful day.

"Damn!" Graham snapped. "You don't do anything halfway, do you?"

"That boss, Glavin? He's a real horse's ass!" I barked from somewhere deep inside.

"Yeah, Lou, he's a real jerk, but he signs all the checks, so you have to play the game, you know? You've got to kiss up just enough to make the man think you really care. Problem is, Lou, you haven't cared for quite a while, and it shows."

Graham was right. I was stuck in some kind of limbo, as if I were living on an isolated island, far away in the Caribbean somewhere. I was going through the motions but not really trying. I knew I wasn't right on. I knew I was producing sub-par, but I really didn't care. Now, Harold Glavin was all over my ass. He wasn't pulling any punches this time when he threatened to fire me. He had a reputation for firing employees with no warning at all and over petty issues. Many were fired over the phone, abruptly. So when he warned me about getting fired, I knew he meant it.

Graham was different from me. He cared. Graham needed his job. He worried about losing it, mostly because he was married with kids. Graham was a young black man who had married a Hispanic woman when he was only twenty years old, and they already had three young children. Talk about pressure! Graham worked all kinds of overtime and even did odd jobs just to make up for being the only wage earner in the home. Clearly, we were different animals. When I felt burned out, I just didn't work hard; I stopped trying. Graham couldn't use any excuses, with five mouths to feed. He was the most mature twenty-seven-year-old I had ever known.

It was three years earlier when we became friends. First, it was by bumping into each other at the coffee shop and in the lobby. Then, after having a few conversations, and after Graham found out that I was a reporter, he immediately put me on a pedestal. I don't know exactly why, but I took to the guy, and Graham soon became a close friend. We talked a lot about the sports teams we both admired, and we always had a lot of laughs, but we rarely hung out at night because he had obligations.

"So, tell me more about this assignment Glavin threatens to take your job away over." Graham put down his sandwich and gave me a mischievous grin.

"Oh, that! I haven't had a quality story to cover in ages. In fact, I can't remember writing anything interesting in months. It's as if I'm being black-balled by His Majesty, King Glavin."

"Really?"

"Really!" I snapped. "I've been covering prominent obituaries, births, and unimportant petty crimes. And to boot, the clown Glavin has the balls to call me in on each story I write, tear it all apart, and make me rewrite it over and over. I feel like he was just egging me on this morning, just so I would resign rather than him firing my ass and having to pay me unemployment!"

"Okay, so what's the new story about?" Graham asked, genuinely interested.

"Oh, get a load of this. The new story is sending me to a nursing home in Maryland to cover a very old lady celebrating a milestone birthday."

"What the . . .?"

"I know, right?!" I said. "They give these kinds of stories to cub reporters just getting their feet wet."

"Why this old lady?" Graham asked.

"It seems that this old lady is the oldest person ever to stay at this nursing home, and she is currently the oldest living person in Maryland."

"How old is that, Lou?"

"The notes Gloria gave me said a hundred and ten years old. Yeah, one hundred and ten years!"

"Holy Samoli! A hundred and ten years old? The oldest person I ever heard about was a hundred and one, and that was my great-grandmother who died just before reaching a hundred and two. I heard that on the day she died, she actually finished a crossword puzzle. She was that sharp." Graham took a bite of his sandwich. "You know, Lou, that sounds like a pretty cool assignment."

"Yeah, maybe. But maybe this old biddy is cold-stone senile. Good luck trying to write a clever story out of something like that." I laughed.

"Hey, dude, you really got to respect anyone who's made it to even eighty today. Think about the odds of living past one hundred. I used to think about that when they spoke about Great-Granny Mable. She never made it out of Africa. But what are the odds, man? All the diseases, accidents, and other junk that could happen to a person. Look at the old person in your story. If she is a hundred and ten, she was born, let's see, in or around the year 1903. I that that's awesome! She has outlasted almost everyone, or at least everyone she ever knew."

Back at my office, while compiling some notes, I thought about the old lady. I thought about Graham and what he had said about his great-grandmother. I wondered if, just possibly, this assignment wasn't some kind of vengeful punishment from Constable Harold Glavin.

I looked at the notes from Gloria on my latest assignment. The old woman's name was Lolita Croome. She had a living relative, a daughter named Jennifer, age eighty-three, who was our contact person. I read on. Jennifer was married to a man named Guy, and both the mother and daughter were very religious and had been their whole lives. Glavin had made a note: "Watch your actions and language, Lou. Don't embarrass the paper!"

Don't embarrass the paper? That's what I'd become in the eyes of the management of the *Washington Gazette*—an embarrassment? I knew I was off my game a bit and uninterested in writing. Maybe I felt burnt out from writing, or maybe I was bored with the low-quality assignments I'd been stuck with for the past year or so. Whatever it was, I realized that I was at the end of the road now. Either I hit a home run with this centenarian assignment or I'd better look through the classifieds for a new job.

For the first time in many years, I was actually scared. I sat at my desk and wondered what kind of work I could perform if not working as a writer. I went through various occupations one by one: waiting tables, driving car service or a truck, painting houses, working at Starbucks doling out caffeine hits to already-nervous people. As I slowly analyzed each scenario, it caused a slight eruption of acid production in my stomach. I realized that I already had the job best suited to my expertise and personality, and one that could pay my bills fairly easily. I sat there for twenty minutes longer staring at the nameplate on my desk, the one that reminded me where I sat, where I belonged each morning, and where I wanted the nameplate to remain for many years to come.

According to Gloria Finn's agenda, I was to arrive in Hagerstown, Maryland, on Wednesday to get acclimated and settled in, and then on Thursday at noon I was to meet Lolita, the subject of my story. The assignment was probably the worst possible assignment I could ever work on at the time. Why couldn't I work on the auto industry, or the building industry, or even unemployment or crime? Anything would be better to get me out of my self-imposed rut than interviewing a centenarian. Boredom is the worst thing for a writer, while inspiration is the exhilarating surge a writer needs. It creates an adrenalin rush that spurs a writer on. Whenever I'd felt inspired, the words had flowed so easily. Inspiration had helped me write the best stories of my career. That internal inspiration had been lacking for many months. I wondered how I could possibly get up the enthusiasm just to travel to Maryland for the depressing trip to that nursing home. I hated nursing homes! The very thought of a nursing home scared me because I envisioned so many elderly people entering alive, only to be carried out as lifeless bodies. Life is really short for many, too long for others, and blessed for a very few—like Lolita.

It was five o'clock on Monday when I entered my favorite watering hole, Brandy's. It is located about five miles from downtown Washington and has a nice mix of patrons. There are the sports jocks who live for every game playing on the large flat-screen TVs in the bar. They root for anything being played: soccer, boxing, baseball, even women's softball. Then there is the younger crowd that is basically there to meet new people; they drink all night just hoping to get lucky with the opposite sex. I often watched some of the young male players vying for an opening to make moves on young women who didn't want to be picked up anyway. It was quite comical and entertaining, almost like a sporting event itself. Then there are the older men who seem to be slowly wasting away at the bar, no doubt widowed or divorced, and clearly too old to be attractive to younger women who want to meet their next romantic interest.

Finally, there are guys like me, a breed of their own, men who drink out of boredom as a way to pass the time and to drown their sorrows, drinking enough to numb the pain of a deep heartache; men who want to be numb enough to fall asleep easily in the wee hours of the morning and sleep like a zombie rather than twisting and turning all night long.

Brandy's features a century-old, solid mahogany bar that is horseshoe shaped and runs about seventy-five feet in length. The bar is historic to Washington, DC, and has been around for ages. Not too many politicians make it into the bar; they frequent the more elaborate ones closer to the Capitol.

I sat at my usual spot with my back to the doorway. The large screens all around the huge bar were showing replays of baseball and golf tournaments. The bar was pretty empty at pre-rush-hour. The bar stool felt good as I settled into it, like an old glove. I had made a good friend of my stool for the past several months. That stool had kept me from falling as I drank too much on far too many occasions. It's a lonely life when a drinker has to leave his stool and face the four unforgiving walls of his home.

Carl is the main bartender. He's always friendly and very knowledgeable in world, business, and current sporting events. Carl is a great listener, and when you vent your troubles to him, he truly cares; he's not faking it. Most drinkers don't vent; they just try to deaden a deep-seated pain and escape home, numb to life's problems.

I stared at Carl, his back to me while he served drinks on the opposite side to two elderly men. Carl is a huge man whom no one would want to test in a wrestling match. He stands about six four and weighs about two hundred fifty pounds. He is quite cheery for a bartender, almost jolly. I only remember him losing his temper once, against a young punk who was too rowdy. Carl's booming voice raised to a lion's roar, and the punk quickly shut up—he was scared quiet.

"Carl, just a Heineken on tap," I said when he made his way over to my side of the bar.

"Ah, no scotch today?"

"No, not today. I've got some real thinking to do."

"I see." Carl winked. "I hope she's gorgeous!"

"No. Oh, no, it's not like that. It's business."

"I see." Carl smiled and waited for more.

"Yeah, I'm kind of on probation on the job. The boss really laid into me for my lack of interest."

"You've been out of it for a while?"

"Well, according to the head honcho, my writing has been sub-par for many months. But, you know, Carl, they've been giving me the worst writing assignments for a long time now, and now he's threatened my job over one last crap story. It's a dog of a story about an old lady in a nursing home."

"I see. It's a story that no one else wants, or is it a form of punishment?"

"Both! The woman is a hundred and ten freaking years old in a nursing home in Maryland ."

"Really? She's that old? Can she hold a conversation still?"

"According to the newspaper, she is cognizant, but she is physically impaired. But they could be lying just to set me up!"

"You know, Lou, that sounds like a story I would like to read—all the history in that woman's life. Can you imagine what her eyes have seen over all those years? All the pain, the joy, the life . . ."

"Carl, you want to go write it for me? I'll gladly fill in for you behind the bar."

"Oh, yeah, that would work real well. We'd have no liquor left for the customers!" He laughed. Then he leaned on the bar, looked straight and long into my eyes, and said, "No, really, Lou, I think you can turn out a quality story there."

"Well, let me put it this way." I smiled nervously. "Either I write a killer story here, or I'll be waiting tables somewhere, and I've never waited tables in my life."

"I'll be right back at you," Carl said as he spun around and rushed over to the other side of the bar where he worked as quickly as a juggler, mixing, cleaning, pouring, washing down, talking, and sipping his own drink of sparkling water with a twist of lime. Carl never drank a drop of liquor. He told me once that his father was an alcoholic and used to beat his mother when he and his brothers and sisters were young. Carl's father died a slow and painful death from the liquor and heavy smoking. Carl vowed as a teen to never drink a drop. I kidded him once about working at a bar, and he said, "That's precisely why I am perfect to tend a bar. Besides, I can stay sharp and listen to my customers' many problems."

And he was right. Carl always sipped his sparkling water and waited on the next story a patron might feel the need to get off his chest, and there were plenty.

Carl moved like a well-oiled machine, almost robot-like. He reminded me of the robots that build cars in Detroit, fast and precise. And he never seemed to spill a drop or over-pour the head of a beer. In five minutes flat, Carl took care of five people, sipped his drink, and was back in front of me focusing once again on my current dilemma. The other patrons at that moment were clearly not conversationalists. They were drinking scotch shots and elaborate martinis, but they were not interested in talking.

As if on autopilot, Carl filled my glass, including a perfectly finished beer head, and then topped off his sparkling water. Carl had kind blue eyes, and could have been a professional football player. He was about fifty-five years old, had been married some thirty years, and had five children—a real family man. He once stated that he was a lot like a psychoanalyst, a great communicator with a habit of listening far more than preaching. I've heard him give advice to widowers who have recently lost their spouses and to older men whose wives were gravely ill. He put everyone at ease.

While he looked me in the eyes again, Carl said, "You know, Lou, I want to make a few friendly observations, if I may. I hope you'll accept them in the vein in which they are intended."

Without waiting for me to respond, Carl said, "Lou, you've been coming here for a few years now, and honestly, I've seen a big change for the past several months now, ever since you broke up with your girlfriend."

"Carl, you don't have to do this . . . ."

"Lou, I do. I owe it to you as a friend."

"I know I've been a little off lately," I said.

"Lou, you've been walking around in a daze. Your boss is right, there's no fire in your belly. You have lost your enthusiasm for life. For months now, you've been coming in here not to have a good time, but rather to get plastered and kill some inner pain. I like you, and I realize it's been only three months since you lost your girl, but it's time to get on with life and stop self-destructing. You know, there's a fine line between social drinking and becoming an alcoholic. I must warn you, right now you are well on your way to becoming an alcoholic. Wake up before it's too late."

"Maybe I do drink a little too much, okay, I'll admit that, but alcoholic? No way!"

"You said that your boss gave you one last shot to retain your reporting job. I am confident that you can turn things around, but you must get serious."

"I'm over Alicia now. She's a distant memory."

"Lou, Alicia isn't a distant memory—don't kid a kidder. I see it in your eyes as you slowly get loaded each time. It will get better, but you've got to let go, or you will be sleeping in the streets and killing yourself over someone who has moved on with her life. Move on, Lou!"

Carl was right on. He knew the pain I wore on my face over Alicia, whose picture was etched into my brain. I could see her as if she were standing in front of me. I saw her tall, slender figure at five-seven, with her long silky dark hair. I saw her hazel eyes that captivated me throughout our yearlong relationship. It was true that I had been devastated when Alicia broke up with me for a physician's assistant at a local hospital. After all, we had planned to marry within a year. Carl had it right: I'd been like a zombie for months, just going through the motions but devoid of passion for the job and for life in general.

Alicia was all I thought about. Sure, I kept telling myself that I was fine, that I was over her, able to move on. But I wasn't. Carl went on to confront me with the fact that when I did meet a woman at the bar, my only goal was to get her to bed and then drop her. And he was right. No woman meant anything to me except as a sex object. And after I had slept with one of them, the inner pain quickly returned. No one could compare to Alicia, and sleeping with the few I had slept with since breaking up with her had convinced me of this.

It finally dawned on me while talking with Carl that my heart had turned as cold as ice. I didn't care for any other women because none of them were a match for the woman I had put high on a pedestal. My job, my life, even my own family meant very little to me anymore. A part of me was dead. Carl was right: zombie was the right word for how I was going through life each day; I was like a robot—without a heart.

But after speaking with Carl, after his telling me what I already knew full well, I realized I had to snap out of the funk I was deeply caught in. After an hour or so, I left the bar and went home to my apartment. With tears in my eyes, I finally had the courage to tear up the eight-by-ten photo of Alicia on my dresser. I used to stare at her picture every night and then fall off to sleep. Even after we broke up, I'd stare for an hour at a time. I was consumed with Alicia. It didn't matter that she had broken my heart, that she hadn't lived up to the perfect angel I had envisioned her to be. My heart had been permanently damaged by that woman. I was sure I would never fall in love that deeply again. More importantly, I could not possibly love that wholeheartedly again, because my heart, I was convinced, was dead. After all, how many times can a man fall that deeply in love?

After destroying the picture, I went out and walked long, hard, and fast, to nowhere in particular, just around my neighborhood. My feet and legs moved unconsciously as my mind raced, calculated, and tried to wipe out the brain cells that still held on to the memories of Alicia—her scent, her smile, her eyes, and her voice.

I calculated how to excel on this last chance of a writing assignment I'd been given. I could hear Harold Glavin, cigar-chomping boss from hell, demanding, "Don't think of coming back, Baba-Louie, without a story fit for the front page!"

When I had asked how long he wanted me to work the story, he screamed, "Forever, 'cause you won't have a job if you write shit! Make it good, not like the crap you've been writing!"

The air was cool and the rain was light as I walked and thought of where I was in my life. I felt somewhat like a ship without an engine, stranded in the middle of the ocean. I had no sense of destination, no ambition to move in any one direction. Yet, Carl's talk had urged me onward and woken something deep inside of me, something that had been dormant for a long time.

So, I thought, *who is this old woman named Lolita Croome?* And this hick town in Maryland? I had known some older people in my past, people in their early nineties, many of whom were not in good physical condition and had failing memories. This Lolita woman, if she had any of her marbles left, might not be able to recollect much of her past. Or, like some centenarians, she might just keep repeating the same story over and over again.

I kept wondering where there was a great story here. Of course, I knew the great achievement she had in merely reaching that advanced age. That alone was a near impossibility. Just the fact that sickness that took so many lives along the way, or accidents that rob so many other lives—she had side-stepped all of those obstacles. I figured I could have had a far worse story to work on. After all, I'd had some real boring stories to cover in my career, like the one about the dog stuck in a sewer for a day that had to be rescued, or the cat stuck in a tree for three days, or the lemonade stand run by a five-year-old girl to raise money for a worthy cause. Writing is not all it's cracked up to be. Sometimes it is much like being a singer with a great voice but only allowed to sing songs and genres you dislike. A writer needs motivation; he needs to be driven with inspiration in order to write from his soul. Oh, sure, a writer can always write *something*, but if it's forced out, it won't be sharp, edgy, and inspired.

By the time I arrived back home, it was time to pack a bag for my trip to Hagerstown the following day. I would need a haircut early in the morning before my drive there. My hair was growing wild in every direction. It had been about three months since my last haircut. Reflecting back, I now realized that I had neglected many things for the past several months, including myself. Of course, this showed through to everyone. At age thirty-one, I didn't like my hair to be long; it's just so hard to keep neat when it is long and out of control. I thought of how funny it was that even very long hair never used to bother me in the least when I was in my early twenties. Maybe I was getting old. I sure felt like a very old thirty-one-year-old, at least mentally.

That night, I couldn't sleep. I just lay on my left side, then my right, for ten minutes each, then switched back to the alternate side. My mind raced but always came back to my boss yelling and threatening to fire my ass. I needed sleep, but in those times when the mind won't rest, there is nothing a person can do to ease the insanity of nonstop thinking,

It was nine-thirty Tuesday morning when I made it to the local Washington Mall where my barber, Fred Karner, works. He owns the same shop where he first started cutting hair some thirty years ago. I've been getting haircuts from Fred for as long as I can remember.

Fred is now in his early fifties, and we've become friends over the years. It's always fun to see Fred, like a form of relaxation therapy. I had neglected my hair for many weeks, but used to go religiously every two weeks. Fred and I used to talk about women, sports, and drinking, pretty much in that order of importance. He is married and has two grown daughters, one a police officer and one the owner of a bridal salon. Fred had been a party animal, a drinker, a smoker of anything he could smoke, anything to make him feel good. But that all came to an abrupt halt a few years back when he was diagnosed with cancer and COPD. His lung capacity had been quickly reduced to thirty percent, so all the partying and drinking suddenly ended. I had felt sorry for Fred, but also for myself, because we used to go out to bars, ball games, and bowling alleys—anywhere they served cold beers. Fred stopped cold turkey. He didn't even look to have an affair any longer, and he had been a womanizer in his younger days. The cancer spot on his lungs had been diagnosed twelve months ago.

But Fred, over the many years, was never judgmental with me, no matter what I told him about work, my romantic status, or my life. He always backed me and made me feel better about my circumstances. Still, I realized I had clearly been suffering from depression for some time because I was even avoiding him. Of course, I lied to him about why I hadn't been around for such a long time because I hated when people felt sorry for me about my breakup with Alicia.

"Lou, holy crap, where've you been? I was getting worried," he said. He shook my hand hard and hugged me.

"Oh, I've been real busy: the job, the apartment, drinking at the bar . . . ."

"Oh, I hear you!" He studied me then repeated, "You look horrible, buddy!"

"Thanks, Fred! Maybe you can turn me back into Prince Charming."

"Even I ain't that good!" he said with a laugh.

Fred looked okay, but he seemed much weaker than I had remembered. He had lost too much weight, mostly due to the chemo and staying away from the alcohol. He told me that there were times when he just couldn't breathe, and he had to use the emergency inhalers and oxygen in addition to the routine inhalers he used every day. He was looking like he was in his late seventies rather than his early fifties. So when he wanted to know how I was doing, I just let on that things were not that bad. God has a way of waking us up sometimes. Just when we think our lives are so bad, we see someone far worse off than we are. I knew Fred wasn't long for this world, as much as I wanted to deny it.

It dawned on me as I watched Fred's face in the mirror that I had so much going for me at that moment, even if I were to get fired from the newspaper. Fred kept clipping and we kept talking. I told him about Glavin's threat to fire me, and the assignment I was heading to after my haircut that day. He wanted to know all the details. He listened intently, and I could see he was deep in thought while I spoke. After I told him all I knew about Lolita Croome, he said nothing for a full thirty seconds. The only sounds came from the snipping of the scissors. I studied Fred.

His hair had always been perfectly styled and colored. But now it was very sparse. He had lost his potbelly over the past several months and now looked much different from the family photo on the counter in front of me, which had been taken a few years earlier. I waited for him to digest it all.

As he cut my hair, all the memories and good times we had shared together raced through my mind. Ever since Fred's diagnosis, I always felt terrible whenever we parted after spending time together, like it was going to be the last time I would see him alive. It was depressing. He was fighting valiantly for his life. God only knows what I would do if I were in his place. *How does he show up every day to work?* I wondered. *It must be that he focuses on the positive future of beating the cancer, while I am silently tortured into believing that he will slowly succumb to the dreadful disease.* I looked closer at Fred in the reflection as he began to smile.

"Louie, you know I think the world of you, but I must be honest. You're going down the toilet!" His smile turned nervous as he continued. "Look at me. When you are dealt a bad hand, it suddenly wakes you up. You see, I wake up each morning, open my eyes, and thank God for a new day, a new opportunity to live. Life means so much more since I was diagnosed. I will beat this thing! It won't be easy, but I have set my mind to focus only on the positives of life and eliminate the negatives. You, Louie, look like you've been beaten down. Wake up, man! You've got the world by the tail! Start to live it, man!"

My reflection showed a stupefied look on my face. He paused for a solid five seconds while I stared into the mirror.

"You have an award-winning story here, Lou! This woman is an icon; she has lived more than a century. That is basically impossible. Do you realize what she has witnessed throughout her lifetime? And guess what? You get to interview her. You get to be closer to her, getting inside her head, than anyone else has in many a year. But here's the thing."

He stopped to shake a finger at me. "Listen up, buddy. You have to straighten up for this here gig! If you don't, this elderly woman, who's seen and experienced it all, will see right through you. Lou, keep in mind that this Lolita woman is wise. She can pick up on the slightest attitude or mood swing you may have. She can tell if you are sincere or just trying to get through an interview, only to get to the finish line. If you want the once-in-a-lifetime story, you must project that through your attitude, your appearance, your love for her and your interest in her and her life story. Anything else will blow up in your face."

Suddenly, Fred reminded me of my father. How I wished my father were still alive. Sometimes we need someone to look at us from the outside and give us an honest survey. Most people will not say anything negative; they just sugarcoat everything and refrain from rocking the boat for fear of hurting your feelings. I had not thought of Lolita Croome in the light that Fred portrayed her.

"And," he added, "I want daily updates at night, buddy."

What else could I do? I agreed.

I left the mall with probably the finest haircut Fred had ever given me. Tears welled up in my eyes as I thought about him. Here was a man fighting the battle of his life, and he was so concerned about *me*. As I left the mall, I asked God why He would want to take a man barely fifty, while allowing an old basically blind woman in a nursing home to live past the age of one hundred ten. We all have so many unanswered questions in life, like my father's death. Why him? Why not someone else, like the homeless alcoholic, or someone old and ready to die? I hope we receive all the answers to these questions after we each leave this earthly home of ours.

Slowly, I pulled my car out of the Irving Street mall lot and headed toward Hagerstown, Maryland. It was a ninety-mile trek that I estimated would take me two-and-a-half hours. The newspaper had arranged for me to meet with Lolita Croome the next day, and I had research to do. I would have the chance to settle into my hotel room, do some navigating of the town, and grab a good meal. I was getting more comfortable with the thought of writing a story about an old lady in a nursing home. I kept reminding myself that it was just another story, but my mind kept telling me that it was to retain my job. My career was now on the line. I was screwed if I messed this one up.

At that moment, it dawned on me that surely Lolita was someone's grandmother. That was how I would approach the story—making believe that the woman was *my* grandmother. I remembered my two grandmothers, who had passed away when I was very young. They were both loving grandmothers, although I didn't much care for them hugging and kissing me—it made me uncomfortable, maybe because I was a young boy.

If my friends, Graham in the office, Carl at the bar, and my barber Fred, all thought the story was special, then I also chose to believe the story could be very unusual. The story I wrote could just possibly be the best story of my career. My attitude was beginning to improve. Perhaps that bulldog of a boss I had was just the motivation I needed to analyze and modify my life. Harold Glavin might well be the all-time editor from hell, but the way I saw it, jobs weren't too plentiful these days.

My drive from Irving Street in Washington, DC, to Hagerstown would allow me to think and reflect on my life. I needed gas, so I filled up with ultra-octane—and, yes, I filled the car also, with regular. The ultra-octane was actually Starbucks brand coffee, a large Pikes Place brew, which has to be the strongest around. Talk about staying awake on the highway! I was in overdrive and the car was still parked. I had bought my friend, Dan Lambert, a large Pikes Place Starbucks once, and he accused me of feeding him engine oil. Guess you have to acquire a taste for strong coffee. I thrive on it. Maybe I need the caffeine rush it gives me.

My route to Hagerstown would be I-270 North to I-70 West, a nice long ride, allowing me to do some real soul-searching to try to get my life back on track.

I'm sure many others have had their lives turned upside down and their hearts broken for various reasons. Some lose a loved one to sickness or an accident or, like me, a breakup. At first, you believe that it is fine, that you will easily forget and move on. After all, she was just another woman, not some movie actress. But the mind won't allow the heart to forget. Like a deep-seated splinter, the mind, all on its own, sporadically sends impulses of painful memories to the heart. The heart feels the pain over and over again. And all you can think is: *How much longer will it take for me to forget?* The alcohol only numbs the brain temporarily, like Novocain, and then it wears off, leaving more heartache and pain.

CHAPTER THREE

The weather was perfect for a long drive—clear, sunny, and warm—and the highway traffic was moving at a good pace. The soft music on the radio was stuck on love ballads. I let it play instead of chasing after other music that would annoy and rattle me. Dolly Parton's famous song "I Will Always Love You" came on the radio, causing me to picture Alicia all over again. I seem to reminisce about the same thing every time. I can't shake that moment in time. It was very early in our relationship when I first realized that I had indeed fallen in love with her.

I remember it all too well. Her eyes drew me in. I studied the irises, and their various hues. The fact is that a person's eyes are so unique and contain so many colors other than the standard blue, green, or brown that we usually use to classify eye color. Her hazel eyes were alive with excitement and so much life. I had no chance. I fell in love quickly with this statuesque goddess. And when she smiled, my heart always skipped a beat. I had never fallen like that before. They say that when someone falls in love, they actually hypnotize themselves. I don't know anything about that, but I do know that it was a powerful love that took over my life in the beginning, in the middle, and at the end, and well after Alicia broke off the engagement.

Two hours into my trip I stopped, mostly to stretch my legs, but also to top off the tank with gas at a reasonable price, at least compared to the prices in Washington, DC. Not everyone in Washington is a politician, but businesses think everyone is wealthy. It is one over-priced city. At the rest stop, I got another coffee and a few cookies and sat for a while with my trusty notebook. I found a nice, quiet table to one side.

"Hagerstown, Maryland" was the title at the top of my notebook. Yesterday I had managed to do a bit of research on Hagerstown, a town I hadn't even heard of before—the history, the charm, the people. It is all quite interesting. It's a quaint little town. The Internet told me that Hagerstown had a population of around 39,000. The town was settled in 1739. It was named after Jonathan Hager, a German immigrant, though it took some time until the town was named. The history books reflect that in 1861, Hagerstown was used as a base in the Civil War by General James Longstreet's troops of the South. The town was very active in the unfolding of the Civil War.

What really grabbed my attention, though, was something I had come upon while searching for Lolita's timeframe. The records showed that in 1923, Lolita was engaged. But it was also the year that a mass murderer executed several young women in the small town execution-style. The murders went unsolved. One of my many questions for Lolita would be what her memories were of that year. In 1923, serial-type killings were rare. My initial research had showed no such killings in the several years before or after that year anywhere in the United States.

So who could have committed such hideous murders of three young women? Was it one killer, or someone copying the lead killer? Were the killers locals or people from outside of Hagerstown? These kinds of murders are usually committed by the same individual. Lolita was young in 1923. Did she and the other young women of the community live in fear that entire year? I'm sure they did. And since the murders went unsolved, no doubt the fear remained into the following year and for some time afterward. I was sure that Lolita, if she still had her senses, would have recollections of that time in her life. It was a memorable time in Hagerstown history.

The website ancestry.com also housed newspaper stories from that specific time. The killings were truly horrific for 1923, and would still be horrific if they were committed today. I learned that the killer or killers were sadistic in their actions surrounding the Hagerstown girls' deaths, because in each instance, the killer would wait exactly one month to the day after the killing and then would prominently display a part of the dead girl's body. It seems that on that day, the killer would take a severed arm of the murdered girl and leave it sticking straight up out of the ground somewhere.

The records showed that one of the arms was sticking straight up out of the front lawn of the Hagerstown Theater, one was sticking up out of the front lawn of the town's only Chevrolet dealership, and the third was found outside the Hagerstown high school. It was sticking straight up in a large flowerpot near the front entrance of the school. Lolita, coincidentally, had worked at that school as a teacher's assistant in 1923, according to my notes.

The killer, back then, was nicknamed "The One-Armed Bandit" by newspapers across the country. The records reflect the outrage and uproar of the local citizens that the "Butcher Killer," as he was known in Hagerstown, was never apprehended, though he was sought for decades.

There have been other notable criminal acts that have gone unsolved over the years. In 1947, a pretty young woman named Elizabeth Short, nicknamed "the Black Dahlia," was found cut in half and mutilated in

Los Angeles. The case remains unsolved and widely publicized. And to date, sixty people have tried to confess to the murder, though no one has been tried for it.

And then there was the Zodiac Killer, who murdered at least five known victims and maybe more in 1968. No one has been tried, even though over 2,500 potential suspects were investigated.

Consider Jack the Ripper, who evidently went to his own grave as an unknown killer. He might have been a well-respected person of the community in his day. No one ever figured out that very famous case. Some speculate that the Ripper was a member of the physician community.

I had made quite a few notes in my notebook, as I had become quite intrigued about the 1923 Hagerstown murders that this special woman, Lolita, had lived through. I likened Lolita to a big old oak tree that had stood for one hundred and ten years. I found it remarkable in a strange comparison that like the oak tree, Lolita had clearly weathered many a storm, and possibly hurricanes and tornadoes.

One hundred and ten years is a ton of time. So many people who were born in the early 1900s days died very young. Some died as infants or young children. Many died before reaching adulthood of various diseases and viruses, sicknesses that today are just minor inconveniences to us. So this woman was indeed unique. My main problem, as I saw it, was how to get any useful information out of someone so old that she may have lost most of her senses.

I pictured myself screaming at the top of my lungs, because she was probably wouldn't be able to hear very well, or waving my hands about, as if she were an immigrant new to America who couldn't speak the language. My mind raced with so many scenarios that I gave myself a headache. All I could visualize was Harold, the boss from hell, with a big smile on his face as he gave me my walking papers while cursing me out as the biggest loser in newspaper reporting history.

A half hour later, I started out again for Hagerstown. Maryland was known for crabs, something I had never acquired the taste for, although their other seafood was reported to be quite fresh and inexpensive. *Something good, hopefully, as I may be eating more than working if my hunches are correct.*

I had joked with Graham that the most exciting thing that ever happens in Hagerstown, Maryland, is probably when the Dunkin' Donuts shop in town puts out the new donuts at 6:00 a.m.

The radio was playing loudly as I drove at a good clip for some twenty minutes, when it happened again. It was a Frank Sinatra song. I recognized it from the bars. Some of Sinatra's songs are sad in one way or another, but this one hit me pretty hard. I remember listening to it in the bars many times, but this time it hit me harder, perhaps because I had no liquor in me to deaden the effects of the stabbing words that penetrated deep inside my brain, awakening once again the pain of losing Alicia and living without her. Lately, most songs felt hurtful because they brought back memories, but not as badly as this one did.

The song was "Cycles." Sinatra sings about a fella who's down and out because he's just lost his girl and been fired around the same time. The words resonated deeply as I heard him sing, "So I'm down and so I'm out, but so are many others. So I feel like trying to hide my head 'neath these covers . . . . So, I'll keep my head up high, although I'm kind of tired. My gal just up and left last week; Friday I got fired. You know, it's almost funny, but things can't get worse than now. So I guess I'll try to sing; but please, just don't ask me now."

I glared at the radio and punched the button to change the station. I hit it so hard that my knuckle stung for about twenty seconds. And in return for my efforts, the station that popped on turned out to be a gospel station playing some crazy song about Jonah and the whale. I slapped at the on-off button to silence the radio as I shouted, "Holy shit!"

I floored the car, trying to make it feel my pain. In return, the car whined as it gunned forward to ninety-five miles per hour. At that moment, I didn't care. I didn't care about a possible ticket, or the cars I was passing and weaving in and out of. After about five minutes, I calmed down and returned my speed to around sixty-five. "Self-control, buddy!" I yelled at myself.

Out of habit, I thought of Alicia. I wondered where she was, what she was doing, and if she ever thought about me. I pictured her at night with the light off, just before she drifted off to sleep. I visualized her smiling with a twinkle in her eyes as she thought about me, wondering if I was all right, even though she had someone new in her life. I saw her as if she was thinking about me with a new woman in my life and wondering if I was happy. Then I snapped back to reality, knowing full well that I was the last person on her mind. And there was no way, with the light out at night, that Alicia would be thinking or caring about my well-being or happiness.

No, it was I who stared blankly into the darkness of the night, every night, after shutting off my light. It was I who thought of nothing but Alicia before falling off to sleep each night. It was I who tortured myself, unable to sleep every night as I lay there in my lonely, dark bedroom, visualizing her and wondering if she was holding on to her new boyfriend in bed at that moment and smiling into his eyes. Each time I visualized her, I plunged that dagger deeper into my heart. And I did this every night without fail. And the memory played forth so vividly, just like a movie.

I knew that I was subjecting myself to suicidal thinking every time I did this, yet I couldn't seem to stop. Her beautiful face was clear as could be in my mind's eye. Her eyes showed more love than ever before, and her smile was finer than anything, just the way I remembered it. Then, after an hour or so, I would fall off to sleep, exhausted and in pain. The next morning, I was still unrested from an endless internal battle of brain-battling dreams that made me wish I had taken some kind of zombie-producing drug. No wonder I'd been a screw-up for months.

I drove on in silence, the kind of silence that can be deafening at times, the kind where you realize that there are sounds actually inside your head that you never thought existed before. My sounds were like the humming that fluorescent lights sometimes give off. So I focused on the sounds of the road against the tires of my car and thought some more about the core of my assignment—the long life of Lolita Croome. I wondered about that phenomenal age of 110. Was it a blessing or a curse?

I thought on. Well, if one made it to the ripe old age of 110 and had his or her senses intact, it was truly a real blessing. But, then again, whoever makes it to 110 with all their senses: hearing, sight, touch, smell, and taste? And what about other issues, such as walking, thinking properly, and being able to communicate? And then there are issues such as being able to feed oneself properly, washing, and taking care of other hygiene issues, such as going to the bathroom by oneself.

Of course, many people over the age of ninety have some, if not many, issues that require full- or part-time caregiver support. But still, I realized that as long as the communication skills remained—talking to, hearing, and comprehending of others—then life might still be pleasurable for the post-ninety population, even if confined to a wheelchair.

My research into senior citizens had showed that today more than 37 million people in the United States are sixty-five or older. In order to live to the ripe old age of 110, a person would have lived on earth for an astounding 40,150 days plus another approximately 270 days in the womb.

I already admired Lolita for nothing more than her amazing longevity. The odds were astounding. I would estimate that hitting a multi-million-dollar jackpot would be easier to achieve than reaching the age of 110.

Hours later, I was touring the old town of Hagerstown, which had been located on the border between the North and the South during the Civil War, making it a prime staging area and supply hub for major campaigns during in the 1860s.

New estimates of deaths attributed to the Civil War are in the area of 750,000. It was a very troubled, painful time for the country. In only four years, three-quarters of a million lives were lost. There were at least five battles in Maryland. I felt sad as I drove down Hagerstown's Main Street and thought about all those who died.

I got the feeling I was in the 1950s based on the architecture. It felt nice to drive around looking at the old concrete structures in the quaint town. I was slowly getting acclimated to the feel of it all. It reminded me a little of Mayberry from *The Andy Griffith Show* of the 1960s—old buildings that last a lifetime.

I drove on, looking for the police station, the local library, the bars, restaurants, and places of worship. I studied the people, who seemed laid back compared to those in Washington, DC or New York, who seem to run a hundred miles per hour in many directions at once.

I parked for a while, keeping the radio's stinging music off, not looking for any additional emotional letdowns for the day. I made some more notes about locations of various important landmarks I would find useful in my investigation and story about Lolita.

I had researched the year 1923 because, according to some vague notes supplied to me by the newspaper, that was when Lolita made certain documentations of her life and times. It is, of course, the job of the reporter to uncover and investigate through watching, talking, and digging up facts pertinent to the story.

The year 1923 was important because of the three young women killed. One of my goals was to learn more about those killings and determine who could have possibly committed them, although I realized that the investigation was colder than an iceberg. Such brutality in a small town in 1923 was unthinkable in those days. There could be a fabulous story for the newspaper in those unsolved 1923 murders.

I drove past the nursing home where Lolita lived. It was a one-floor, L-shaped, brick complex. My research showed that around 300 residents lived there, and although simple in design, the ratings of care and cleanliness were excellent, according to various independent firms in the health industry. It was one of the better facilities for hundreds of miles, according to a healthcare newspaper published online to mostly seniors. I had never been inside a nursing home and didn't know what to expect.

The next day, I had an appointment to meet with representatives of Lolita, and with Lolita herself after her afternoon nap. I had to abide by certain rules, according to my specific instructions from the home and from my newspaper. They stressed that I not keep Lolita too long, and if she appeared tired, I should come back another time. Lolita's daughter would be available for my meeting with her mother.

The daughter—Jennifer—was over eighty and would be there to assist me, although I understood that she was nervous about any interviews or publicity. She felt it was too much of a strain on her mother. I, of course, had no knowledge of Lolita's physical condition, except that she was frail and in need of round-the-clock care.

I tried to think of whom I had ever known who was close to being that old, or even in their nineties. No one came to mind. Everyone I had ever known had died in their early eighties. My grandmothers had died at eighty and eighty-one, and both were in poor health. My mother's mother suffered for years from Alzheimer's disease; that mind-robbing disease ate away at my grandmother's memory over a long period of time. Alzheimer's can change a person's personality, and it makes some people aggressive. And there comes a time, like in my grandmother's case, when the patient doesn't even recognize her own family members any longer. I imagine that the worst theft to happen to an older person is the theft of their mind; many other physical ailments can be managed with medical care, but the mind is what makes a person unique. To be robbed of their mind is a really cruel death in disguise.

Was Lolita a mere shell of the true person she once was, or had she retained her mind for such an advanced age? One thinks of their own mortality at such times. What would my mind be like as I grew older? Life comes with no guarantees, and many people die well in advance of reaching the age of eighty. I think life expectancy is somewhere around seventy-eight or so. I guess if we could take out a contract when born to reach an age of eighty—with all of our senses intact and in relatively good health—we would gladly sign on. Lolita, it turned out, had glided past eighty by thirty additional years. The more I thought about it, the more I marveled at the achievement!

Many contend that they would never want to go to a nursing home, and would rather be dead than be a resident in "one of those places." I kind of agree. But I don't believe I will make it to such an extended age to have to be concerned about such a decision. My drinking alone will no doubt shorten my life, and men usually die at a younger age than women do anyway.

The sidewalks of the Hagerstown shopping district were not crowded. People strolled casually, smiling and conversing with one another. Total strangers seemed to be quite friendly toward one another. I studied everything closely, taking in as much as I could as I aimlessly drove the streets in a five-block radius a few times, seeing if anything unusual caught my eye. Nothing did. It was the *Mayberry R.F.D.* show all over again but in the present day.

Even the gas station I entered seemed old-fashioned in many ways, and not as modern as the huge stations of today that seem almost like mini-supermarkets. I stopped to top off my tank and get a soda from the vending machine in front of the auto garage that had one stall and one mechanic. The station reminded me of the ones in the old black-and-white movies of many years ago.

The pimply-faced, blond teenager whose nametag read "Brian" stood around six-two and weighed no more than 140. He was very talkative and had an accent typical of the area. He was very interested in what I was doing there and where I was from. He resembled an older version of Opie from *The Andy Griffith Show,* jutting ears and all.

Brian's eyes lit up when he found out I was a newspaper reporter from DC and was doing a story on one of the most famous people in modern-day Hagerstown.

"Of course, I know of Lolita! She is a real celebrity here. Everyone talks about her because no one here ever lives that long." He beamed as he spoke, and his ears turned red.

When I asked more about her, he said, "I've never met her, but I've seen her pictures in the newspapers since she turned one hundred. I think she is sickly, but she still understands things for an old lady. And there have been many stories and even a few newscasts about her."

The station had a few gas customers, and Brian hustled off to attend to them, excusing himself politely each time as he ran off. I parked my car to the side of the station and watched the grease monkey in the garage working deep inside an old car's engine. There was an old-fashioned vending machine from what appeared to be many years ago. It contained real ten-ounce retro bottles. I put in my dollar's worth of coins and pressed down the handle for a Diet Coke, which dropped down to the opening lower chute. I opened it using the bottle opener built into the machine and found a place to sit.

The bench on the right side of the station was nicely shaded and a good spot to continue my background information session with Brian about this little town that I already liked. Brian kept running back and forth between fill-ups. I think he was impressed with the reporter aspect of my angle.

We spoke about the history of Hagerstown and about the crime rate, which was almost nonexistent, according to young Brian. That prompted me to ask the all-important question I had been dying for answers to: "Brian, what do you know about the historic murders of 1923, the murders that went unsolved all these years?"

"Oh, yeah!" he said with a puzzled look. "I've heard about that from the old-timers in town."

Brian ran off again to pump gas as I sat resting comfortably, sipping and thinking of additional questions to ask this eager young man. He had a couple of regulars that he was chatting with. One gentleman was standing outside the car and talking to him. Brian pointed in my direction, and I saw the older man nod. When Brian was finished with the two cars, he ran to the garage mechanic and chatted with him for a few minutes.

Brian hurried back and sat on the bench next to me, all excited. "The old guy at the pump knew about the killings and said that no one was ever charged, although there was suspicion about a couple of people—one was a doctor at the local hospital, and one was a widowed farmer. But no one ever served any time. It was a huge story back then, but no one even talks about it anymore because it was so long ago. Wally, the owner and mechanic, says his grandfather was one of the investigating officers in the case, and he believes there were three girls killed, all school-aged. He said they were mutilated, and some people thought that maybe a butcher or a wanderer from another state had something to do with it."

We discussed the case some more. I gave my thoughts on the killer; Brian gave me directions to the library and the town hall. I left him sitting on the bench as I went to use the bathroom on the other side of the station.

As I was exiting the restroom, all hell broke loose. I heard screaming but didn't know at first where it was coming from. Then I saw quick movements at the gas pumps and heard more yelling. Then I saw the tall attendant, Brian, getting clocked on the head with what appeared to be the butt of a rifle. As he went down hard, there were the loudest explosions I had ever heard—four explosions in succession. I quickly hit the deck and instinctively covered my head with my hands against the ear-shattering blasts.

If I could have disappeared into the pavement I was covering, I would have. I don't think I was ever so flat against the ground in my life. It felt like an eternity, those thirty seconds, as I heard two more rounds being fired somewhere in the vicinity of the mechanic's garage. I could hear the pinging of the ricocheting bullets and the screeching of the spinning, burning tires of the escaping culprit in what appeared to be an old convertible sports car.

I quickly rose as the getaway car swerved from side to side as it peeled away. I couldn't make out much as I stood up slowly, a little too late to get a good look. I ran to Brian as quickly as I could and reached the gas pumps and the collapsed attendant. I got there a full second before the trotting mechanic, Wally, arrived. We quickly tried to lift Brian to his feet, but he had been knocked unconscious. We sat him up and leaned him against the front of the gas pumps as Wally kept screaming his name. I slowly inspected the general area. There was a lot of blood and some cash strewn around where Brian had come to rest. It was perhaps another thirty seconds before the dazed and confused boy blinked his eyes, first, ever so slightly; then slowly, he opened them wide. "What the hell . . . ?" he stammered.

Wally was already connected to 911 on his cell phone and was pleading for an ambulance. The operator asked a million questions.

"Now I remember . . . ." Brian said weakly. "I remember fighting with some guy who was trying to rob me. Then he hit me in the back of the head and it all went black."

"Brian, did you get a good look at him?" I asked.

"I, uh, I think he was Hispanic, with long black hair. I think he was around thirty, but I've never seen him around here before. One thing I know is that he had a great car. It was a black Mustang. It looked like a 1965 model, all souped up!"

"I agree," I said as Wally was quickly and anxiously relaying information to the police. "All I could catch was a black blur, tires screeching and smoking, leaving a black track."

It was a full ten minutes before the police and ambulance arrived, almost simultaneously, sirens blaring, lights revolving wildly. The paramedics quickly wrapped Brian's head to control the bleeding, all the while asking him questions as they took his vitals. The police officers spoke with Wally and me while waiting to speak with Brian, although the paramedics told the police that Brian still wasn't coherent enough to give a report. So the police agreed to postpone their preliminary investigation until he had been evaluated at the hospital.

CHAPTER FOUR

The trip to the hospital took ten minutes. I was slightly uncomfortable as I rode in a police cruiser for the first time ever. I looked around the rear seat of the police car as we drove at a rather high speed, weaving in and out of traffic. I wondered how a criminal felt being arrested and transported. I looked at the back of the officers' heads as we drove. Officer Robert Cianci, a twenty-something, tall, dark young man, made small talk with me while another officer drove. He asked a few questions about me and my trip to Hagerstown. I guessed that non-residents were slightly suspect in their little town. I smiled and complied.

Being an inquisitive investigator myself, and knowing I was on the balls of my ass with my boss, I kept asking questions to fulfill my dual mission of interviewing Lolita and learning more about the murders of 1923. Bits and pieces were being sewn together like a patchwork quilt as I gathered information.

Officer Robert was helpful and considerate with my questions and lack of knowledge about the location of key sites in town. I wrote various locations down, such as the library, hotels, bar, diner, and nursing home.

Officer Robert also suggested that I visit the local newspaper, where they might be able to shed some light on the historic murders of 1923. As for Lolita, the officer advised me that he had seen her close up a few times while visiting his aunt in the home. He said that Lolita was like a special celebrity of the home, not just for her advanced age, but because she was admired for her vast knowledge about how to live a life to the fullest extent.

Built in 1914, the Hagerstown Hospital was a large brick complex that consisted of three stories. The officers left me in the emergency room waiting area as they joined some other officers and walked right through the admittance entranceway. I sat in the empty waiting room reviewing and adding to the many notes in my small notebook. The once-boring assignment of reporting about some old person in a nursing home had turned into an intriguing and mysterious case of a very unique 110-year-old, well-respected woman, and an unsolved multiple murder case that had run out of leads long ago. Adding to the mystery was that someone had attacked Brian at the gas station minutes after I'd asked him about those murders.

The ringing cell phone showed the face and name of the ballbuster editor of the *Washington Gazette*. I knew I had to answer the phone, although I dreaded talking to Harold, as I was already skating on very thin ice with him.

"Insane asylum," I said, answering the phone with some humor to lighten Harold's mood, I hoped. It didn't work.

"Listen, smartass," Harold snapped. "I want an update on your progress."

"Progress? Are you kidding? I just got here a short while ago!"

"Do I sound like I'm kidding? You're on a short leash here, boy. I'm watching you. Get some action, and fast!"

"Hey, boss! I almost got shot in a shoot-out a few minutes ago at . . . ."

"Now that's a story I could use, you getting shot up."

"Seriously, boss, there were shots fired at a gas station where I had just filled up my car, and the attendant I was interviewing got hurt. I'm in the waiting room of the hospital to see if he is okay."

"How's the Lolita story going, numb-nuts?" he screamed, uncaring.

"Don't worry, I'm working on it," I snapped.

"Don't tell me not to worry. You've been totally useless for months now, and this is your final shot to keep your job."

"Boss, I feel real good about this Lolita story so far, but it's brewing into something even bigger: the unsolved Hagerstown murders of 1923. I will have a much bigger story for you, but it will take longer."

"Don't think of coming back without an award-winning story, or else you'll wish that gunshot had hit you!" He slammed the phone in my ear.

"Asshole! Potato head!" I shouted, out loud, before I saw the police officer approaching out of the corner of my eye.

"What's your problem?" he glared at me. The officer stared at me with piercing, cold blue eyes. He was slim, about five-seven, sporting a marine-style crew cut, along with a face that made him appear tough.

"Oh, hi." I smiled. "I, uh, was just talking to my boss at the . . . ."

"Do you have any identification?" he asked as he stood over me, glaring.

I noticed that his nametag read "Sgt. Thomas Pawler." I stood slowly and reached for my wallet.

He peered at my driver's license then looked me up and down with expressionless eyes. "What business do you have in our town, Mr. Gerhani?"

"I am a reporter for the *Washington Gazette*, and I am doing a story on Lolita Croome, the oldest woman ever to live in Hagerstown."

"Sure, you are," he said sarcastically. "Really, now, specifically, what are you doing here, and when do you plan to leave?"

"Sergeant, I really am here on that assignment; you can check with my paper on that."

"Gerhani, you know we don't like your kind here!" He smirked a sick little grin. "You pencil pushers bring too much attention to our quiet little town. Your kind of people start vicious rumors and give us bad press." He stared at me long and hard.

"Bad press?" I said in defense of myself, not caring that he already disliked me. "I'm here to draw positive attention to a bright spot in your town, a 110-year-old woman who has survived all kinds of risks since the year she was born in 1903. That's an amazing story for your little town. By the way, Lolita lived through the historic murders of 1923. I'm trying to research the unsolved murders of that year. Do you have any knowledge of those murders that you can share with me?" I asked, not caring that he already disliked me.

"Yeah, well that's the problem," he snapped. "That's what I mean about stirring up a hornet's nest." He glared at me again. "Listen here, you little shit, stop asking so many questions, and just go back to the cesspool of reporters you came from."

"What?"

"You heard me. All of you reporters are nothing but leeches!" His eyes got bigger, like he was just itching for a fight.

I wasn't that stupid, although many people might argue that claim, especially as of late.

"Well, I won't be here much longer, Sergeant," I countered, trying to get on with my life.

"You're going to the station house anyway. The captain wants to talk with you."

"The captain?"

"Yes, Captain Joel Krolm. He's running the investigation of the shooting at Wally's place. Maybe the gunman was after you."

"Maybe." I smiled a big grin.

It was thirty minutes before Brian walked through the emergency room doors into the waiting area. He smiled at me as he explained that he had a concussion and had needed five stitches in the back of his head. But he didn't care; as he put it, "I've had plenty of stitches in my life; when I was a kid I was always whacking everything!" He had to take it easy for a week because of the concussion.

I felt somewhat responsible that he'd been clobbered, although I knew it had nothing to do with me. But still, I had been asking him all those questions, and he was so excited about the line of work I was in. Maybe he could have dealt better with the gunman if he hadn't been so focused on getting back to me so that we could continue our conversation. Maybe if I hadn't been in the bathroom so long, I could have helped stop the crazed gunman. But then I realized that everything had happened as it was meant to. After all, I could have wound up being shot or killed if I had been a few feet closer. Maybe even that would get me fired by the gorilla of a boss I have.

My hands shook for a few seconds as I contemplated being shot dead. My mind played back the sounds of the gunshots and the ricochet of bullets. Sometimes death is only inches away from us, and most of us don't realize just how precious life is.

Brian was hurried off to a private area where he was to be interviewed by the police. We said our goodbyes, and he told me that his older sister would be meeting him at the hospital to give him a ride home and to watch him closely for the next twenty-four hours per the doctor's orders.

Sergeant Pawler disappeared with Brian after he instructed two young officers to deliver me to the Hagerstown Police Station to meet with Captain Krolm. It was apparent that Sergeant Pawler would be interviewing Brian. I felt sorry for him, knowing Pawler's lack of sympathy for anyone or anything. That cop was a real hard-ass.

The same two officers who had driven me to the hospital drove me to the police station. It was a fifteen-minute trip, as the traffic was its worst in that area. Once again, I had this weird feeling sitting in the rear of a police cruiser. Officer Carl Moeller, a redheaded two-hundred-plus-pound young guy of about five-foot-seven drove while Officer Robert Cianci and I discussed Brian, the shooting at the station, and the killings of 1923.

"I made a call to my grandfather for you about the murders of '23," Robert said. "He told me that for a few years there was much speculation that a doctor working out of the hospital was to blame. I believe he was a surgeon, never married, a little eccentric, and a little weird for the 1920s. Then there was a local pharmacist, a middle-aged man, who came under suspicion. Years later, the pharmacist was mugged and nearly killed. It was believed one of the dead girls' family members tried to kill the pharmacist. But, of course, no one was ever charged for his murder. The case has been dead for many years, and most of the people from that time are dead."

The Hagerstown Police Station was located at 50 North Burhaus Boulevard. As we pulled up in front of the station house, I looked closely at the very old structure. It appeared to be around two-hundred years old, a tall, red brick building with heavy ten-foot-tall wooden doors. The property was protected by a heavy, old-fashioned cast-iron fence.

I marveled, as I always do, at the history that was surely a part of the structure, as I pictured people of the area some hundred years earlier. The Lolita assignment finally rang clear with me. Lolita would have been a ten-year-old a hundred years ago.

As I entered the station house, I observed a décor that didn't seem to have changed in many years. There were old-fashioned gray metal desks, dark lighting, drab wall colors, and embossed metal block ceilings from many years ago.

Only a few workers were present. I asked the girl at the front desk for Captain Krolm, explaining that he was expecting me. She left, and I waited several minutes for her to return. "The captain will see you now, sir. Please follow me," she said, as she led the way to a room at the end of a long hallway. I followed the slim woman of twenty-five with freckles and long red hair that hung to the small of her back. I was almost tempted to ask her what kind of shampoo she used to result in the silkiest hair I had ever seen, but decided against it.

As I passed through the doorway, I noticed the door plaque that read "Captain Joel S. Krolm." He rose quickly with a big friendly smile. He was a hulk of a man at six-three and about two-eighty, with uncharacteristically long hair. He was around forty-five with a round, reddish face.

"Hi, I'm Captain Krolm. Thanks for coming in today," he smiled.

"Captain," I said as we shook hands, "glad to be of any assistance I can."

"Please." He pointed to a wooden chair in front of his large, old gray, metal desk. "Let's cut to the chase, shall we? What business do you have here, Mr. Gerhani?" It was a direct question, but his face was friendly and open.

"As I told your sergeant, I'm with the newspaper, the *Washington Gazette*. I'm on assignment in Hagerstown, doing a story on one of your most famous citizens, Lolita Croome."

"Ah, yes, Lolita. She's a real gem—a wonderful testament to this great town of ours. But when will you be leaving?" he asked impatiently.

"I may not," I laughed. "I like this old town."

"Yeah, right! Did you get a good look at the suspect?"

"Not really. I had just exited the gas station restroom when all hell broke loose."

"What did you see?"

"I saw a man with long, dark hair, and then a dark sports car tearing out. I later learned it was a Mustang, souped up some."

The captain said I might be needed to look at a lineup later, as they had apprehended the suspect a few minutes ago and were booking him as we spoke. The suspect's name was Billy Blaine, an out-of-towner with a criminal past.

The captain and I spoke for five minutes more, and I asked him about the 1923 murder case. He was a little defensive when I asked why there were no leads. He explained that no unsolved case in Hagerstown was ever closed, and asked why I should be so interested in that case in particular.

"I just figured that since Lolita Croome is old enough to have lived through those murders, it would be interesting to revisit the case as part of my story. It would make a nice story." He didn't appreciate my idea of running a story on the murders, but was cordial when I asked for some assistance in background information. He allowed the front desk girl, Loretta, the redhead, to help me do a bit of research in the back-office records room.

I was allowed to take some notes but no photocopies, and no files were to leave the room. A security camera was on me the whole time anyway, I noticed.

It was ten minutes into our reviewing of the files when we both almost jumped out of our skins at the sound of explosions and screams. Loretta yelled, "Get under the table, now! Get under the table! That was gunfire!"

"Shit! Not again!" I yelled as I hit my head hard on the edge of the table.

Loretta crawled over to the door and locked it, then crawled quickly back under the long table. We listened to more gunfire; there must have been around twelve to fifteen loud explosions along with screaming and a lot of yelling. There was a lot of movement and then a man yelling, "Officer down! Officer down! Get an ambulance, now! We need an ambulance, now!"

Loretta whispered so low I could hardly hear her. "Stay perfectly still. Don't say a word. Don't cough, sneeze, or move a muscle."

All I did was nod, as we were sharing a space no bigger than six feet by three. As I breathed in slowly, all I could think of was what a nice fragrance Loretta's hair was giving off. A woman's hair can sometimes smell so nice—not overwhelming, just nice. Then I quickly snapped back to reality as I heard other voices, all at the same time. All I could make out was someone yelling, "He's been shot, and the prisoner has escaped! All points, the prisoner has escaped!"

Loretta looked at me as I stared at her with a blank expression, then she shook her head. We stayed put for a full five minutes until another clerk, a woman, knocked at the door and said, "Loretta, it's Gail. It's all clear out here. It's safe now. You can come out, sweetie. It's okay now."

"Gail," Loretta shouted, "what's my favorite coffee drink?"

"Caramel macchiato grande, Starbucks, with extra caramel!" Gail said in rapid response.

With that, Loretta quickly climbed out from under the table and opened the door. She looked back at me with a glance of reassurance that all was safe, and I quickly scrambled up, gathered my research of the '23 murder investigation, and tried to see what had happened.

An upset and very embarrassed Captain Krolm explained. "It appears that Billy Blaine, after being fingerprinted and having his mug shot taken, said he needed to relieve himself. Officer Carmine Flund, as is customary, accompanied the suspect to the men's room, and somehow Blaine overpowered the officer. Blaine then shot the officer in the leg, puncturing a main artery pretty severely, and escaped in a squad car out front. He fired several shots, and the officer remaining on duty, Dooney, returned fire and tried to give chase, but returned to care for Officer

Flund, who was down. The paramedics are attending to our officer now and have stopped the bleeding. It appears that the bullet went clear through Flund's leg, and he should be fine in a few days.

"It is a shame, though," the captain continued. "Officer Flund was only months away from retiring. It could have been much worse, and usually is, after an officer's gun is wrestled away by a prisoner." The captain shook his head in disgust.

I felt for the captain and the officer, but wondered if someone had put some kind of curse on me. *Maybe*, I thought, *my boss is behind this; that man has a heart of stone. Maybe he did some voodoo on me. Maybe he had a doll and was sticking needles in it.* I wondered what the hell could possibly be in store for me, as I had only begun the stinking assignment hours earlier. There was no way I would call in and report this latest turn of events to the "editor from hell," for surely he would fire me on the spot, somehow convinced that the entire fiasco of the day thus far was all my doing.

Loretta told me that the Hagerstown library, on West Washington Street, would have microfiche about the murders of '23. The library, according to Loretta, was only ten minutes away, and it had just been renovated for the first time in many years. She also told me that the only newspaper in town, the *Hagerstown New News*, was only ten minutes away in the opposite direction. The newspaper had been around for over one hundred years and was still located in the very spot where it had been erected way back then. Loretta said, "I'll call my cousin Sylvia, who works there. I'll tell her about you."

We watched as the paramedics wheeled out Officer Flund, who was clearly in a lot of pain. An officer accompanied him, along with the two medics. I could see a lot of blood splattered on the officer, as well as his blood-soaked, wrapped right leg, as he slowly passed by. Captain Krolm spoke some words of encouragement to the officer as he was wheeled quickly past him.

It had been quite an eventful day thus far, and I was craving a few strong drinks. And just as quickly as the pictures of the drinks entered my mind, they were replaced with the picture of my crazed boss-man, Glavin, his head beet-red as he screamed some obscene words and threatened to fire my "sorry ass" once again. I decided the drinks at the bar would have to wait. I closed my eyes, hoping Glavin's image would be wiped out of my mind, at least for the time being. He was like a bad dream, the kind of nightmare you wake up from all wet with perspiration, the kind of nightmare that is so believable that you just can't shake it, a nightmare that you keep reliving over again.

Even though my hands were still shaking, and had been since the gas station shoot-'em-up, I needed a few cups of strong coffee. I knew the caffeine rush wouldn't calm my nerves like alcohol would do, but alcohol at this time would be like suicide for my assignment.

Captain Krolm escorted me out of the station house, clearly a very pissed-off man. "You know we will recapture that son of a bitch very shortly, don't you?"

"Sure," I said. "I'm sure you will, Captain."

"But in the meantime, be alert about your surroundings. The suspect is armed and very dangerous. He would have no problem killing anyone who gets in his way. And if he sees you nosing around, he may recognize you or your car from the gas station and try to take you out permanently. Eliminate witnesses, you know?"

"Uh, I guess. I'm already shell-shocked, though, and I've only been around your town for a few hours now."

"Well, I can't say that I'll miss you when you leave," he said with a friendly smile. "But when will you be leaving?"

"I might stay, Captain. Loretta and I hit it off big under the table back there a while ago. We might get hitched!" I laughed.

"Yeah, right. Smart ass!" He smirked.

"See you around," I said as I walked past him toward the door.

"I hope not! Stop asking so many questions. I'll have my officers keep an eye on you, anyway, just for good measure."

The wind was blowing strong, but the sun was shining bright and the afternoon had warmed considerably. I looked around the perimeter of the station house; it was like a ghost town. There wasn't an officer to be found. No doubt they were all in frantic pursuit of one Billy Blaine. No matter what town or city you're in, there's no getting off easy when you shoot at, wound, or kill a local police officer. They will hunt you down to the ends of the earth. Billy Blaine would be caught, there was no doubt about it, but what else might he do before he was recaptured? He was capable of killing, and he might not be willing to be taken alive. Like a cornered rat, he might strike out. I would heed the captain's advice and be very aware of my surroundings. After all, I had had enough action for a lifetime already.

CHAPTER FIVE

I t was almost 4:30 p.m. when I pulled into the parking lot of Millie's Diner on East Washington Street, a nice, tree-lined street in an old neighborhood. The trees were huge in height and circumference, and appeared to be oak trees.

I wasn't due to tour the nursing home until the next day, and I had an interview set up with Lolita shortly thereafter. My agenda for the rest of today was to get something to eat, nose around some more, go to the library, which was open late, and hit a bar to have a few brews, pretty much in that order. I decided I would only have a couple of drinks. All I needed at this point was to get bombed, arrested, and then released to a representative of the newspaper—and then get canned for good. No, I would be on my best behavior no matter how much it killed me. I pictured myself in the back of a police car, but this time cockeyed drunk. Glavin would have my ass for sure.

Millie's Diner stood directly across the street from the Hagerstown Home for the Aged where Lolita lived. The nursing home was a one-story structure of red brick. As I pulled up the street, I had noticed that the home was U-shaped and had a huge property. The grounds were landscaped beautifully and trimmed meticulously.

As I looked over the diner, it appeared from the front to be retro-style, but unlike other diners I had seen, this one was much deeper in size.

I noticed from my view of the side of the building that some years ago, a big addition had been put on the diner. The large neon sign out front read "Millie's, est. 1930, serving the best pancakes in MD."

I laughed at the boast about pancakes, and wondered how many diners across the country claimed to have the best pancakes around.

I once claimed that I was the best lover in America; the only problem was, no one else ever believed it.

The front of the old diner was graced with gray stone, which ran up some four feet from the ground, with plate-glass windows that spanned the length of the building on all sides but the back. A red cloth canopy shielded the windows from the sun. It appeared that the owners had converted what had once been an old-fashioned all-metal diner to a stone and wood front, making it look more like a traditional modern restaurant.

I later learned that Millie's was named after its original owner, Mildred Farner, who started the diner with her husband Clarence in 1930. The diner had remained in the Farner family until it was sold in 1980 to its present owner, Sylvester Trylan, son of the minister of the largest church in Hagerstown. Sy had been the head cook since purchasing the diner. Millie's was a Hagerstown landmark, and many residents frequented it regularly. I parked in the diner's huge lot.

My stomach was churning, making me wonder if it was more than just a matter of hunger. Maybe being around gunfire had set off stomach acid. Gunfire has strange effects on a body. *This might just be the assignment from hell*, I thought as I glanced around cautiously. After all, Blaine, the crazed gunman who had thought nothing of shooting up a police officer and the station, was still running loose somewhere. I thought about Billy Blaine. I wondered what drove young men to perform such stupid and destructive acts. Did they actually plan things out or just wing it? Hopefully, Billy was far, far away by now. But then again, he had already demonstrated that he really didn't have any brains. I felt sorry for him in a strange way, mostly because I realized that people make stupid decisions then compound the problem with drastic additional choices.

The attractive-looking diner was as impressive on the inside as it was on the outside. There were the old-fashioned stools at the counter that diners of the past were known for, and huge, plush booths throughout the large, open space, and what appeared to be a large room used for parties.

The hostess greeted me and sat me in a booth that was set for four. I quickly ordered a coffee and dialed my newspaper in Washington. I wanted to make sure that I was still on to meet with Lolita the next day. I was told to meet her at one p.m. sharp, right after lunch. Harold's assistant, Gloria, reminded me that my job was on the line and that Harold wanted routine updates. *Gloria's a bitch on wheels!* I groused to myself. *Everyone thinks that she and the boss are sleeping together, but sometimes I wonder about that. Who would want him?*

Gloria had that librarian look: thick glasses, long hair, lots of makeup, heels much too high, and skirts too short for her age. She was clearly trying too hard. And her bitchiness, snappy answers, and lack of any personality made her less attractive. She always seemed mad at the world; it was no wonder she was divorced.

Gloria told me that Lolita was known to love homemade pistachio ice cream, which the nursing home rarely stocked, and fresh-made chocolates. She also told me again about an old diary Lolita sometimes shares with guests that covers an entire year of her life from the 1920s. I made some more quick notes as Gloria spoke. She asked me if I would like to speak with the boss.

"Harold?" I asked sarcastically. "I would rather have a triple root canal without any Novocain."

"I'll tell him you had to run quickly . . ."

"Yeah, into oncoming traffic!" I laughed.

Gloria hung the phone up rather hard. I had to chuckle at that. *At least she didn't try to suck up to me.*

The waitress—Kristen, according to her name tag—returned for my order. "What'll it be, sweetie?" She smiled at me with perfectly straight, white teeth.

"How's the meatloaf special? Honestly, is it worth it?"

"Oh, sure! That's one of my favorites!" She beamed. Her hazel eyes shined as she smiled invitingly, waiting for my approval. I waited, looked her over. She was all of twenty-one, with long brown hair, naturally curling a little. She must have been about six feet tall and was very thin; she looked like she could use a couple of home-cooked meals herself.

"Kristen, I'll take your advice."

"Oh, you'll love it!" she said as she rushed off, looking like she had hit the jackpot. She returned quickly with a pot of coffee. As she poured me a refill, she asked, "Are you a writer? I see you taking notes in that book."

"No, I'm a reporter from Washington, doing a story on Lolita, the most senior citizen of Hagerstown."

"Oh, wow! I don't know her real well, but I've heard of her. A reporter? Really?"

"Really."

"Like television reporter, cameras, action?"

"No, not that exciting. Just boring newspapers."

"Still!" She giggled.

I smiled and said, "Kristen, have you ever heard anything about the old Hagerstown murders from 1923?"

"No, but I know someone who is an expert about anything Hagerstown," she said as she rushed off all happy, screaming out as she hurried into the kitchen, "Sy, Sy, we have a real live reporter here! Do you know anything about the famous murders of 1923?" Her voice trailed off. Kristen was young, innocent, a little bit of an airhead, but genuine and likable. And now the entire diner knew that I was a reporter and that I was looking into a famous case from 1923. I felt the eyes of the Hagerstown locals looking at me, studying me as if I might be famous from television. I tried to concentrate on my notebook, reviewing and modifying my notes. I saw two black women at a table close to mine staring intently at me for a solid minute. I find it amazing how a person can tell when someone is staring at them, even though they aren't looking at the person staring. It's as if the person staring has eyes like laser beams.

I looked up at the two women and smiled politely. One of them popped up out of her seat and came over. She was a big-breasted, big-boned woman. When she smiled shyly and said "Hello," I saw a gold front tooth.

"Oh, hi," I said.

"I overheard you speaking with the young one about the old one, Lolita. We work at the nursing home," she said in a heavy Jamaican accent. "We know her." She waved for her friend to come over as she helped herself to a seat in my booth. "Come on here, Nancy," she yelled over to the other one, while clearly speaking with a heavy Jamaican accent.

Nancy rushed over with a big excited smile. "Hi, there," she said with a nervous laugh, her accent matching that of her friend.

"We are food service workers at the home. I'm Mary," the first woman said. "We have known Lolita for many years."

"Oh, great! You want to join me and share some stories?" I asked, now more excited as I felt I could finally get some insight into the mysterious old woman the whole town seemed to know.

Nancy smiled. "We ate already, but we were just going to have some coffee."

"The Wise One," Mary said. "Miss Lolita, as we call her, is known as the Wise One. She is very much respected by all the residents, and even the residents' family members. She has been there many years now, ever since she fell and broke her hip, and got pneumonia. Must be over ten years now, huh, Nancy?" She looked at her co-worker, who had a close-cut haircut and a gold tooth like Mary's. Nancy was also heavyset, but shorter than Mary.

"Yes, be sure of it. Miss Lolita is the Wise One. She is always sought after for advice of all sorts: love, marital issues, job problems, and so much more."

"I gather that Miss Lolita has all her marbles?"

"Be sure of that!" Mary giggled. "She is so sharp that no one can put anything over on her! She wins all the trivia contests at the home."

"And stubborn," Nancy chimed in. "If there is a meal Miss Lolita doesn't care for, you can stand on your head, but she won't take a taste of it! She knows what she wants, and she won't settle for less!"

"Oh, yes. I heard that Miss Lolita likes ice cream, and in particular, pistachio; is that right?"

"She loves pistachio ice cream," Nancy confirmed. "Always has. But it is very rare that anyone brings some, and we don't offer it at the home. You see, most residents want only vanilla or chocolate."

"I'd like to bring her some," I responded.

"You know," Nancy said, "the very best ice cream around—and Lolita loves theirs—is from the farm. They make all their ice cream fresh from scratch." She gave me the name and location of the farm, which sold only organic fruits and vegetables, and which also specialized in dairy products, including the freshest ice cream in Maryland.

Mary and Nancy both departed, wishing me well with my interviews with Lolita and her family. They had not been able to shed much light on the 1923 Hagerstown murders, but told me all about an older resident, Josephine, who volunteered at the nursing home and came to Millie's every night for dinner. Perhaps she would show up while I was there. They said she was born and raised in Hagerstown.

Kristen brought my meatloaf dinner to the table, and she sat down across from me as I began to eat. She stared at me and smiled with big bright eyes. "I think you have a very exciting job, Mr. Lou. You get to see all kinds of famous people all the time."

"Not really, Kristen. It's not like that at all. There's an awful lot of ground work, investigative reporting, and mostly it is boring. I write news stories about a great many things and people, and some of the stories aren't even interesting. But it's a job. Then again, some of it is quite satisfying."

"Well, I like it!" Kristen laughed. "Oh, by the way, I have some information on those old killings. It seems that Sy does remember a couple of things he heard while growing up."

"I see," I said, as I reached for my notebook.

"Yes. He said when he was growing up, he heard rumors that two men were suspected in the murders years earlier. Sy tells me that one of them was a young doctor who worked at the Hagerstown Hospital. He wasn't a married man; he was a playboy type, a heavy partier, a good dancer, and he had a different girl each night. The second person of interest was an older pharmacist who was married but had no children."

Just at that moment, I saw a middle-aged man come out of the kitchen, looking my way. He was taller than six feet, slim, with a dark mustache, crew cut, and piercing dark eyes. I asked Kristen if she had to get back to work.

"Oh, that's just Big Sy there. He's owned Millie's forever. I can stay another minute. Where was I? Oh, yeah, the pharmacist. It seems a couple of years after the murders he was mugged real bad, almost killed, and forced to retire and move away. He died a few years later." She stood up and headed quickly back to the kitchen, calling loudly over her shoulder, "Neither of the two men was ever charged," she yelled a little loudly as she was running back to the kitchen.

Sy gave me one last long look as if he were studying me, and then he disappeared into the kitchen after Kristen. The meatloaf wasn't bad. The mashed potatoes were a little lumpy, but the extra butter I added helped a lot.

It was ten minutes later when an older woman walked in and came over to my table. "You must be Lou. Mary told me to stop by and speak with you. I'm Josephine Cleary."

"So nice to meet you," I said as I stood to shake her hand. "I heard about your many years with the home."

"It feels like my whole life I've worked at the nursing home. I've loved every minute of it, and made so many friends over the years. I even volunteer now after taking my retirement." She had a loving motherly look about her.

"So, you must know everything there is to know about the nursing home, its residents, and, in particular, Lolita."

Josephine was a slim woman of about eighty. She walked with a cane made of what appeared to be the rough limb of a tree. She explained that her husband of more than fifty-five years had died a few years ago, and that's when she had retired. But she soon realized that she needed to volunteer at the home because she was just too bored and missed the interaction with the residents. She explained that she also ate every day at the diner, mostly out of habit, but also because she didn't like to eat alone at home. Josephine stressed how lonely life was when a spouse was suddenly gone from one's home. "I could swear my husband speaks to me every so often."

When I gently directed the conversation to Lolita, Josephine said with a big smile, "She is the most amazing patient in the home. I think she is the smartest person I have ever known—Miss Lolita. Everyone calls her Miss Lolita."

"The Wise One?"

"Absolutely! Miss Lolita is very wise, understanding, and compassionate. She has a philosophy she lives by, and she even has it printed and hanging on the wall above her bed at the home. And for the past twelve years or so that she has been there, I have seen it almost every day. It reads, 'When it's all over, all said and done, what impact will my life have had on this world?'"

In my mind I quickly played back the words Josephine had said and responded, "What an amazing, deep statement that is," I replied. "Such a great motivator to live one's life to the fullest." I quickly jotted it down.

"Exactly! Miss Lolita has many more statements like that, and in the last twelve years, I must have heard them all."

"So, Lolita is doing well for one hundred and ten?"

"Yes, she is doing fabulous!" Josephine smiled. "Oh, sure, she can't get around without someone pushing her in her wheelchair. And, yes, she is considered legally blind. You have to get up real close to her before she can make out who you are. But, really, for one hundred and ten, she's doing remarkably well."

"It is amazing," I said. "I know no one even close to that age. It really is quite a special milestone. That's why the newspaper sent me."

"The world will finally get to know Miss Lolita," Josephine said with a happy sigh and a big smile. "They should do a movie on her."

"Speaking of stories that would make great movies, what do you know about the historic murders of Hagerstown in 1923?"

"Oh, yes, the famous murders of 1923. What a sad time for Hagerstown and all of Maryland. It was many years before people finally gave up trying for a solution to the mystery. There were suspects, both in the minds of the authorities and in the minds of the citizens of Hagerstown. One was a local doctor, one was a pharmacist, and one was a retired police sergeant."

"A police sergeant?" I perked up and began writing again. "Tell me more about that suspect, Josephine."

"Well, the talk from many years ago—and that's all I can recall is talk, because I was born ten years after the murders—but the talk was that the police sergeant committed suicide shortly after the second girl's murder. It was thought for sure that the police sergeant was the killer. And it remained that way until the next girl was murdered in the same fashion as the other two."

"So why would he take his own life?"

"Well, it came out that he had a terminal disease of some sort and was almost broke. So he spared his family the anguish of a long, drawn-out death and leaving them in poverty from spending the rest of his money on medical care. So he took his life. The family collected his pension and a sizable life insurance policy. And all these years later . . . . In fact, it's the ninetieth anniversary this year, and they never caught the person or persons responsible for the murders of those poor young women."

"Do you know anything about the girls who were murdered?" I asked, my notebook at the ready.

"It is so long ago, but because of the anniversary of the murders, the story has been getting a little attention lately. The girls were all high school students. Two of the young ladies went to the all-girls school, The Hagerstown High School for Girls. The other girl went to Hagerstown Coles High, a mixed boy-girl high school.

"One girl's father owned an automobile repair shop in town. She was the only one of the three who had her head cut off, God bless her!" She made the sign of the cross.

"This killer was insane!" I replied.

"Worse than insane: sadistic, heartless, and much like the cold-blooded terrorists of today. But for 1923, this kind of butchering was unheard of. The entire state was in mourning for these young women." She now had tears in her eyes.

"Please try to remember, Josephine," I said after waiting a minute. "I need to know more."

"Well, the first girl—she was only fifteen—her head was found on the side of the road that was usually traveled by students on their way to school each day, and her body was found a month later in a car at the town's Chevrolet dealership. One of the killer's trademarks was to cut the bodies up and leave a piece in a prominent spot to be found exactly one month after each girl was murdered."

"What a sick bastard!" I said. "And especially brutal for the Twenties. What could have possibly been the killer's motive?"

"Many law enforcement people worked on the case," Josephine said, shaking her head. "The FBI was involved. The place was swarming with police. The few suspects were quickly discounted, and after a number of years, Hagerstown slowly recovered from that very depressing time."

"The three girls were killed over what time frame?" I asked.

"The first one, Lori, was killed on February tenth. The second, Ingram, on June tenth, and the third, Amanda, on October tenth. The second girl was seventeen. Her body was floating in the pond at the same time they found her arm sticking out of the flowerpot at the entranceway to her school. The third girl was only fourteen. Her father had died the year before from a boating accident. Her mother had to clean the homes of rich people to care for her family. They found the girl's remains one month later at the movie house, propped up in one of the seats. Her arm was found sticking straight out of the ground at the local park. No one would let their children walk to school alone or walk home alone. Keep in mind, this was in 1923, when everyone left their windows open wide and their doors unlocked. Family and friends would routinely just drop in on one another's homes. No need for locks. No fear of strangers, as everyone basically knew one another. Suddenly all that changed."

"So, Josephine, any ideas how I can get the latest scoop on any new leads or anything recent that might be related to the murders?"

"Well, I have some friends at the newspaper, the *Hagerstown New News*. I'll make a few calls for you tonight. You know, the *New News* is the oldest paper in Maryland; it was started in 1890. It's over on Summit Avenue. You can ask for Harriet Newman; she's been there forever. She'll help you. And I'll fill her in about your story on Lolita and your interest in 1923."

CHAPTER SIX

Harriet Newman had deep blue eyes, a short haircut with bangs, and a plump, roundish frame. She looked to be in her late seventies. She had a warm, pleasant personality as she greeted me.

"Josephine told me about you," she said with a welcoming smile. "We have a boring and quiet town, so you are a welcome diversion for us here."

"It's been far from boring so far."

"Well, the newspapers here don't have much to write about. Hagerstown has the lowest crime rate in Maryland. You'd be surprised what we consider a story these days—at least compared to the big cities like DC and New York."

We spoke about the nursing home I was to visit the next day, and we spoke more about the town, the historic movie theater I wanted to visit, and Miss Lolita's amazing longevity. Harriet introduced me to a girl of around nineteen, named Julie, in the newsroom, which was nothing more than a small office. In fact, the newspaper building was old and quite small overall. Julie was as slim as they come and had long, blonde hair and dark eyes.

"Harriet told me you were looking for old news stories about the 1923 murders and Lolita's press of late."

I took plenty of notes but didn't uncover too much useful information that I didn't already know from my own research and interviews. Julie, as with almost everyone I had met in Hagerstown, was extremely friendly and helpful.

I did see some current pictures of Miss Lolita, in a story their paper had run on her nearing her 110th birthday. Miss Lolita did look old, as I had expected, but rather good for her age, although I had no one to compare her to. She wore glasses with thick Coke-bottle lenses, had all of her hair, and a few extra pounds on her. The pictures depicted a smiling, happy-looking person. I'd venture to say that Miss Lolita could pass for a woman of eighty-five, and as for the few extra pounds, I had recently read that a few extra pounds can add to longevity. There must be some secrets there; I would try to find out from the wonder woman herself when I interviewed her for the first time.

Julie was able to pull up pictures of the three young women from the 1923 murders. Lori Gellate, Ingram Stuart, and Amanda Harrison all looked so young, so innocent. And all I could think as I looked over the various pictures from the many news stories was that these girls could have been anyone's sisters or daughters. How sad. How sick. What a waste of three young lives that never got the chance to shine; young women who never got the opportunity to forge a life or a career for themselves. Sad that these young women never got to be wives, mothers, grandmothers. I felt mad as well as sad, and drained of all energy as I sat there reading about the taking of their young lives in such a sadistic manner. And then to think that the killer or killers got away with it just sickened me.

I could read no more. I could take no more notes. I had had my fill of sadness, but I had a newfound sense of responsibility to find at least some new clue yet uncovered. I felt too close to these girls now, and could only imagine the sense of grief that Hagerstown and the whole state of Maryland must have felt in 1923 and for many years after that.

I wondered how some people could turn into human monsters. We are all born pure, loving, and without prejudice. At what point in a person's life does his personality abruptly—or gradually—change, turning him into a vicious animal, willing to tear people to pieces? When does that once-pure creation from God decide he can take another life that was also given by God? What really disturbed me the most was that ruthless killers of this sort didn't seem even a little scared about dying one day and having to answer to the highest judge of all. Don't they believe in God?

As I exited the news building, the day's activity and stress finally hit me. I was exhausted, mentally more than physically. My legs felt like they had heavy weights attached, and my back felt like I had just played a full game of football against the Dallas Cowboys.

The air was warm and breezy as I crossed the street to where my car was parked. My mind was working overtime in calculations and thoughts of the entire day, of murder victims, of Lolita, and my newfound acquaintances who had been so helpful in my investigation.

As I crossed the empty and dead-quiet street, a dark car suddenly swerved toward me with a screech of tires that shocked me to attention. My eyes quickly focused on the vehicle, tires smoking as it raced right at me. The split second I had to think convinced me that I was a dead man. My first reaction was to run, but tired feet cannot outrun a car gunned full-out with a head of steam.

Before I could move a muscle, I heard a loud slapping sound of hands, arms, body; I saw bright lights . . . and then total blackness.

It's amazing how fast a calculation the human brain can make in a life-or-death situation, convincing the person in that tenth of a second that their chances of surviving their current severe situation are almost zero percent. My situation was no different. My mind came up with me hitting a half-billion-dollar lottery faster than surviving that oncoming car.

The darkness quickly turned bright, and I saw my mother and deceased father as they looked when they had just been married. They were smiling at me as they were illuminated in very bright light, as if a spotlight was shining on them. All I could do was stare. No words were spoken; there was just brightness, happiness, calmness, and peace—perfectly quiet peace. *Heavenly,* I thought, and then, *Me? Heaven? Now? No way! But if this isn't heaven, what is it?*

We all hear about tunnels of bright light, of relatives greeting the new arrivals, and some convincing the person who's near death that it isn't their time yet and they must go back. I waited, but there was no sign, no communication, no tunnel, and no movement. Just peace and quiet like I'd never experienced before.

Then suddenly, the bright light grew brighter, blinding, as my parents disappeared and were replaced with just pure light. I wasn't scared or worried about hell or heaven. I didn't want to wake up, or go back home, or do anything but bask in the glorious bright light and perfect silence—a silence I had always yearned for but had never found, a silence that solved all the problems of the world. *Maybe this is it!* I thought, hoping that heaven was waiting for me.

But suddenly I heard a noise that shattered the silence, though I couldn't decipher the sounds or even where they were coming from. They grew louder, and the light grew intensely bright in my eyes. Louder still, a man's voice spoke: "Okay . . . it's okay . . . ."

My eyes slowly opened and focused on a man with a beard—a doctor. I was groggy. I stared at him and at the bright light he was shining in my eyes. "Welcome back, Lou," he said, as he shined the light into and away from one eye and then the other.

"You're doing fine now," he said.

Slowly, I looked around at the hospital bed and room I was in, and just then, pain shot from the back of my head, and I let out a groan.

"Yes, you have a nice big bump on your head," he said. "But you'll be fine. My name is Dr. Frederickson."

He must have been at least seventy-five, tall, slim, with a full head of white hair and a beard. His glasses gave off a reflection from the overhead fluorescents.

"You've been unconscious for a little over thirty minutes now. Do you remember anything, son?"

"All I remember is a car, a fast car," I said, and my voice cracked a bit out of weakness.

"It was a hit-and-run."

"Oh, great," I muttered in disbelief.

Dr. Frederickson assured me that all my vitals were fine, that the X-rays all were negative, and that I had only a slight concussion. He suggested that I remain for the night as a precaution. I would be monitored closely and released in the morning.

My head felt like it was split in two, and my hands and arms were scratched up a bit. The doctor put me on some pain medication for discomfort, and then he left the room.

A few minutes later, the police captain dropped by to check on me. Just as I saw him approach, I felt the back of my head. I had a baseball-sized bump that hurt like hell. The doctor's pain medication hadn't had a chance to kick in yet. I knew I needed a tall, strong drink, but that wasn't going to happen in this gown-infested happy-land, which was my prison for the night.

As I looked up, Captain Joel Krolm towered over my bed. I studied his six-three, two-hundred-eighty-pound frame.

Of course, the captain was way past football-playing age, but he would have been a force to be reckoned with. He came close to me and placed a hand on my shoulder. "You are one lucky young man; you know you could have easily been killed out there."

"Captain, it's not like I was playing marbles in the middle of the street . . . ."

"Funny. No, but someone wants you out of the way in the worst way. And you know, I want you out of my town, too." He smiled a sarcastic smile.

"I'm not having a good time in your little town, Captain. Why would anyone want to hurt me?"

"You are snooping around, rustling up a hornets' nest, but the sting will kill you for sure. Stop asking questions and go back to your own little world. We can't protect you here, not with you asking all your questions about a very sore subject in our history. Someone is clearly disturbed by you."

"Captain Krolm, I'm just writing a story about a sweet old lady and . . . ."

"You're writing your own obituary, my man. You're pissing someone off, and Billy Blaine is still on the loose with a gun, a rifle, and one of our police cruisers. He is extremely dangerous."

"You don't think he . . . ?"

"I don't think anything. But he almost killed two men, in case you've already forgotten about that, and he won't think twice about taking you out. Now, what do you remember?"

"I had the meatloaf and lumpy mashed potatoes. It wasn't that bad."

"Right, smart ass! Anything stand out?"

"Just a big, dark-colored car, very fast, screeching tires, smoking, swerving, aimed right at me. I blacked out, hit my head, and didn't see anyone."

"Great help you are." He smirked. "Feel better, but get out of my town."

"Or else?"

The captain looked me in the eyes long and hard. "Or else we'll send you back to your boss, Harold Glavin, in a body bag."

"You know Glavin?" I asked, stunned.

"Yeah! He called to check up on you. I think he was disappointed you were still alive!" He laughed. "He'd have a great story: 'Reporter Investigating Famous 1923 Hagerstown Murders Gets Knocked Off'."

"Captain, you're in the wrong business."

"Just watch your ass, son. And remember, I'm watching your every move!" he snapped as he quickly turned to leave, and as he opened the door, he repeated in a trailing voice, "Watching your every move!"

Evidently, the hospital was not busy because I had no one sharing my semi-private room. I was glad, because hospitals freak me out—all the germs and all. The food is probably equal to prison food, and unless you are severely ill, it's good to run out of there as soon as possible.

The limited-channel television bored me silly, so I walked the empty halls. I touched base with the newspaper and left a detailed message for my cold-hearted boss, letting him know that although I had experienced a hell of a day, I was still alive and well, or as well as could be. The secretary at the paper said she would type a full report for the boss and have it on his desk for the morning. He was a real hard-ass, but I wondered how he would react if I had been killed. The ones that talk the toughest are sometimes lambs deep down inside. But I knew one thing for sure: Unless I did die, I'd better write the story of my life and have something new and exciting about the murders of 1923. Glavin would get a real thrill out of firing my ass and watching me clean out my desk, jeering that I would be lucky to get a job at a movie theater making popcorn. I finally eased back into bed and had just dozed off when—speak of the devil!—the bedside phone rang.

The hardest part of the day to get through after a person's heart has been broken is when one tries to fall asleep at night. Their eyes are closed tight, yet the imagined light still seeps through to the brain. The silence of the night is as noisy as the busiest highway. Sleep is almost impossible as the brain goes into a frenzy of calculations as to why the breakup was all your fault. In the end, sleep comes only out of sheer exhaustion, and every night the mind's calculations are different, confusing, yet so important.

The mind seems keener when my eyes are closed on this evening's torturous battle, trying to forget and fall off to sleep. I was analyzing my self-destructive decline after that woman left my life. I realized just how little life really meant to me. Oh, sure, I got up and went through the motions: the shower, the shaving, the smelling good, and trying to work a normal day. But it meant nothing. In fact, no one and nothing meant anything to me. I went to work, ate lunch, and went home, but in reality I was like a zombie just faking his way through the day, only to punish himself when his eyes closed tightly against a bright light of guilt.

In reality, everyone knew I was a fraud of a person. I was trying to scam everyone into thinking that life was good and I was still a caring person able to produce quality work on a daily basis. My boss was right. I had been a disaster for a while. Sure, he was still an ass and always had been. A robot had more compassion than he did, but he was right: I had crashed and burned as a productive professional. My heart had suddenly become frozen after the breakup. Frozen to life, love, everyone, and the world around me.

On this night, the torture went on forever. Then finally, there was the hallucination that the mind does for a few minutes, and then the bright seeping light finally dimmed into the blackness of sleep.

"Hey, nipple head," I heard as I picked up.

"Who? What? Who is this?" I said, half awake.

"This is your worst nightmare!" he blurted.

"Oh, Harold, how are you?"

"Evidently, better than my newspaper reporter, who can't cross a street. Were you drinking? 'Cause I'll fire your sorry ass right now!"

"Boss, someone tried to scare me. And no, I wasn't drinking. I've been good as gold."

"Gold is crap lately; don't count on gold."

"Harold, I told you I was onto something with this 1923 murder investigation here."

"The only thing I know is you are pissing off the Hagerstown Police Department, and it's about time someone other than me wants to kick your ass all around town. They want you out of their town. Funny thing is, I don't want you back. Why don't you find a job on a farm somewhere near Hagerstown; you'd fit in real good with the cows and pigs."

"Thanks for your support, boss."

"Don't mention it, hammer-head."

"I can't hear you too good," I lied.

"Well, hear this!" He screamed so loud I could have heard him from DC without the benefit of a phone. "I want a positive and full report of activity tomorrow evening, and don't pull any of your shit! You hear?" He slammed down the phone so hard it hurt my ear.

"Bastard!" I shouted loudly, just as the nurse entered my room.

"Excuse me?"

"No. I was just yelling at my boss . . . ."

A short time later, I fell off to sleep. It had to be the drugs. Finally, sleep.

CHAPTER SEVEN

We know it sometimes when we are dreaming; we remind ourselves that we are asleep as the visions pass quickly through our brain. Problem is, many times we forget our dreams after we wake up. The ones I usually remember are the weird dreams, the ones where someone is shooting at me or chasing me with a baseball bat, or I'm drowning in the ocean somewhere. I usually wake up full of sweat, almost certain that I'm bleeding profusely. Of course, it takes me a full five minutes to realize it was only a dream.

But this night was different. This night was as real as could be—eerily real. It was scary, because it was so unique.

I had learned through my research that Miss Lolita's uncle was a very wealthy man, a doctor named Walter Klug. The entire hospital wing I was in had been financed with a bequest from the hospital many years ago by the good family doctor, who was loved by all the Hagerstown natives.

Lolita's uncle appeared to me that night in my sleep. I was sure it was Dr. Klug because a large painting of the doctor is on the wall right next to the elevator on the floor I was on. In my dream, the doctor looked much like he does in the portrait: tall, slim, with a full white beard, and a full head of white hair. He appeared to be in his late eighties and was smoking a pipe. Appearing with him in my dream were three young women—the murder victims, I reasoned, although upon waking up, I couldn't remember their faces. Dr. Klug was showing me some items, such as a large, bloody knife, a red brick with a chunk missing from the middle, and a dark-colored women's scarf. He said nothing; just looked at me as he smoked his pipe.

Lolita's uncle was smiling, wordlessly inviting me to help uncover the killer. As quickly as the vision appeared to me in my dream, I was awake again, lying in the hospital bed in the dead of night, staring at the ceiling. I was wet with perspiration, even though the room was rather cold, I believed the perspiration was from such a deep sleep and the visions I had experienced. I stared long and hard at the ceiling, trying in vain to make sense of all I had seen in the dream. I made sure to replay every second of it in full detail because I was certain it would be forgotten if I didn't plant it firmly in my brain, frame by frame. The faces of the girls were already a blur, but I decided that their faces were not important at this time. Uncle Walter had shown me all I needed to know for the time being: the deformed red brick, the large, bloody butcher knife, and the dark-colored women's scarf. I wondered how these details could help me. I realized then that there was a real purpose for my being in Hagerstown, Maryland, and Miss Lolita's uncle had made sure I realized it.

The next morning I was released from the hospital after what the hospital called a full and nutritious breakfast, but what I called "punishment food." It was oatmeal that had dried up, toast that could be used as leather soles for shoes, and coffee that could wake the dead. If my body had complied with my intention, I would have run for the exit, but I was sore all over. My scraped hands, arms, and legs hurt, and my body ached all over. As is customary, I was wheeled out of the hospital to a waiting taxi the hospital provided, which took me to my car across from the *Hagerstown New News* building.

I reported in at the Washington newspaper. Gloria Finn, Glavin's assistant, was her usual sarcastic, smart-ass self. She insinuated that I had asked to be hit by the car and fired upon by a crazed gunman. I was sure Glavin was sleeping with her, though it turned my stomach to picture them being romantic in any way. She said that Harold Glavin had instructed her to confirm my appointment to interview Lolita at one p.m. that afternoon. She passed on a message from my boss: "Screw this one up and you might as well leave the country for good." Gloria laughed a long, sinister laugh as she said, "Check in later, Lou, or you'll be shining shoes in the subway on Monday as your new career."

It bothered me a lot that no one seemed to have confidence in my ability to investigate and report a story. I realized that for months I had let people down and been off my game. But now, with my back against the wall, I was motivated to show everyone what kind of newspaper reporter I could be. This was my chance to shine again, even though it had been a long time since I had last shined at anything.

My cell phone had a couple of messages on it that I needed to get back to. One was my buddy Graham from the office; another was from Fred, the barber; and finally, there was one from my bartender friend at my favorite watering hole. Clearly, people were concerned that I might be screwing up the assignment. They knew this was my very last chance to prove myself, as I had been on the road to hell for some time.

My body was sore and dragging, and in need of its usual caffeine fix. So I found a Starbucks coffee shop. They sell the freshest, most powerful coffee I know of, just what I needed to kick-start the long day ahead of me. I would return the calls as I sat in the coffee shop some three blocks away.

The first new message was from the newspaper's secretary, Gloria. Her voice on a phone message grated on me, like scratching one's fingernails on a blackboard. She had further informed me that she had adjusted my stay at the hotel in Hagerstown and informed them about the night before, and had kept the departure date open for as long as I needed. Also, I was pre-checked in, and only had to pick up my room key at the front desk.

The coffee was hot and as strong as ever. Maybe it had been sitting for a long time, as there were no other patrons in the Starbucks but me. The quaint town of Hagerstown was growing on me.

I returned my buddy Graham's call, and then Fred the barber's. Both went to voice mail. I basically told them both the same thing: that I was doing well, that Hagerstown was a quaint little town, that there had been some gunfire but I was fine, and that today I would interview the older woman my story was about. I let them know I would be staying on longer in Hagerstown, investigating another story for the newspaper, and that I would contact them once I returned to Washington.

My stomach churned, and I knew it wasn't the crappy breakfast the hospital had served or even the motor oil they call coffee at Starbucks. I was still uneasy about my job, my newspaper, and my boss, Harold. I was also very uneasy about getting a good story out of Miss Lolita. And for the first time in my life, I felt like I had a target on my back. Sure, I was probably just paranoid, and my very active imagination was now in overdrive, but something deep inside was tugging at my brain, making me believe that the 1923 murders were still bothering someone in Hagerstown. Of course, the killer (or killers) from 1923 couldn't still be living now, could they? No, they would have to have been dead for a great many years. But someone somewhere was spooked, or at least that was what my gut was telling me. In any event, I downed a couple of butter cookies to calm the acid, or the coffee, or the worry.

From now on, I planned to observe my surroundings and the people in this town just a little more closely than I had done before.

My next stop was the Hagerstown Library on East Washington Street. As I had learned from Loretta, the redheaded girl I spent time with under the police station table, the library was a good source of information. It had just been remodeled and updated on the inside, but the exterior was retro, looking the way it must have a hundred years earlier. I pictured Lolita in her twenties, coming to the huge brick building to borrow some books. As was the case with most buildings in Hagerstown, this one was old and well preserved. Evidently, brick could last forever. And just then the brick from my dream once again entered my mind: old, red, and with a chunk missing from the center. I stopped and stared for a moment at the exterior brick of the library, wondering if it matched the brick that Lolita's uncle had shown me in the dream. I shook my head and continued into the library. Its tall ceilings and huge rooms were overwhelming.

Immediately, I recognized Emily Swift, the woman Loretta had told me to look up. She was about eighty-five years old, slim, and good-looking, with glasses and long gray hair. Loretta had told me that Emily had worked at the library some fifty-five years and knew many things about historic Hagerstown.

As soon as I approached her desk, Emily looked up, smiled a friendly, almost motherly smile, and said, "Well, let me guess. You are Lou, the man Loretta has been talking about. You're the newspaper reporter, aren't you?"

"Yes. And you must be Emily, the well-respected librarian who knows all about Hagerstown and its history."

"I can help you with some information," she said.

"Great! As you're probably aware, I am here for the most celebrated resident of Hagerstown, one Miss Lolita Croome."

"Well, yes, Miss Lolita is very famous these days. She was born a Klug. Her father owned a huge farm on the hill and raised some cattle. Her uncle was a well-known family doctor. Walter Klug was a very wealthy and respected member of the community. Miss Lolita was a teacher for a few years until she married her childhood sweetheart, D. K. Croome, an auto mechanic. They had one child, a daughter."

I smiled at such a trove of information in one sentence. "Loretta said you were like a historian of Hagerstown."

"Well, I don't know about that, but here is a little-known fact about Miss Lolita: She has a special trait that most people don't have. It's called hyperthymesia."

"What is that?"

"Hyperthymesia is the ability to recall all memories from her past, including early childhood, in complete detail."

"Amazing! Even at her advanced age?"

"Oh, sure! She can recite full verses, poems, and speeches she heard as a young child. It is fairly rare that a person is born with this gift."

Emily was indeed quite knowledgeable about the town, the nursing home, and even Millie's Diner. Emily told me that Millie's was founded in 1930 and was known as the best pancake house in all of Maryland. "It was started by Mildred Farner and sold in 1980 to Sy Trylan, who refurbished the restaurant. Now it's a popular eatery of Hagerstown. Many old timers frequent Millie's."

I asked Emily about Sy, the owner I had seen at Millie's.

"Oh, good old Sy? He's all right, just has a tough exterior, but he's harmless once he gets to know you. He just barks a lot, like an old pit bull."

"So, his father is the minister of the church?"

"No, his father *was* the minister of the church. He died some thirty years ago, and Sy's older brother, Mitchell, is the current minister. Sy and Mitchell's father, Seymour, and Seymour's father before him, were ministers of the oldest church in Maryland for many years. Miss Lolita was a parishioner, as were her entire clan, and she even sang in the church choir for many years. Miss Lolita also was very active, dancing many times a week as a teen after school, and even as a young teacher she would dance with other female teachers and the students. Dance was very popular in the 1920s, as was going to the movies. Lolita was a movie fanatic and used to receive the movie magazines on a regular basis. There was no television, so dancing, clubs, movies, and soda fountains were very big with young people, as was canoeing and swimming, or just plain sitting on a backyard swing. Every home had a piano, and Lolita entertained her immediate family as well as uncles, aunts, cousins, and friends by playing the piano.

"The families would bake all kinds of breads, pies, and cakes regularly, and everyone would visit one another's homes and sit around the piano, singing and playing games. It really was a pleasant time to be a child. Of course, the drawback of the time was sickness. Many people died far too early from various viruses—or even from colds and fevers in those days. Sicknesses we have basically eradicated in today's society would take the young and the weak. It was very common to bury many family members. And if you were fortunate enough to beat the latest virus strain, you might still be laid up for weeks at a time, requiring daily visits from the doctor, who made house calls."

In a half hour or so, I received an in-depth education about the life and times of Miss Lolita Croome during the 1920s. Emily's insight was far better than any book or DVD. She made me feel like I was alive in those days as she laid out what life was like back then. It sounded so much simpler than the high-tech, fast-paced world we live in today. For a while, as she spoke, I wished I had been alive back then, or at least could be transported in time for a week or so, like in the *Star Trek* shows.

The microfiche gave me even more insight into Hagerstown in the 1920s, including the murders of the three young women, but it shed no light on any new leads. To me, it seemed like a dead end. But to someone out there, it was still alive. Someone was clearly nervous as a result of my visit, which I thought was somewhat comical. After all, what could a simple newspaper reporter uncover, compared to the town's police department, which, since the 1920s, had been following and investigating the cold case?

Still, I felt a weird connection to the 1923 murders, as I had when I first started looking into the information Gloria had given me about Miss Lolita and what I had found on the internet. I felt a strange bond, as if I were supposed to care and be affected. And something told me to keep digging, though my better judgment told me to get a story about the wonderful old lady and tear ass out of the old town that had been nothing but painful headaches for me, in more ways than one.

CHAPTER EIGHT

I t was eleven o'clock when I pulled into the parking lot of the Hagerstown Home for the Aged. It was a huge horseshoe-shaped one-story brick building, modern with many windows, and several people were sitting on the front lawn and around the sides, some by themselves in wheelchairs and others with aides or family members. The air was warm and inviting, and the sky was a picture-perfect blue.

I had the strange feeling that I had been followed and observed from a distance. But every time I looked around, there were no cars or people who appeared to be tailing me. My imagination was working in overdrive, and had been ever since the glancing blow I had taken from that car and the nice egg of a bump I had received. Everything still hurt, and I took some more of the pain medication the hospital had given me. I was to take no more than three of the horse pills per day, as they could make me drowsy. They were strong enough to ease my worst pain.

The landscaping around the nursing home was beautiful. The various colorful flowers and neatly trimmed shrubbery made it a very attractive place for its residents to relax outside and admire it all. I studied the residents as I approached the building. None seemed uncomfortable or in any kind of pain. Indeed, most seemed content. Many had someone, family or staff, accompanying them.

As I continued to observe, I tried to imagine myself in a home similar to this one. I imagined what it would be like to know I might never be released to live freely on my own again. It felt strange to me and somewhat sad as I pictured myself unable to ever leave. Oh, sure, many people do recuperate and ultimately rehab, and are released. But as I looked around, I knew most of these people would never be able to leave. I stared. I wondered.

As I walked past the residents, many smiled at me and said, "Hello," just hoping I would strike up a conversation with them. I felt bad that I couldn't. I could see how easily one could become a volunteer in a home like this, giving hope, attention, and love to many in need of a little extra compassion.

I walked through the entranceway and signed the guest register, filling in the purpose of my visit. First, I was to meet the director of admissions, Jeremy Roberts. A young lady escorted me and introduced me to Mr. Roberts.

"Ah, Mr. Gerhani, I have been expecting you."

"Am I late?"

"No, right on time," he said with a warm smile. "But it's not every day that our facility is graced with a reporter from the great Washington, DC, and as fine a newspaper as the *Washington Gazette*."

"Thank you, Mr. Roberts, but we're just a friendly little newspaper looking for newsworthy stories, and your town's Miss Lolita Croome is a very worthy story indeed."

"Yes, Miss Lolita is one very special and unique person. We treasure her every day. I'd venture to say that there has been no one in all of Maryland, or even the United States, like Miss Lolita She is probably sharper and has a better memory than both of us combined. And don't try to outshine her in a trivia contest; she'll run circles around you!" He smiled.

"What is her secret to such longevity?" I asked the pressing question I had been pondering for many hours.

"Well, many people want the magic potion that has kept Miss Lolita going for more years than ninety-nine percent of all the people in the world. And studying Miss Lolita for so long now, I have come to a certain conclusion."

"And that would be?" I waited patiently, my notepad and pen at the ready.

"Well, the way I see it, Miss Lolita loves life. She loves people, and she never holds a grudge. She never has a negative thought or gets angry at anyone. But most importantly, Miss Lolita lives to help others unselfishly. She will go to great lengths to get into someone's head and truly help them to help themselves. And over the years she has improved many people's lives by offering encouragement, motivation, and, most importantly, pure love." He had a distant look in his eyes, like he was digging deep inside for the words.

I interrupted him. "The Wise One?"

"Ah, yes, and most certainly, the Wise One."

"It is amazing. People are living so much longer these days." I shook my head.

"Medical technology today is magnificent," Mr. Roberts added. "Medications can extend life far longer than ever. We have more residents who have achieved the milestone of one hundred than ever before. And the truly amazing thing is, they are far sharper than a centenarian from years back. Oh, sure, many residents who are nearing one hundred have senility. We will always have that, but we have over twenty who are one hundred or better. But no one here has made it to Lolita's milestone of that amazing one hundred ten," he boasted, as I scribbled notes.

Mr. Roberts proudly gave me a tour of his facility, because Lolita was at her hour-long physical therapy session; she was scheduled for at least three times per week. I was somewhat surprised that a person of her age could do any physical therapy. But Roberts advised me that it was not the same physical therapy a younger person would partake in. Miss Lolita's physical therapy might consist of arm and leg movements, and walking with the help of a walker and a therapist, as she was otherwise confined to a wheelchair. And she would perform movements of all of her joints and some muscle flexes.

We continued our tour of the dining area, the lobby, and the kitchen. Everyone I met was outgoing and very compassionate toward the residents. Overall, the nursing home seemed like a pleasant place to reside if one had the need for the specialty care and rehabilitation provided there.

Next, Mr. Roberts took me to the most sought-out place of all, where the residents and their families often gathered when visiting with one another: the garden sunroom. It was a lovely room—bright from the sun that streamed in through the overhead glass panels and from the array of beautiful flowers and plants that decorated the space. The room was filled with residents and their families and friends who were visiting. Many were admiring and commenting on the varieties of colorful flowers.

I studied these people carefully, noting the many smiles and the calming effect the room seemed to have on everyone. It was a form of therapy, I thought, as I walked through the very large room with Mr. Roberts. There were very old and frail people, as well as younger, incapacitated residents, and it all affected me. I walked past a resident of maybe forty strapped into a wheelchair, and he spoke to me. He asked me for something, but I couldn't understand him. He asked again.

Mr. Roberts said that his name was Ken, and that he was a little hard to understand. Once again, Ken spoke to me, but Mr. Roberts helped me out, saying, "Ken wants you to lift his leg and rest it on the wheelchair footrest."

"Oh," I said, feeling quite foolish. "Sure, Ken," I smiled as I tried, with difficulty, to lift the man's leg. After about fifteen seconds, I was able to place his foot onto the footrest of his wheelchair, which clearly made Ken more comfortable. Total dead weight, and heavy—that was Ken's leg.

"Ken has a brain injury from a car accident he had when he was nineteen years old. He was thrown from the car. Ken has no use of almost anything but his fingers and facial muscles," Roberts explained.

As I watched Ken zip around in his motorized wheelchair, all I could do was feel terrible. Here was someone who had almost been killed at age nineteen, and had been incapacitated ever since. What kind of life was that? Still, Ken and others go on living life.

"That's terrible!" I said out loud, not realizing I had said it.

"Yes. There are some with even worse situations here," Mr. Roberts said. "We have a very young man of twenty-one who is completely paralyzed due to a diving accident in a pool. He can move nothing but his eyes. His mother is here every day to help feed him and wheel him around the property grounds. He cannot speak and has a great deal of trouble swallowing. But we make him as comfortable as possible."

Mr. Roberts continued the tour, I caught some of what he was saying. He was talking about the huge strides they were making with their state-of-the-art physical therapy program. But I was thinking of other things. First off, I felt terrible for ever feeling sorry for myself at times whenever my back, feet, or teeth hurt.

Next, I wondered why God ever allows such suffering to exist here on earth. Why allow a young man of nineteen or even forty to stagnate in a wheelchair with almost no life, or at least not the way life was meant to be lived? I suddenly felt very fortunate to be able to speak properly and to walk anywhere I wanted to and at any time I wanted to.

I thought about some research I had done on longevity. People have been living longer than ever before in human history. A French woman most recently held the world record as the longest-living person in the world, until she died at age 122. Amazing; 122 years old! Then I researched further and found documentation on the Internet listing the oldest people who are still alive and the oldest people who have passed on. There must have been a hundred people on the list who made it to more than 110 years old. And I'd venture to guess that most of these people had fairly good health and their senses for most of their lives.

So, I wondered again, *Why? Why make those people live so long, and others like the two poor souls who were merely a mind in a useless body, suffer so greatly?* Then, I realized that I had a possible explanation.

My reasoning was this: God lets us experience different things, though some may be horrific, sad, or heartbreaking, for a reason, like the young man who had both legs and arms blown off in battle, or a baby who falls out of a window and dies. I believe that we are exposed to many sad things in life to remind us of the precious gift we each have in our own lives.

I realized how very blessed I was, though I routinely took that blessing for granted.

"We should get ready to see Miss Lolita," Mr. Roberts interrupted my daydreaming and philosophy session.

"Yes, that's a good idea," I said, as I took a good look around at some more residents, realizing we all have to play the hand of cards we are dealt with by the good Lord. Most of the people I observed in the home appeared to be resilient, rolling with any punches life had thrown at them through illness, accident, or old age.

We walked down a long corridor past many rooms, some with residents laid up in bed or sitting in chairs next to the bed. The home was large, and I wondered how it was all kept so organized. How could the staff possible give the proper attention to each individual?

"This way," Roberts said, as he made a right turn into a large room. The room looked like a lounge area. There were tables and comfortable chairs, and it was half filled with people.

A small group of people was gathered around an older woman in a wheelchair. We headed toward them. I studied her from a distance: an old face with coke-bottle glasses. She had a full head of hair, fixed short and neat, a woman with just a few extra pounds and not frail like many older women I had seen. Miss Lolita was laughing with the women near her as we approached.

"Miss Lolita, we have a special treat for you," Mr. Roberts said with a warm smile for his honored resident.

"Who said that?" Miss Lolita smiled a big wide grin.

"Mom, it's the director, Mr. Roberts," an older woman said.

"Who is there; I can't see?""

"Oh, great!" I said in a low annoyed voice, thinking my whole trip and assignment was going down for the count. *She must be senile.*

"Of course, it's Jeremy Roberts, director of operations. I know that! But I can't make out the person with him. Is it a man or a woman?" she asked, impatient with herself.

"Mom," her daughter said, "it is a young man, the reporter from the newspaper out of Washington DC that we were expecting.

The daughter was a slim woman in her late eighties. Her hair was gray but impeccably cut and neat. She was a fine looking woman now, and I can only imagine how good she must have looked years earlier. And Miss Lolita, being her mother, must have been a looker in her day, too.

"Come close," Miss Lolita said. "I can't see you."

"Uh, sure. Okay," I agreed.

"Closer, please!"

I went within three inches of her glasses before she said, "Oh, that's so much better."

I felt kind of silly being that close, and I slowly withdrew to a more comfortable distance.

"Come close again, sir, so I can get a good look at you," she said impatiently.

"Oh, I'm sorry," I said, as I went up to her face again.

"You know, I'm legally blind, not deaf, Sonny!"

Now I felt worse for when I had said, "Oh, great!"

"My hearing is so good that it makes up for my lack of vision."

I was suddenly impressed with this ancient woman who had all of her marbles. It appeared to me that Lolita was a straight shooter; she didn't pull any punches and spoke her mind freely. And why shouldn't she at her age?

"You are a handsome lad, now that I can see you."

"Not really, I . . . uh . . . ."

"Listen, Sonny, I'm old. Don't waste an old lady's time. Just agree and accept a compliment, okay?" She smiled with a motherly look.

I laughed and she smiled. "Okay, Miss . . ."

"Call me Lolita, please."

"Okay, Miss Lolita. How do you feel at achieving such a milestone of one hundred and ten years?"

"I really don't think about it much, since it is all out of my hands now, isn't it?" She smiled and looked up as if gazing at the heavens above.

"I guess, but there must be a secret to your longevity."

"Listen here, Sonny, you already know a lot about me. I know nothing about you except that you are a reporter, a handsome lad, and you have brown eyes."

"Mom, now be nice," her daughter said, but she couldn't help laughing at her mom's outspokenness.

I smiled and went right up to her face. "Miss Lolita, what would you like to know about me? I'm an open book."

Lolita looked deep into my eyes and asked, "Why are you here?"

"I am here to tell the world about an amazing woman who has led an amazingly long life."

"No, why are you really here?"

"Your fabulous story . . . ."

"Don't lie to me, Sonny. Why are you here? I see it in your eyes."

Feeling uncomfortable and seeing Mr. Roberts look at Lolita and then her daughter, I let the question remain in the air for two seconds before I answered. "I am trying to save my job with your story."

"Now that's more like it." She smiled lovingly. "Do you have a girlfriend?"

"None," I said hesitantly, looking at the floor. "I was engaged, but we broke up a few months ago."

"I know," she said with a loving smile. "I can see it in your face and eyes, and hear it in your voice."

Was she clairvoyant? I thought she was very insightful. *The Wise One* resonated in my mind.

We spoke about my family, my father, how he died early, and how much I missed him. She felt the pain of my breakup with my fiancée. She studied me carefully and then said, "You remind me of the wounded bear that becomes vicious because he is hurt. You must let it go, Sonny. Breathe in deeply and exhale all the pain. I want you to try this later. It works wonders."

Just then, her nurse dropped by, a good-looking, dark-haired woman with very interesting eyes. Her name was Felicia. It was time for Miss Lolita's snack and Ensure. Lolita asked Felicia to take her outside to sit in the warm air. She wanted only me to accompany them and continue our interview. Miss Lolita's daughter, Jennifer, and Mr. Roberts would be discussing Lolita's medical care and nursing home matters.

The sun was warm, the sky was royal blue, and there was a soft breeze—a beautiful afternoon in Maryland. I watched closely as Miss Lolita carefully sipped the vanilla vitamin-enriched drink. She had a little trouble drinking and eating things, I learned. They had to feed her slowly and in small amounts, but she was doing fabulously at her age. I watched in amazement.

Anyone aged ninety was amazing, especially if they had their health and wits about them. The few ninety-year olds I had ever seen were in fairly good shape. Here I was witnessing real history. I was communicating with the Wise One, a woman I had soon realized was a real treasure to everyone who came to her for advice. But what really struck me was that, compared to the ninety-year olds, this woman was twenty years their senior.

I had so much to ask her and so little time. Felicia told me that Miss Lolita would need a nap in another half hour. It was her "energy" nap, and she never missed it.

Who was I to interrupt a 110-year old woman's nap?

We talked freely in the open air. It was better that no one was crowding around us and maybe influencing Miss Lolita's answers. Although I had a feeling that she would speak her mind regardless of who might be near.

Felicia kept smiling at me, encouraging me. The people of Hagerstown were in awe of me, or anyone, I thought, from a big city with the allure of being a member of the media—that is, everyone except someone with a gun and a car aimed right for me.

Miss Lolita wanted to look into my eyes again, real close. I said, "What? Are you trying to hypnotize me, Miss Lolita?" I laughed.

She laughed and said, "Listen here, Sonny, I don't know how or why, but I can see through a person's eyes into their soul. I want to know you better, especially if you are coming back tomorrow with some ice cream for me! And, Sonny, you can call me Miss Lolita only because I like you."

I cracked up and said, "Anything you want! And, Miss Lolita, I'm going today to buy pistachio ice cream because I know you like it."

"That's her favorite!" Felicia said. "And those homemade chocolates they sell in town, well, she's crazy about those, too. We're trying to fatten her up." She laughed.

"It's all right for her?"

"Oh, sure. She just has to eat everything in smaller pieces, and eat slow. But medically she can eat all the sweets she wants, though not too many people visit with pistachio ice cream and chocolates."

I looked into Felicia's eyes and realized that they were unique, not the standard issue basic brown. Her skin was of olive complexion, and her hair was long and black. She had cute bangs, which always make a woman appear younger and cuter.

While looking her over, trying to calculate her age, I fumbled with my notebook and dropped it on the ground. I quickly bent to retrieve it at the same moment she bent to get it. We almost hit heads as I quickly grabbed it and we both came up and locked eyes. Embarrassed, I said, "Oh, sorry, are they gray? Your eyes, I mean."

"Why, yes!" She smiled.

"Very unique . . . very pretty—your eyes, I mean."

"She's a sweet girl," Miss Lolita said. "And I can see through your eyes, Sonny. I see that you have a sincere soul and a loving heart. You're just bitter and in need of some loving care." She nodded her head a few times and looked me over.

"Miss Lolita, I am here for you." I smiled. "I have to formulate a great story about you, or I'll be flipping hamburgers at McDonald's!" I chuckled.

"They'll never take you; you're too old to work there, Sonny," she said with a girlish giggle.

Felicia laughed, and as she did, I gazed at her beautiful and loving smile.

"Felicia, my love, please go get that red book we look at every now and then. It's in my dresser drawer." Miss Lolita motioned.

"Yes, Miss Lolita," Felicia said, and disappeared quickly.

"You know, young man, I've been around for basically two life spans, and I can size a person up pretty good. You, down deep, are a loving, caring soul. You have some issues right now that need some working on. But you'll fix it all. You see, I am entrusting you with a most prized possession of mine, my yearlong diary of 1923. If you want to know more about me and where I came from, you'll gain a great insight there. But if I don't get the diary back in its same condition, I will personally kick you all the way to that newspaper you call home! We understand each other, Sonny?" Her eyes locked onto mine.

"Miss Lolita, it will be a great honor to study your diary. It will be like a history lesson into your life and the times so many years ago." I smiled as I gave Lolita a hug.

"Now don't get all mushy on me, Sonny. It isn't that big a deal!"

"Your eyes ain't all that bad!" I said, as I blinked away at my moistened eyes.

"I'm an old woman," she said as she took my hand, "but if you could find someone as loving as Felicia, it would do you a world of good." She squeezed my hand gently, just as Felicia returned with a hardcover red book.

"This is awesome!" I said as I opened an almost pristine book to its first page in January 1923 and read, "January first. Today is the beginning of my new life in 1923."

Felicia and I delivered Miss Lolita back to her room for her energy nap, and I said my goodbyes for the day, but not before asking Mr. Roberts if I could continue my interview about Lolita with Felicia over a cup of coffee at Millie's next door. He was quick to agree, and I could swear that Miss Lolita gave me a saucy little wink. I reminded Miss Lolita that I would see her the next day at the same time.

"Don't even think about coming without that pistachio ice cream, young man!" She laughed, and everyone joined in.

CHAPTER NINE

Half an hour later, Felicia met me at Millie's. I was wired after three quick cups of coffee that had seen fresher hours. I was busy taking notes and flipping through the diary. Felicia smiled at me with sparkling eyes, and I could swear that my heart skipped a beat.

Men love different parts of a woman's anatomy. I personally notice first the eyes, then the hair, and then a sincere smile. All the rest of a woman is, of course, noticed and adored, but those first three can win me over. I study eyes carefully. Most men couldn't care less about a woman's eyes, but they are extremely important to me.

As I observed Felicia, I estimated her height to be around five-seven and her weight to be one-twenty, on the slimmer side. When a man is suddenly attracted to a beautiful woman, he has a hard time looking too long at her. Staring into her eyes for a prolonged period is almost impossible. It has something to do with rejection, I believe. We don't want the other person to know we are interested in them for fear of their rejecting us. What's more, I was still reeling from an emotional breakup with my ex. I had no problem making love to a woman for the sake of sex, but I was still shell-shocked when it came to anyone really special and attractive.

"So, Felicia, what is so special about the Wise One, Miss Lolita?" I asked, with my notebook at the ready.

"Well, sir . . ."

"Oh, please, just call me Lou. All my close friends call me Lou." I smiled and looked into her wonderfully amazing gray eyes.

She smiled and said, "Okay then, Lou," and then she hesitated and looked back at me, apparently studying my standard brown eyes. Two seconds of silence can be a lifetime. I waited. I melted.

"Oh, yes, Miss Lolita. She is like a full-time shrink every day. She is so full of knowledge and positive energy. She knows what to say at precisely the right time. She reminds me of the sign hanging above her bed every day. It is so inspiring. It reads *When it's all over, all said and done, what impact will my life have had on this world?*"

I had heard the words before. As I wrote her words in my notebook, it made all the sense in the world. I read the saying to Felicia, making sure I had it just right: "When it's all over, all said and done, what impact will my life have had on this world?"

"Yes, that is it," she said. "It is very inspiring to me and many others in the home."

"Well, if interpreted correctly, it is a very powerful motivator. Is it her own statement?"

"Yes, indeed," Felicia said. "She has many. But this is something she has lived by her entire life."

"The way I understand that statement," I responded, "it means that we must maximize our lives each day, be all we can be, knowing full well that we will be leaving this world and being remembered after we are gone for as much good as possible. Did we make a difference, an improvement, or did we just pass through, only taking up space in the world?"

We spoke for over an hour. I got to know more about Lolita and also more about Felicia, who, remarkably, was unattached and available.

"So, how could someone so cute be unattached?" I asked.

"Oh, I don't know. Maybe there's something wrong with me." She giggled.

"Oh, I don't think so."

Then with tears in her eyes, she said, "I'm actually divorced. Lolita convinced me to divorce Harold almost two years ago. It was a very bad time in my life."

I found out that Felicia and Harold had been married when she was twenty-four, and remained so for less than a year. He was a construction worker who stood six-three and weighed nearly three hundred pounds. He would drink after work, heavily, and then he would beat her out of jealousy, until Lolita convinced her to get an order of protection and divorce the creep. She still hadn't dated again.

Felicia looked more attractive to me as the minutes ticked away. I knew it wasn't the liquor, because I hadn't had a drink for days—and after hearing about Harold and his drinking problems and anger issues, I almost swore off alcohol forever right there and then. I knew drinking could be destructive, and that it made whatever depression I felt even worse. There was no benefit in heavy drinking except to deaden all pain and reasoning for a short time, but then it only seemed to compound my sadness.

Lolita was right. There was no substitute for a caring, loving woman who would be your best friend and partner in a lifelong relationship.

As we talked more, I learned that Felicia drove a red Mini Cooper vehicle, which is great on gas, though she admitted it looked like a clown car. She rented a studio apartment because she couldn't afford the high rents in town. She was a Scorpio, while I'm an Aries, which was supposedly like fire and water, but I discounted that.

Her smile told me that she liked me. There are telltale signs in a woman's body language, facial expressions, and laughter, sometimes nervous but cute nevertheless. They laugh nervously at stupid things we say out of our own nervousness. If all this could be played back on video, it would make for a good comedy. But every new relationship goes through such awkwardness. She told me how she loves to sing, mostly behind closed doors, and that she is shy by nature.

"Getting back to Lolita," Felicia said, "she is so philosophical, and most of the nursing home staff stops by every so often for advice, or merely to spend time with her. They admire her for her advanced age, of course, but also just for who she is—her personality."

She confirmed what Emily had told me earlier that day, that Lolita's family had owned a huge farm. As a child, Lolita had many chores to fulfill around the farm before and after school each day. Her father died at an early age. Lolita used to get fairly sick and would take weeks to get better. What we call routine sickness today was major to the people back in those days.

Lolita's uncle, the doctor, had an office, but he spent his days making house calls or making rounds at the hospital.

Lolita was a teacher for a few years, loved dancing, and was a big fan of the motion pictures. She frequented the theater, which was still in use today, though it had been completely renovated.

Felicia asked me if she could look through Lolita's diary.

"Lolita has shared this with me over the years," she said, as she carefully paged through it. "It is filled with so much history that it's like you are magically transported back in time as you read it." Felicia made a few points about different sections of the diary, but I was largely tuned out to what she was saying. Oh, sure, I heard her voice and even some of her words, but mostly, I was looking into those magical, sparkling gray eyes that had me mesmerized. Where had this woman been my whole life?

I studied this woman as I tried to formulate in my mind the character, the heart, the sensitivity of Felicia. Here was a wounded woman being observed by an equally wounded man, a man with a heart that had been split in two. No doubt this fine woman, with such a loving heart, had lost all motivation to allow a man to get close to her.

I looked at her silky, long, black hair with perfectly trimmed bangs, which contrasted beautifully with her olive complexion, and those unique eyes, such as I had never seen before. I kept saying "yes" and "that's amazing" as she talked, while secretly stealing in-depth scans of the entire woman. I made special notes, etching deep in my brain pictures of this woman for later retrieval. It lasted perhaps ten minutes before I was shocked back to reality.

"Lou, didn't you hear what I said?" Her voice was higher-pitched than usual and startled me to attention.

"Excuse me, I was thinking of something I had to do." I lied and hoped my smile was convincing.

"I was just making a point about the 1923 murders Lolita mentioned here. She doesn't like to speak about them much because she knew all the girls very well. She used to dance with them after school a few times a week. It was a very painful time, and Miss Lolita told me once that all the women were deathly scared that they could be the next victim of the vicious Hagerstown madman killer."

The fear, according to Felicia's conversations with Miss Lolita, went on for years because no one was ever apprehended for the killings. The diary told about the pain and sadness of the teachers and students as one death turned into two and then three.

Felicia and I exchanged cell phone numbers, and she agreed to meet me for dinner at eight o'clock that night at a little Italian restaurant called Maurino's Authentic Italian, right in the center of town. I was ecstatic inside, but I maintained a cool, calm exterior.

Felicia went back to work. I had told her to remind Miss Lolita that I would see her the next day, and would like to discuss some of her diary with her.

My hotel was a few blocks away. The Cosmopolitan Inn Suites is located on Route 40 Dual Highway and Cleveland Avenue. Gloria had assured me that a suite would be waiting for me no matter what time I got around to checking in; it had been booked from the day before and was available indefinitely.

The Cosmopolitan was not the finest hotel around but had reasonable rates and offered all suites. The hotel was only a few years old and not in the historic section of town. But all the major sites in Hagerstown were only a few blocks away except for Elizabeth's Farms. The farm and creamery were located several miles outside of Hagerstown, and had been a family-owned business for many years. I would be visiting the farm the next day just before seeing Lolita again.

Once again, I thought about how attractive Felicia was. That smile and those gray eyes just kept popping into my mind. Felicia's eyes were not only unique in color; they were so alive with life and excitement as she spoke and when she smiled. I was far from an expert on women, at least respectable women, but I felt Felicia might be attracted to me, too. Then again, I'd been wrong before.

Sure, I had made love to many women, or maybe it wasn't love but rather just animalistic sex. But respectable women like Felicia— well, they are rare. So I was unsure exactly how to read the signals she was sending. Miss Lolita was right: I was a wounded animal acting out accordingly.

A fine woman must be treated differently from the women I would regularly see for a fling. My only thoughts about Felicia were to hold her in my arms, look into her eyes, and softly kiss her full lips—

nothing more, nothing too fast, and nothing that would offend this extraordinary beauty.

It is amazing, that intense emotion that works on the mind. It won't let you forget if you are very attracted to a person, especially in the very beginning of a relationship, when it is almost impossible to concentrate on other things. The brain just keeps tapping away in your head like the flashing of a strobe light, and the thought I kept having was *Felicia, Felicia, gorgeous gray eyes, awesome smile, twinkle in her eyes . . . .*

CHAPTER TEN

T he room in the Cosmopolitan Suites hotel was huge. I could have thrown a party in that suite. It was two bedrooms and two living rooms separated by huge sliding pocket doors made of thick, solid walnut. The beds were both king sized, and the living rooms had modern, L-shaped leather sofas with power recliners built into them. Top it off with a giant-screen entertainment center and a fifth-floor view of hills full of trees, and you have a great party animal's paradise.

It was four-thirty when I was checked in by a very courteous hotel staff person, and an equally courteous bellman brought my luggage to the suite.

As soon as I had settled in the room, I took a nice long walk on the grounds of the hotel around the pool area, the gym, the restaurant, and the lawns. I made a couple of phone calls while sitting by the pool and taking in some of the day's best rays of sunshine. I had to return two calls to people who had left me voicemail messages. There was Graham, my buddy from work who reminded me of a very young Eddie Murphy when he was on *Saturday Night Live*. He had left two messages. No doubt, Graham was concerned about me. He knew that for several months I had been on a slow course toward crashing and burning, and he wanted to make sure that I was all right, and that I was taking hold of the reins of this opportunity to keep my reporter's job with the prestigious newspaper.

I kept the call to just under five minutes, convincing Graham that everything was going real well. I only touched on the fact that there had been gunfire at the gas station and the precinct headquarters. I told him that I had almost gotten run down in the street, but that everything had calmed down now.

"You know, bro, you were safer when you were drinking heavily. The worst back then was falling off the bar stool!" He laughed then told me to stay in touch and watch my ass.

Then I returned Gloria Finn's call. Speaking with her was like walking on red-hot burning coals.

"Harold wants a full accounting of your day, young man," she snapped.

"Tell him I went for an Asian massage where they walk on your back. It went well except for the fat one . . . ."

"Listen, you! You are on thin ice already; don't push the envelope. I'll tell Mr. Glavin."

"Gloria, everything went well with Lolita and Mr. Roberts. Everyone there was super nice. Roberts showed me all around."

"Yes, he told me."

Holy crap! Then don't ask me, I thought. She always pissed me off with her holier-than-thou attitude, like she worked for the Queen of England instead of some cone-headed drill sergeant. Harold had to be banging her. No secretary was that intense for the boss unless there was something else going on. I was sure of this.

Ever since old Harold got thrown out of the house and divorced by his third wife for sleeping with some forty-something fat bimbo, Gloria'd been up his rear end, hoping old Harold would ask her to be wife number four. Together they would make a vicious pit bull tag team.

"I'll be returning again tomorrow to continue Lolita's interview."

"I know that already, young man. You didn't return my call fast enough."

"Well, then, Gloria, maybe you can tell me how my day went," I said sarcastically.

"Mr. Glavin wants a full—"

"Massage? I recommend the fat Asian woman who walks on your back. Just make sure he doesn't have that Wendy's chili beforehand, or there could be a real explosion!" I laughed.

"That's it! I'm telling Mr. Glavin that you are not—"

I missed her next words because I turned off the cell phone and kept it off. After all, she knew everything she needed to know, and I hadn't even had a drink in days now. Sober is good, but I wasn't staying that way by choice. I was just too busy to take a drink. Although Harold Glavin and Gloria Finn were enough to drive the pope to drink until he fell over.

It was six o'clock when I made it back to my room. I was tired and needed to take a break. I still ached all over, though I had ignored the body pain and headaches all day long. It is amazing how the aches and pains seem to multiply when the day calms down. Maybe the mind can cut out pain when it needs to concentrate on tasks.

As soon as I opened the door to the suite, I was surprised to hear the surround sound entertainment center playing soft rock music. On the dresser top was a fresh bucket of ice along with three bottles of cold water. It was great to have complimentary water—a nice touch by the hotel. Most places make you purchase a bottle of water for two or three bucks. The water was ice-cold, like it had just come out of one of the vending machines the hotel featured on each floor. I quickly poured a glass and drank it down. It was a warm day, and I hadn't had any water all afternoon. My dinner engagement was for eight, and I wanted to look my best, so I took a quick shower and had a fresh shave.

As I stepped out of the shower, my legs suddenly buckled, and I had to grab hold of the countertop to steady myself. My head was spinning and I was nauseous, as if I were really drunk. I held on to the counter until I felt strong enough to sit on the toilet. I thought maybe I needed to go to the bathroom. I sat still with my eyes closed for a full five minutes.

With my eyes closed, the room's spinning decreased to the speed of a slow carousel. I waited, breathing deeply, trying to calm my racing heart, but it wouldn't settle down. So I tried to get to the bedroom and lie down, but that didn't work. As soon as I stood and walked five steps, I passed out and fell to the floor.

I must have been out cold for half an hour, but it could have been a minute or two. I had no idea. I was able to crawl slowly, and then stagger, and then crawl again to the bed and slowly lift myself enough to lie down sideways on the mattress. The room was spinning out of control as I closed my eyes again and tried to calm myself. Instead, I threw up in the bed and passed out once more.

The ringing of the phone scared me as if someone had stabbed me awake. I looked around the revolving room and saw that my cell phone was on the nightstand. I hit the button and tried to speak, but only gibberish came forth, and I blacked out again.

CHAPTER ELEVEN

The killer's face was indistinguishable as I watched him stabbing the screaming girl. There was blood all over the girl's face, glasses, hair, and neck, and her clothes were torn. The man was viciously and repeatedly slashing at the girl without any hesitation like a robot programmed to slice a side of beef. The girl slumped to the ground, apparently dead. She had glasses and long hair that I couldn't tell the color.

Even as I slept, somehow I knew it was a dream; still, I tried to notice the man's features. All I could see was a big man of stocky build wearing an overcoat or raincoat, and he was stabbing the girl with a long butcher-style knife. I could make out nothing further amid the dark of night.

It was apparent that the dream was a reenactment of one of the murders from 1923. I knew this, and remarkably, I was very calm, as if I were watching an old movie. I knew I could do nothing to change the outcome. Still, I needed to see more, to study every detail I was being shown.

Off in the distance was another young woman, someone who, like me, was just a distant observer. She was attractive, in her twenties, with long curly hair, and she just stood there staring at the scene. I knew this had to be Lolita when she looked in my direction. The scene was frozen in time. The man held the knife straight up in the air, completely still. The girl sprawled unevenly on the ground. Lolita looked as if she were staring at something special, like she was trying to tell me something.

I studied it all over again, looking for any telltale signs, anything unusual: shoes, hat, overcoat, hair—nothing, though Lolita's eyes didn't move. Finally, I saw it. I saw what Lolita was trying to get me to look at. It was a ring on the middle finger of the man's right hand—not a normal ring, but rather a very large ring. But what was strange was that that large ring was in the shape of a lion's head. As soon as I noticed the ring, its size, and its shape, Lolita looked my way as if to say, "It's about time!" And at that precise moment, the movie-like dream came screeching to a halt.

The light entered my eyes ever so slowly as I blinked a few times. I felt stoned, like I had been on an all-night binge, and my head was tapping out a very loud drumbeat. When I realized where I was, I recognized the doctor. It was Dr. Samuel Frederickson, and, somehow, I was once again occupying a bed at the Washington County Hospital.

"There you are," the doctor said.

"Is this a dream?" I asked, dumbfounded. I kind of realized it wasn't, but still didn't quite know for sure.

"No. This is live and in color, my friend. How do you feel?" He studied my face.

"Like a train ran me over," I said weakly.

"You'll feel better shortly. Do you know what happened to you?" the doctor asked patiently.

"I'm not sure, but I think I fainted, maybe from exhaustion."

"You were helped tremendously with a dose of poison," the doctor said, and his eyes focused long and hard on mine.

"You've got to be kidding!"

"Yes, Lou," the doctor said with a wry smile. "It was some strong stuff!"

Just then, I saw Captain Joel Krolm out of the corner of my eye as he walked through the door. His face was stern as he stared at the doctor, who just nodded in response.

"You cheated death again, Mr. Gerhani," Krolm said, staring long and hard at me. He was clearly pissed.

"I . . . uh . . . ."

"It's official. The poison used was thallium, an odorless, tasteless poison that is usually very deadly."

"But how? Who?"

"It was Billy Blaine, at the hotel," said the captain. "We have him on hotel surveillance. He planted the water bottles, the poisoned ice, and the poison-rimmed glasses. It appears that you didn't touch the ice, but you did drink a little from the poisoned glass. But he was counting on you using the ice. If you had, you would have died for sure. What saved you was a young woman, Felicia, who called 911 and informed us that something was terribly wrong."

The captain was clearly pissed, though I didn't know exactly why. Nor did I care. It could be because they had a shooter and would-be murderer still on the loose, which was a disgrace for his department. He also could have been pissed at me, as if everything was my fault. I was too groggy to care.

"Louis," the doctor said, "you are going to be fine. Once you were picked up by the ambulance, they administered intravenous drugs right away, and we suspected some kind of drugging. We quickly tested the blood and found thallium, a very powerful compound that, as the captain touched on, usually kills its victims. You consumed too little to kill you quickly, which gave us time to administer the proper drugs needed. We also sedated you heavily for several hours, giving your body a chance to clear out the poison. You are very fortunate. It seems you are like a cat with nine lives. Thank God you're young.

"And yes, the captain was correct in the fact that the lady friend was sharp enough to realize that you were not yourself, and called 911 for assistance. If perhaps a few more hours had elapsed, your organs would have shut down one after the other, and you would not have been able to survive."

"That poison is that potent?"

"Louis, it is indistinguishable to someone ingesting it, so you have no clue that you have been poisoned until it is too late. It also takes such a minute amount to do someone in. Your only saving grace is that you didn't take any ice," the doctor said.

"Right. I have a sensitivity problem with ice."

"Again, your ass was spared," the captain said.

"I guess I have friends in high places." I managed to produce a weak smile.

"Well, not in Hagerstown, my friend. Someone wants you dead in a fierce way, and a quick and painful death at that. You are just too gullible or stupid to get the message."

"Captain, I'm sorry, but I've got a job to do here. My ass is on the line."

"Yeah?" he snapped with a fierce glare. "Your ass will be going for a one-way trip in a hearse if you hang around!"

"I'm not leaving," I said, and I looked the captain square in the eyes. "I'll leave when my story is complete. I do believe that Billy Blaine, or someone with him, is spooked by my investigation into the murders. And also, my interviewing Lolita is rubbing someone all wrong. I'm convinced there is some tie-in to the 1923 murders and Lolita."

"Are you implying that Lolita has some knowledge about the murders or the killer responsible?"

"Captain, with all due respect, I have had more action in a couple of days than your department has had in decades."

"Listen, you little . . ."

"Okay, gentlemen, I think Louis needs some rest right now," the doctor said, and he put his hand on the captain's back and steered him toward the doorway.

"One second, Dr. Frederickson," Captain Krolm snapped. "Louis, since you won't heed my warnings, I am assigning my best officer to watch your every move. From now on, consider Sergeant Thomas Pawler your permanent shadow. He will report to me on your every move. So, have a nice stay in our fair town of Hagerstown.!" he said as he headed out the door.

"Great! That hammerhead!" I snapped.

"I heard that!" the captain said, leaning around the doorframe. "Still not going to change anything." His voice trailed off.

Dr. Frederickson smiled nervously at me. It was clear that he was uncomfortable with the exchanges between the captain and me, but was mostly concerned about my overall health.

"Doctor, when can I blow this joint?" I asked.

"Well, you can blow this fine establishment in a few hours if all your new blood work comes back negative for toxins and infections."

"Infections?"

"Yes, you see, that poison wreaked havoc on your immune system, and we have to monitor the blood carefully. I'm betting that all is back to normal, but your liver functions were through the roof on the results of the first blood work. So just relax, enjoy our gourmet breakfast, and we'll try to get you out of this joint by around ten thirty." He laughed good-naturedly.

"Thanks for everything, Doc. But that breakfast you serve may be more potent than the thallium!"

"Funny! I have to remember that one. Oh, by the way, there is a young lady who is patiently waiting to see you. She's been waiting for a couple of hours. I'll let her in now. See you in a little bit, Louis."

Within two minutes, Felicia entered the room, and I swear the entire room got brighter. She was absolutely beautiful in her nursing uniform. I used to fantasize about a gorgeous woman dressed in a nurse's costume, but, of course, she would always slowly strip. But that's another story for another time. Maybe it's the white pants or the pure white shoes they wear, but I find something sexy about nurses in general.

As she came closer, I had no problem this time looking deep into her sparkly gray eyes. Felicia was smiling as she said, "What, are you trying out for the next Superman movie? First the gas station shooting, then the police precinct shooting, then the wrestling match with an oncoming car, and now poison?"

"Someone up there likes me, I guess. Not too many friends here in Hagerstown, though!"

"You have one right here," she said, and she walked closer to my bed.

I stared long and eagerly at her ruby-red lips as she bent slowly toward me, looking tenderly into my eyes. She moved closer to me, and then closer still.

A fabulous tingling feeling came over me as we almost touched lips. Suddenly, I was startled when I heard, "Son of a bitch! I can't believe you are still breathing!"

I turned quickly to see Sergeant Thomas Pawler glaring at me.

Great! What timing. I'm about to make the move of my life with Felicia, and this lug-head macho-man has to ruin it all.

"Get used to it, Professor, I'm your new shadow. I got orders to keep you alive, although I don't know why. You keep barking up trees that hold grizzly bears."

"Nice to see you, too," I said. "Felicia, this is Sergeant Pawler. Sergeant, this is Felicia, from the nursing home."

"I heard. She saved your sorry ass, huh, buddy?"

"Would you believe?"

"He is very lucky, isn't he?" Felicia asked.

The sergeant looked Felicia up and down then said, "Lucky is the operative word, my dear!"

Taking a hint from the way I was glaring at him, Pawler slowly withdrew from the room. "I'll be right outside the door, bud. Your prison food is here," he said with a sinister laugh.

It was too late. The look on his face and the sound of his voice had destroyed the moment between Felicia and me. It was replaced with cold scrambled eggs, wheat toast, and piss-tasting coffee.

I could eat nothing but a few bites as my appetite hadn't returned and the food turned my stomach. I wanted nothing more than to leave the hospital and get back to the work at hand.

Felicia had to get to work, so we said our goodbyes as two nurses' aides were futzing around my hospital room. I was still set to see Lolita at one that afternoon. Felicia said she would be there along with Lolita and Mr. Roberts. I reminded her that I was going to run to the farm to pick up that fresh-made ice cream for Lolita.

Dr. Frederickson returned and asked why I hadn't touched my breakfast. I asked him, "Did you ever taste this slop?"

"No, can't say I've had the pleasure."

"I've seen dog food more appetizing than this food!" I laughed.

By ten o'clock, I had received my release and was hugging my newfound friend, Dr. Frederickson.

Sergeant Pawler, my sarcastic, arrogant, and reluctant chaperone, wheeled me out of the hospital to his police cruiser. He was working his shift with me alone. We sat in the car and spoke for a while.

"I had a conversation with your boss, Harold Glavin," Pawler said. "He didn't sound upset that you got poisoned." He laughed. "Sounds to me like he wishes he had beaten Billy Blaine to the punch. What the hell did you do to that man?" He smirked.

"Glavin's just pissed at the whole world. I'm just a punching bag for him. I think if I was knocked off, he would actually cry."

"Sounds like he'd cry for joy, bud," Pawler snapped.

"You could be right. His assistant is a real bitch."

We spoke about my schedule for the day— going to the farm for ice cream and returning to the nursing home to talk with Miss Lolita again.

"Your car is at the hotel?"

"I'm in the back parking lot."

"Well, I will be following you to the farm."

"Come on, now . . . ."

"Don't even try that crap! I'll be following you everywhere. Don't you understand that someone wants you out of the way? They think you know something valuable, though I don't think you know anything useful. Someone will stop at nothing to eliminate you. We know Billy Blaine is involved, but we are sure someone else is involved. And so far we have no leads as to Blaine's whereabouts."

"Sergeant, who is this Billy Blaine character?" I asked.

"Blaine is a young career criminal. All small stuff—assault and battery, larceny, harassment, stalking—but never any killing. No ties between him and Hagerstown at all. He's been in and out of prison since the age of seventeen, never holds down a job, but he never shot up a gas station and a police officer before. So, he's now graduated to a new level of threat and is armed and extremely dangerous.

"Why me?"

"Well, he clearly thinks you have leads on the murders of 1923, and he is either protecting someone connected to the murders, or someone hired him to take you out. Keep in mind that he isn't just trying to spook you; he wants you six feet under. And remember, Felicia may also be a target, and anyone else you chum up with until you come to your senses and leave us all alone in our normally boring little town. Either you are very stupid or you want to be a front-page martyr in your own newspaper. But stop risking other people's lives in Hagerstown."

"I'll be gone soon, Sarge."

"Maybe in a body bag." He laughed coldly.

"Well, right now I want to get on the road to the farm if it's all right with you."

"Not so fast, bubba. We have to look that car of yours over real well before you take off in it."

"What?"

"You heard me right. To a killer, that car could be an extended weapon, a way for them to murder you without touching you directly."

"I hadn't thought of that."

"I didn't think so. I'll explain on the way."

The sergeant told me that killers can rig a car to blow up when the ignition switch is activated.

"Okay, my car is right in back of the hotel, in the parking lot. It's the red Malibu late model with some damage on the bumper."

"Oh, you're a drunk driver, too?"

"Not exactly, though I do drink a little too much. No, I got rear-ended by a Lincoln Navigator the other day."

"So you're one of those heavy-footed brake drivers?"

"You think I stopped short and caused my own accident? What, are you crazy?" I yelled, now frustrated.

The sergeant made his way over to my car and got under it to look around. He walked all around the car, noticing the damage from the accident, then looked me up and down, sizing me up.

"Okay, it was my fault, the accident." I laughed.

He squinted at me then moved on. For a solid five minutes, he inspected my car, opening the doors, looking inside and under the seats. He popped the hood and looked at everything inside.

"See, I told you everything is fine, Sergeant," I said. "Who wants to screw around with a Chevy Malibu?"

The sergeant promptly radioed in a request for a tow truck to pick up the car.

"Hold on there, Sergeant Pawler. You can't do that!"

"Oh, please excuse me, Mr. Gerhani," he said sarcastically. "Listen here, Gerhani, I am ordered by Captain Krolm to keep your ass safe. It's not something I want to do, but I must. So, until you take your sorry ass out of my town and go back to the most corrupt city in the world, you're stuck with me. Get it?" he snarled.

"Oh, I got it, all right."

In five minutes, the tow truck pulled up. It was Wally from the station that I was at the other day when Billy Blaine went on his shooting spree.

"Are you in trouble again?" Wally joked. "What, are you stuck?"

Pawler took control of the conversation, and Wally quickly attached my car to the lift on the tow truck.

"Sergeant, I'll give it a good going-over back at the shop. We'll see if anything is out of whack," Wally said.

We drove behind Wally back to the station, where he had my car up on the lift within a few minutes. The station was relatively empty except for the occasional gas customer passing through. It was nice to see that Brian Fawlta, the gas station attendant, had returned to work. He told me that he was back to normal except for a large bump on the back of his head that was taking its time to go away.

"How's the story going?" he asked excitedly.

I told him very little, mostly just about Lolita and the nursing home.

"I've never been inside that nursing home," he said.

"That's probably a good thing," I remarked.

I was happy for Brian because a nursing home can be a very depressing place to visit. On the other hand, some people feel that young people should be exposed to the sick and elderly in order to be awakened to the brevity of life and encouraged to make the most of their time.

Wally inspected my car as if the president were going to be riding in it, while Pawler looked on and Brian bent my ear.

"So, how long you staying? Oh, and I heard there was a shooting at the police station by that Billy Blaine creep."

"Yeah, Brian, can you believe that hard-on Blaine shot an officer in the station house? That's some real big balls!"

"It's all been in the papers, you know. Shame you didn't write the stories. They even wrote about someone trying to run you down. Think it was Blaine, Lou?"

We spoke for a few minutes more. I found out that Brian was going to night school. He wanted to be an architect. I commended him on his choice, telling him to stick it out and that it is far better to choose a career that uses your brain rather than your body, as a body will break down and become less reliable as one ages; eventually it'll get hard to continue with merely muscle instead of brains.

He listened intently, again putting me on a pedestal, as many in his town had done, except, of course, for Billy Blaine and the town's law enforcement.

Wally had motioned for Pawler and me to come stand underneath the car on the lift. I looked first at the lift, then at my car, and then I slowly made my way underneath it. I was always paranoid about extremely heavy objects raised right above my head. I hoped Wally would talk fast. I couldn't take another hit in the head.

"Lou," Wally began, "someone clearly wants you dead. I've seen many instances of someone putting the fear of God in a person by modifying and rigging something on his vehicle, but in this case, someone wanted to do you in for sure!"

"So, Sergeant Pawler was correct," I said, as I glanced apologetically at Pawler, then at Wally, and waited.

"Oh, he was right on!" Wally smiled.

Pawler looked at me and said, "When we were at the hotel parking lot, I thought I saw a drop of brake fluid on a rear brake line, so as a precaution I had the vehicle pulled in without anyone starting it up."

With that, Pawler called the station house for the fingerprint officer to come to Wally's to print the car.

"Someone knew what they were doing here," Wally said, with a little admiration for the culprit. "They sliced the brake line just enough for your brakes to fail, perhaps on a highway or steep incline some minutes after your next car trip began. And that's not all. Look here." He pointed to the insides of the two front tires.

"That's a bubble!" I snapped, as I shook my head in disbelief. "Holy crap, that's ready to blow!"

"That, too, was brilliant," Wally declared, a devilish smile on his face.

Nice that he's being entertained at my expense.

"You see," he continued, "as the tires heat up like they do after a few miles, the air pressure rises in the tires and the bubble has a great chance of causing a major blowout. This is someone who clearly has done this sort of thing before."

"I was going to head to the farm off the highway . . . ."

"I bet you would have come back in a body bag." Wally shook his head with a very serious expression on his face.

"The only way you're going to any farm is in the back of a police cruiser, Bub," Sergeant Pawler snapped.

"I'll have this baby fixed up as good as new, as soon as I receive the go-ahead from the authorities," Wally said. "And after they lift all prints, I'll dive under the hood and inspect everything, including the full electric system and fuel lines. But, gentlemen, I fully expect to find nothing additional. After all, with both tires bubbling from being sliced, and the brake line already oozing precious brake fluid, the job would have been successful in causing a horrific accident. But more likely, an overturned vehicle and then a flipping car. Sorry to be the bearer of bad news, but I'm glad you men had me do a quick look-see."

"I'll be dipped!" Brian exclaimed as he, too, came under the lifted car. "A real-life execution hit!" he marveled.

Brian ran for coffees and donuts while we waited for the fingerprint officer to arrive. I listened to voicemail messages while I waited. Graham Griffiths had left another message, and Felicia had left me a couple as well. She wanted to lift my spirits and make me laugh, which her messages did. I returned Graham's call before he could get too worried and raise suspicion at the newspaper's main office.

"Where have you been, buddy? I was—"

"Listen, Graham, I can't talk. I am fine now, but it's been rough. Someone tried to take me out, run me down, then poison me, and now cut the brake lines and tires on my car."

"Son of a bitch! They're out for you, my man!"

"I'm fine. Don't tell anyone at the newspaper, especially Harold the hard-on!"

"But what are you going to do? You need protection."

"Listen," I said, "I'm fine. The police captain assigned an officer to me full-time. I'm as safe as anyone could be. Trust me, Graham. I'm cutting out of this town in a day or two, so please don't call anymore.

I'll call you when I have some more time. Take care. I'll see you later," I rushed the call.

"Watch your ass, okay?"

"Okay, bye," I said and disconnected the call.

While we waited, we enjoyed the coffee and donuts Brian had picked up, and Wally explained what needed to be done to rectify the damage to my car.

"Lou, you realize that once a tire is compromised the way your two tires were, we have to replace them. Unlike with a regular hole from a nail or even a screw, we cannot just seal up a hole of this kind with a plug. The tires were cut purposely so they would blow at any high-speed heat-up, the perfect scenario for a nasty accident. The brake line can be replaced real easy. After I get an okay from the police, I can have your car ready in about an hour and a half."

"He won't be needing it for a while," the sergeant chimed in. "I'll be taking him for a ride." He laughed and looked directly at me. "I made him an offer he can't refuse!"

I hated to have to rely on anyone. For my entire life, I have been independent to a fault. I feel somewhat helpless when another person has to drive me around. But I realized I had no choice. I needed to get to Elizabeth's Market Farm and Creamery. We needed to pick up the pistachio ice cream for Lolita, or I'd look like a fool.

So, I was stuck with Sergeant Pawler, who had absolutely no way about him. I didn't know if it was just me he hated, or maybe the world. I knew little about him or his personal life except that he had served in the military with the Marines. He also was divorced a few years back, and had been with the police force for over ten years. I could tell that he was tough as nails and went real hard on criminals, taking his job perhaps too seriously. I knew one thing: I wasn't going to ruffle his feathers knowing that he wanted nothing to do with babysitting me and being my shadow. He, no doubt, would celebrate with Captain Krolm upon my departure from Hagerstown.

It was around ten thirty that morning when Sergeant Pawler drove me to the farm to purchase the pistachio ice cream.

I remembered the few times I had eaten pistachio ice cream. It was a little funky compared to other flavors, but still very good. I was curious why the farm creamery's ice cream was so much better than other brands. No doubt, Lolita was an expert after 110 years of life. She had known food back when it didn't have preservatives, additives, and fat-free low everything in it. I hoped the farm would enlighten me as to how they made the fresh, homemade ice cream and how it differed from store brands.

The farm was fifteen minutes away by highway. All I could picture was the major blowout I would've had if I had been driving my own car. I thought about the motive to knock me off. It finally sank in: Someone wanted me dead. It's a very unnerving feeling to know there is someone who wants you dead so badly that nothing will stop their attempts.

First, your stomach tightens into a knot once your mind accepts that the threat is real. Your eyes may start twitching uncontrollably, as mine did, and worse, you start looking around at your surroundings non-stop and uncontrollably, because anyone could be the killer. No one was exempt. Even old people were suspected potential killers, as disguises can make anyone look entirely different. And lastly, whenever you eat or drink anything, it immediately turns into acid in the stomach, and the stomach emulates a simmering volcano.

Sleep is impossible for the potential mark of a killer. The mind revolves faster than a spinning top, calculating all the ways you could ultimately be killed in full, gory detail. And the detail plays back in the mind as if it were a movie on an endless loop.

So, here I was, riding along with Sergeant Pawler, once again in the back of his cruiser. I was supposed to feel safe, but my mind convinced me differently. After all, for someone to poison me with thallium and, on top of that, to slice my tires and brake lines, they meant business. Anyone can take out another person if they want to badly enough. No one can ever be fully protected. No one can be put into a protective bubble. Car bombs can be planted. High-powered rifles can be shot from great distances. Poisons can be added to foods or drinks. Walk-by stabbings can't be defended against if you're caught unaware.

No, I would have to get out of town, and quick. Fear is a very strange emotion. It eats away at you, driving you insane to the point where your mind stops working properly and your thinking becomes clouded. This was where I was at that precise moment. I could concentrate on nothing but death, and even envisioned my own wake, coffin, color of the casket, and the pillow inside it, and all the mourners around it. Unfortunately, there weren't many mourners. It crossed my mind that maybe I should try to do something about that from this point on. I had never thought of my own funeral before, but as I envisioned it, there were so few cars lined up behind the hearse that it really bothered me, not that a hundred cars in procession would make me much happier at that moment.

I was suddenly shocked back to reality as Sergeant Pawler blurted out, "Don't look now, but I think someone is following us."

Of course, I spun around and looked. What I saw was a large black car with no license plate on the front, still a good distance behind us. *They're following a police officer? Now that is strange.* Then again, almost everything I had experienced in Hagerstown had been strange, dangerous, or unusual.

As soon as we passed the next exit, the sergeant put on his siren and flashing lights. I watched closely as the large black car made a sharp turn off at the exit and left rubber in a quick getaway. I strained as I tried to see the driver.

"They were uncovered!" Pawler said, as he called into the precinct and ordered a cruiser to the exit in pursuit of the black car. I thought that chasing the car ourselves would have been a better idea, but the sergeant clearly thought it could be a trap of some kind, and his number one priority and his orders were to protect me. So he asked for a cruiser to trace the black car's tracks just in case they were careless. I thought it was fruitless.

But now I was convinced that I had to wrap up my investigation of the 1923 murders real soon, or I could be the next obituary in the local paper. I could just drop the investigation; after all, I had only come to interview Lolita and write a nice story about her. Still, why should I cave in to someone who was spooked because I was nosing around about some murders that took place ninety-one years ago?

After all, what did I really have? I had spoken with a few people and uncovered mostly old news about the murders, their victims, and some suspects who were never found guilty. I had seen clippings about the murders, and I'd read about the victims. There was nothing concrete to indicate that I was closing in on any real leads, thus I wasn't a threat. Why kill me? What good would that do? No one had been able to solve the murders for almost a century. What made anyone think that I could do any better?

I turned quickly around to look behind us, studying the road. Nothing. No one was behind us or even close to us. Then it hit me. The only variable, I figured, that someone had deciphered was that this nosy reporter, who was investigating a 1923 murder case, also was interviewing Lolita Croome, the oldest person in America and, more importantly, the oldest living Hagerstown resident, a woman who lived through all the murders and knew all the victims. Still, I wondered, where was the connection to the killer? And who today could possibly care so much that they, too, were willing to kill to keep the truth from coming out?

Sergeant Pawler didn't talk. It was like driving with a mummy. Well, he wasn't very pleasant to speak with anyway, so I probably was better off in my own world. After all, my mind is always so active that sometimes I have to scream internally to stop thinking so much. It doesn't usually work, and today was no different. I kept wondering if someone was waiting with a machine gun or a grenade around the next bend. Anything was possible.

Ice cream, think ice cream, please! In return, my mind sent out the thought, *You could wind up on ice—as a corpse!*

Nice thought, Lou.

"Sergeant," I said, against better judgment, "you think we're safe now?"

"I am. Don't know about your sorry ass. At least I have a gun to protect myself." He laughed, and I couldn't help noticing that it sounded almost sinister.

"Oh, that's real encouraging!" I snapped, as I looked all around the highway, searching for anything slightly suspicious, just in case.

CHAPTER TWELVE

We arrived at the creamery in about twenty minutes. It reminded me of a very big ranch, the kind in the old western movies. Cows and horses were grazing on a huge tract of land. We drove up a very long driveway past trees and farmland, under and past a huge old wooden sign that read Elizabeth's Market Farm and Creamery.

"Don't get out until I give the order!" Pawler yelled as if I were deaf.

I always wanted to be a Marine, I thought.

"Let me look around. Stay down and stay put."

"I'm as put as can be, sir!" I replied.

"You know, I should shoot you right here myself and save everyone the trouble. I would, too, if I knew there was a bounty on your head, you know."

"Aw, you love me!" I smiled a real big smile.

"You little turd!" he snapped as he exited the car and walked all around the parking area to view the large property. Then I saw him wave for me to come out.

We were met at the entranceway by the owner of the farm who was waiting for us. She was very concerned to see a police officer, and mistook me for a detective. The sergeant reassured her that there was no police matter concerning the farm. He told her about my assignment and the need to bring the Hagerstown celebrity, Lolita, some fresh-made ice cream.

I explained to Sherri that Lolita was 110 and loved fresh-made pistachio ice cream, and that I wanted to make her happy. But I also wanted to know more about how the ice cream was made and why it was so much better than store-bought ice cream.

Sherri took us on a tour and let us taste a few flavors.

"We've never had a big-city reporter here," she said. "Let me tell you the history of the farm. It was founded in 1893 by the Burnett family, and it stayed in that family until my husband's father purchased it in 1978. He added in the fresh ice-creamery addition. It was an instant success. Of course, we raise and sell fresh fruits and vegetables, but we also produce fresh dairy products right at the farm. We use the fresh cream in our products."

"What is involved in the process of ice-cream making?" I asked, as Sergeant Pawler gave me an impatient look.

"Well, our ice cream has a different fat content than most store brands and has twenty-five percent air in it as opposed to fifty percent in store-bought. Ours is also made in an Italian-style batch freezer, and we use a blast freezer set at minus thirty-five degrees so that the tiny ice crystals don't have a chance to form chunks. To make the pistachio flavor, we mix in a pistachio paste, similar in consistency to peanut butter. Then we fold in the fresh pistachios after the ice cream comes out of the batch freezer. You can easily taste the difference from the store-bought kind."

Pawler's eyes were glazing over. He probably wanted his donut fix. Too bad for him. I was doing research.

We tasted the pistachio and quickly knew why Lolita loved homemade.

I found out that pistachio ice cream was created 1940s. They were cultivated over 7,000 years ago, and were loved by the queen of Sheba.

I purchased three two-gallon buckets of pistachio ice cream, and we were on our way. I could tell that Pawler was ready to kick my ass, so I cut it rather short.

Once outside, the sergeant inspected the general area again, while I looked out over the horses that were grazing in the fields. Pawler inspected the police cruiser very carefully, even lifting the hood and getting underneath the car and looking closely at all four tires.

He finally gave me the okay to climb into the back seat, and we took off at a rather fast speed. He was annoyed, but I didn't really care. Pawler always seemed pissed off at something or somebody. What a way to live your life.

On the drive back, I pulled out Lolita's diary and thought, *God forbid I should lose it. I would never be able to face Lolita or her daughter ever again.* I think I would just disappear and not even go back to my job. And what if someone injured or killed me and stole the diary? It was just too much to think about.

I flipped through the 365 perfectly handwritten pages that looked like they had been written yesterday, even though Lolita had written it all in pencil. The year 1923 was a long time ago, but certain world events mentioned in the diary stuck out. They had crazy weather back then, too, just like today. For instance, on July 10 of that year, Russia had a hailstorm with two-pound hailstones that killed twenty-three people and many cattle.

On August 2, Warren G. Harding, the twenty-ninth president of the United States, suddenly dropped dead. He was only fifty-seven. The next day, Calvin Coolidge was sworn in as the thirtieth president. *Only fifty-seven,* I thought, *and here I am reading the diary of a 110-year-old woman.* And on September 1 of 1923, a 7.9 earthquake hit Tokyo and Yokohama, killing 142,000 people. Imagine—142,000 dead! That's three stadiums full at Yankee Stadium—a little hard to comprehend. Life is so precious. Some never live to age twenty-one, while others live, unscathed, to age 110. It all boggles the mind. Life, I feel, is like walking through a minefield; one never knows which step could end their life. And then you have the crazies, like madman Blaine, going around and blasting at people. No wonder I drink. Which reminded me, I hadn't had a drop of alcohol in two days, and I was still functioning. Not bad!

Suddenly, I came across a quote that was underlined in the diary: "An old Cherokee Indian told his grandson, 'My son, there is a battle between two wolves inside us all. One is Evil. It is anger, jealousy, greed, resentment, inferiority, lies, and ego. The other is Good. It is joy, peace, love, hope, humility, kindness, empathy, and truth.' The boy thought about it and asked, 'Grandfather, which wolf wins?' The old man quietly replied, 'The one you feed.'"

It was a powerful statement that hit me hard. Two wolves inside us in constant battle: Good and Evil.

Following the quote, Lolita had noted that her Uncle Walter Klug, the doctor, had told her the quote and that she was very impressed by it.

I was astounded at how many times Lolita was sick in that one year. In one instance, she was laid up for ten days, and her uncle made house calls almost every day, as town doctors did in those days. Of course, the minor sicknesses of today were major sicknesses in 1923, and in some cases were even deadly. Then there were the flu viruses that killed many people of that time, including many children.

Besides going to the movies and to dances, the drugstore was another hangout Lolita frequented, as well as a shop that sold fresh-made chocolates. I read that canoeing and swimming locally were a big outing for her friends and family, but the cars of the day frequently broke down. Someone in most homes played the piano, and nearly every house had one. The family members and friends would all gather around and listen to the songs being played. It all sounded so attractive to me, and I envisioned myself in 1923 through Lolita's writings. It was a simpler time in life and a calmer time in our history, a time when family meant everything and people had time for one another.

Lolita noted a number of additional profound quotes in the diary, some of which had been shared by her Uncle Walter, who was apparently a very strong influence on her. He was very spiritual, as was Lolita, even very early in her life, as demonstrated throughout the diary. I decided to bring up Lolita's uncle to her when I spoke with her again later that day.

One of the quotes really stood out to me: "When God leads you to the edge of a cliff, trust Him fully and let go. Only one of two things will happen—either He will catch you when you fall, or He will teach you how to fly!"

Then there were others: "Be noble! And the nobleness that lies in other men, sleeping, but never dead, will rise in majesty to meet thine own."

"Every word of God is pure; He is a shield unto those that put their trust in Him."

"Boast not thyself of tomorrow, for thou knowest not what a day may bring forth."

This last quote came from Lolita's Bible, as shared with her by her uncle. Lolita stated in the diary, "Uncle Walter and I once again read the family Bible while on the swing seat in the yard under the shady tree."

It was clear that Uncle Walter was also a very wise man who passed a lot of knowledge on to Lolita, knowledge that stayed with her throughout her long life. Even at her young age in 1923, Lolita understood that life was unpredictable and that there were no guarantees of a tomorrow. That last quote etched itself in my mind. Before the Hagerstown trip, I had taken each day for granted, fully expecting a tomorrow as if it were due me in some secret contact I had with God. Not until I almost lost my life did I realize that today is a blessing that each of us is given by the big guy upstairs. We must capitalize on today, because tomorrow is not guaranteed. Lolita's diary made great reading.

I was shocked back to reality as Sergeant Pawler made a sharp turn going a little too fast. At first, I thought he was falling asleep at the wheel, but I quickly realized that he wanted to spook me away from my deep, thoughtful reading. He succeeded.

"Hey, Sarge, I'll buy you a cup of coffee when we get back, at Millie's Diner."

"You're gonna buy lunch, you tightwad!"

"Sergeant, I'll buy anytime you want me to!" I laughed.

He went back to driving normal again but kept studying me in the rearview mirror. I couldn't put my finger on his personality. Either he was tough as nails and just all-around rude, or he had a slight mental problem, or maybe a learning disability. Or perhaps he had some of that PTSD, post-traumatic stress disorder, that servicemen suffer from after the war. Some veterans come back all messed up, and their personalities are changed for life. Either way, he was weird in a scary way.

Anyway, I kept skimming through the diary for tidbits of information, anything that would help me understand Lolita, her personality in her younger days, the times and customs of the day, and anything relating to the 1923 murders.

It was heart wrenching to read her reflection of the girls' murders one by one throughout the diary. First there was Lori Gellate, then Ingram Stuart, and then Amanda Harrison. Lolita didn't get into all the gruesome details, just the tremendous heartache and pain that everyone in the town was enduring.

What caught my eye in particular, toward the end of the diary, were her notes about the many dreams she'd had depicting the dead girls. Lolita had been friends with all of them. "But why so many realistic types of dreams?" she wondered. A couple of her dreams showed a large butcher's knife and women's clothing. Then, amazingly, she recounted that a couple of dreams showed chipped red bricks, a religious cross, and the face of a lion.

How much of a coincidence was that? The damaged red brick, the cross, the lion's head, the large butcher's knife—I had seen them all in my dream, but I hadn't read about these details in the diary until today.

But when I had talked to Lolita, she had stated emphatically that she did not want to go back in her mind to speak about the 1923 murders.

In the diary, Lolita commented on her very troubling and graphic dreams of the dead girls. She had tried to confide in the doctor, her Uncle Walter, about the meaning of the dreams. The uncle had a very special talent for seeing some future and past events himself. He told her to keep track of all her dreams, log them somewhere, and not try to over-analyze them. He said that one day, maybe years later, it might all make perfect sense.

As Sergeant Pawler pulled into the parking lot of Millie's Diner, I wondered whether Dr. Walter Klug had a way of sending dreams to Lolita and me. Or perhaps the three dead girls were trying to send messages from beyond the grave to solve their murders.

My days in Hagerstown were now really numbered, and I was worried that I would leave with no new leads on the Hagerstown murders. Granted, I was not sent to solve the murders that had been unsolved since 1923, but something deep inside me, a force I hadn't felt before, was pushing me to keep investigating. Maybe it was the faces of the dead girls I had seen in the newspapers, or maybe it was that when I dreamed about the girls, their faces had become etched in my brain.

Maybe it was because I had gotten so pissed at how so many people seemed to get away with murder. I knew that the killer was dead. But someone was troubled by all the attention the case was getting.

Very soon, I would have to return to the Washington newspaper where I prayed I would still have a job. Until then, I was consumed with the murders, and worried that my compulsion to solve them might affect my health.

CHAPTER THIRTEEN

I
t was 11:50 that morning when we sat down in Millie's Diner. Maybe it was nerves or the lousy food I had been eating of late, but I was starving. And when I'm starving, I want one of everything on the menu. Kristen, the hazel-eyed, somewhat flippy waitress, came running over to our table. She was as excited as if she'd just found out that she'd hit the lottery.

"Oh, Lou, I have been thinking all about you and your news story! I've been telling everyone who comes in all about you. You're a big celebrity here in town!"

"Who, him?" Pawler asked. "What, are you kidding?"

"Hey, Sarge! Yes, he is so important, all the way from Washington where the president lives. I've told everyone all about your stories about the old lady and those nasty murders!"

She took our orders and scooted away, rushing into the kitchen, yelling out to the owner, "Hey, Sy! He's back, the reporter! Go look! Maybe he will put us in the Washington news. Hey, Sy, look!"

"What did you tell that nitwit?" the sergeant asked. "What'd you fill her head with?"

"Nothing much."

Just then, I saw Sy sneak a peek out through the kitchen doors. He looked me over, kind of inspecting me as if I had a contagious disease. Then he slowly made his way over to the table to say hello to Pawler. They shook hands and made some small talk for a minute before he acknowledged me. "And you're that hotshot reporter everyone's been blabbing about. You ask a lot of questions." He narrowed his eyes as if trying to size me up. Sy was a big, imposing kind of man, the kind that sticks out in your mind.

"Only trying to write an award-winning news story," I said.

"You know what they say, don't you? Curiosity killed the cat." He laughed loudly.

"I've heard that before. But I've never taken to cats. Besides, I'm allergic . . . ."

"Well, best of luck, young man. I've got some cooking to do." Sy returned to the kitchen.

Some people just don't take to me. Maybe Sy is related to Sergeant Pawler. Sy was a big, imposing kind of man, the kind that sticks out in your mind.

Kristen's eyes were wide and bright as she brought our food. She smiled her big smile and said, "Do you think you could sign your placemat for me?"

Pawler laughed loudly. "Give me a stinking break!"

"You want my autograph?" I asked, shocked.

"Yes. You're going to be famous one day."

Pawler laughed even harder. "Him?"

"Please, pretty please . . . ."

"Fine!" I snapped, trying to end Pawler's entertainment. I signed the placement to her as follows: "To Kristen, the happiest girl in Hagerstown. Don't ever change! Louis J. Gerhani."

She ran into the kitchen like she had found gold, clutching the placemat and yelling, "Sy, look what I have!"

I felt like a fool. Then I felt even dumber as Sergeant Pawler looked at me with a sarcastic grin.

"Hey, Pawler, sit on a tack!"

Kristen had been such a sweetheart, and had stored my containers of pistachio ice cream in the diner's large freezer. I was only too happy to comply with her silly request for an autograph. She would make someone very happy someday. *There is a childlike innocence in that girl,* I thought. Just thinking of her brought a smile to my face. *You know, innocence beats out over-educated haughtiness in a woman any day. There should be the right mix.* That brought Felicia to mind, and I could swear that my heart skipped a beat.

As we entered the nursing home, Jeremy Roberts, the administrator, was waiting for us. He greeted Pawler and me and was thrilled to learn that I had brought three containers of fresh-made ice cream for Lolita and her friends. He gladly asked someone to store them in the kitchen's freezers for me.

Residents, seated around the room, seemed to stare at people as they arrived. Smiling and waiting for you to smile at them, hoping you would say a kind word to them.

Clearly, some of them were lonely, even though there were so many other residents to mingle with. It was quite sad to study their faces, observing the real sick ones, the lonely ones, and the ones not even sure where they were.

Pawler said, "Hope someone puts a bullet in my head before they dump me in a glue factory like this."

"I'm sure someone will help you out with that wish one day!" I joked. I understood his thinking, and that scared me too, more than anything. Sometimes the ones with the hardest outer shell are the softest inside, and deep down they have a good heart, though it may go undetected for many years.

"So, Sergeant," Roberts said, "what brings you to our senior home?" He studied the sergeant.

"Just a precaution; someone has escaped captivity. We should have him back in custody shortly. I'll be guarding the front entrance, and as soon as Lou here is finished, I'll be on my way."

The sergeant stood by the entranceway, observing everyone who came and went. I could tell he was bored out of his bird. But I never asked for his help. Still, it was comforting having a gun nearby for my defense.

I smiled a stupid grin at the sergeant and then followed Jeremy Roberts to the meeting room where Lolita would be waiting for us. It was around one, after her lunchtime and the physical therapy she did each day. Roberts explained that they exercised the leg and arm muscles to ward off atrophy, which could freeze up an older person's joints and muscles. "Then they kind of waste away," Roberts explained. "'Use it or lose it,' is what we say."

Miss Lolita was sitting in a comfortable reclining chair and had her eyes closed. There were a few other residents in the recreation room where family members came to gather with their loved ones.

Roberts and I spoke for a few minutes about the kind of care that his home could provide. I didn't want to disturb Miss Lolita. Along with other elderly residents I saw, she slept in the chair. It's a wakeup call to someone like me. I couldn't wait to leave and appreciate the freedom I have. I don't think I could work in a nursing home. It would be heartbreaking when someone I had come to love passed away, as surely happens regularly. I was acting paranoid and I knew it, but the place really affected me.

I was looking around for Lolita's family members, but Roberts told me that they would be coming by that evening. We waited a few more minutes, and Roberts gave me a bottle of spring water to drink. Of course, I had to discuss the 1923 murders with him. But he shed no additional information on the investigation, just reinforcing all the previous facts I had come to learn from various sources about past suspects.

In Roberts's opinion, whoever committed the murders had some connection to the young women—either a jealous boyfriend, a jilted lover, or perhaps a loser of some sort—someone who always struck out with the girls. Some men can't get a date and have been hurt many times in their efforts to get close to a woman and, thus, according to Roberts, who had some knowledge of psychology, might lash out at women due to their sense of inferiority.

It made perfect sense to me, and I absorbed his theories and filed them away in my mind for later reference.

Some ten minutes later, Lolita awoke. I didn't rush in to speak with her right away, as I wanted to give her a chance to fully awaken. From a distance, I saw a beautiful Felicia, in her white uniform, go in and attend to Lolita. She adjusted Lolita's position in her soft chair, fixing a pillow behind her and making sure she was comfortable. Miss Lolita's hair was combed, and Felicia made sure her makeup and lipstick were touched up.

I realized at that point that I had serious feelings for Felicia. She was the most stunning woman I had ever laid eyes on. And although her gray eyes were a knockout, her smile floored me every time I saw it. She was trim and fit, and her hair was long and dark, and was perfect for her gorgeous face. She was a ten out of ten for me. It is amazing how someone can fall pretty deeply for another person so soon after meeting him or her. I suppose that's love at first sight, which I had never really believed in—not until I came eye to eye with Felicia that very first time.

My life would not be enjoyable without Felicia being a part of it, though I had no idea how we could or should move forward from this very early and intense infatuation we had for one another. Once I got my assignment finished and the 1923 murder investigation all sewed up, I would talk to Felicia about the possibility of a relationship going forward. I prayed that I would do nothing to risk losing my job or to screw up the Lolita story. After all, it was my only opportunity to keep a very good-paying job. And who wants to date a poor, unemployed, homeless guy, even if he is cute? Yes, I had to add cute to the list. I have to hold on to a shred of self-confidence, after all! Love begins within, or so I tell myself.

Felicia and I made eye contact for two full seconds, then we said our hellos without showing any special interest outwardly. We knew that she could lose her job if she was discovered flirting with or dating anyone connected to the nursing home.

Jeremy Roberts was right on the scene, and I made a special point not to stare at sweet Felicia. But it was killing me. When you are very attracted to a very beautiful woman, it is almost impossible not to look at her.

Roberts whispered in Miss Lolita's ear, "Lou, the reporter from the Washington newspaper, is here again, and he brought your favorite homemade ice cream!" Miss Lolita's eyes lit right up when she finally realized I was there.

"Show that young whippersnapper in! Don't make anyone with pistachio ice cream wait. Time's a-wasting!" She giggled.

As I got close to her, she said, "Now you know the deal: get real close so that these old eyes can see your baby face in all its glory!"

I got real close and kissed her gently on her cheek.

"Look, how sweet is that?" Felicia said.

"Careful, young man, there must be three hundred old women here who will fight me for you. I may have to beat them off of you!" Lolita laughed with a roar. "Did you go out of your way to that farm and get fresh-made ice cream for little old me?"

"Oh, no!" I bluffed. "You wanted pistachio, too? Some woman who's only ninety-nine took it from me . . . ."

"Listen, Sonny, I still can put you over my knee for a spanking! Don't let the white hair and lack of some fool you!" She laughed.

We all laughed with her, including some other residents in the lounge area who were enjoying our banter.

I pulled up a chair and sat almost up to her face. With my notepad at the ready, we talked more seriously to each other.

"Miss Lolita, I read the many great quotes in your wonderfully insightful diary. I was amazed at a woman so young, in her early twenties, being so philosophical."

She smiled at me and said, "Come a little closer. I want to see your eyes better. You're a handsome lad!"

I felt a little self-conscious about having Lolita study my eyes, but I moved my chair close enough that I could have kissed her. Felicia smiled a loving smile. I could tell that Felicia was a sensitive and loving person as soon as I met her. People can fake that sensitive caring stuff only so long. A person can see through you and find the real person rather quickly. Body language and a person's eyes can give away a person's attitude quickly. Perhaps that was why Lolita wanted to see my eyes up close.

"You know, Louis," Miss Lolita began, "my Uncle Walter was a doctor, and he was also a very positive, philosophical man who influenced my early days a great deal."

"Yes, I gathered that from your journal entries," I said.

"We used to read the Bible together, and then he, along with Minister Trylan of our church, along with the minister's son, Seymour, would discuss the meaning of the words and the real messages behind the verses of the Bible. It was like the minister wanted his son to learn while we were learning. The minister's son was a bookworm, and he could recite large sections of the Bible from memory. We learned so much with Minister Trylan. So, I had great influences early on and kept it going for life."

"Amazing. There were so many motivating sections in your diary. What really caught my eye, Miss Lolita, was the part about being the greatest living miracle. Can you elaborate on that for me?"

"Oh, yes. You see, we are each born as the greatest living miracle in the world. Most of us don't realize this or appreciate how much of a miracle we really are. I have been explaining this to everyone for my entire adult life. The odds of your being born with your exact personality are millions to one. And if you analyze the human heart, lungs, and brain, they contain over sixty thousand miles of blood vessels. The greatest living miracle in the world? Yes. You see, whether you are a millionaire or a homeless, penniless person, you are equally the greatest living miracle in the world. And you should never forget that!" She smiled lovingly.

"Miss Lolita, I have taken that for granted my entire life. I've been down and out, and sometimes at the top of my game, but I've never realized that we are each the greatest living miracle in the world. We are each as amazing, in reality, as each of the Seven Wonders of the World. In fact, the headline for my story about you will be 'The Greatest Living Miracle in the World.' And, Miss Lolita, can you touch on your self-suggestion statements?"

"I'd love to share an affirmation, or self-suggestion statement, with you. You must keep in mind that I have been saying the same statements for most of my life."

She began, "Thank you, Lord, for this new and glorious day. As I look out my window, I see a beautiful blue sky with gorgeous white clouds slowly passing by. I thank you for this new and glorious gift of a new day of life. But I don't realize why I have been chosen to receive this gift of life while so many others have been taken away. I will not waste this day. I will squeeze from the grapes you have given me, Lord, every drop of juice, not wasting one drop, as this could very possibly be my last day on earth. And if it is my last day on earth, it will be my finest day. I thank you, Lord, for all of the precious gifts you have given me throughout my life, but most of all I thank you for this extra precious gift of a new day of life." She smiled at me and said, "There is more, but I gave you the meat of it."

"You call them self-suggestion statements. You really are the Wise One, as people call you!"

"I am as equal in value as anyone else is," she said lovingly. "The reason they are self-suggestions is because as you repeat the statements to yourself, your inner mind accepts them and retains them in your brain for later retrieval. You see, it's easy for us to dwell on negative thoughts, as eighty percent of all things around us daily are negative in nature. So, to combat the negativity, I call it adding mental blinders to protect my mind from negativity. The positive statements create the mental blinders, and the negativity bounces off."

"You know, Miss Lolita, what you say makes perfect sense. But you have a special way of explaining things in easy-to-understand language."

"Miss Lolita, tell him the other morning statement you taught everyone," Felicia chimed in.

"Okay, sweetheart. Here is another positive statement I repeat a couple of times per day: 'I feel healthy, I feel happy, I feel terrific. I like myself. I like myself, I like myself. I will be successful; it's inevitable, because my aggressiveness will lead to opportunities for my success. I can, I will, I want to. All things are possible through belief in myself and the Lord, and with His help, I can accomplish anything.

'I feel great, I feel wonderful, I've got the world by the tail. If I start acting enthusiastic, I'll become enthusiastic; if I start acting positive, I will become positive; and if I start acting happy, I will become happy. It is amazing, but when I act enthusiastic, others around me become enthusiastic. When I act positive, others around me become positive. And when I act happy, others around me become happy. Life is rewarding, and we all have choices in life; we can choose to act positive or negative. I choose to act positive. We can act happy or we can act sad; I choose to act happy. Why would anyone in their right mind want to act sad? The Lord is my Shepherd, I shall not fear. After all, I was born into this life as God's greatest living miracle in the world. I owe it to Him, my family, and myself to be all I can be. Thank you, Lord. Amen.'

As Miss Lolita finished her daily positive statement, all I could do was look at her eyes and stare for a few seconds. Then I looked at Felicia, who had been mouthing the words along with Lolita. I realized just how powerful those words were. She had a smile on her face, and it all made perfect sense to me. There was silence in our area. I looked around the room at the elderly residents who were either sleeping in their wheelchairs or sitting and staring at nothing, self-absorbed in their own world.

This was truly an amazing 110-year-old woman who fully understood life. Miss Lolita understood what life really meant, while most of us are baffled by life's purpose. Miss Lolita knew that to waste a life would be an insult to our Creator. Now it made perfect sense to me. God always has a master plan. Why else would Miss Lolita have entered the record books for longevity in Maryland and many other states? She had no doubt helped thousands of people with her philosophy of life and her motivation in general.

My story about Lolita was taking form. It would portray an extraordinary woman who changes people's lives. But it would also portray a woman who lived through the three murders of 1923. I believed that event alone had changed Lolita's life, as 1923 was when she had first realized that every life was the greatest living miracle in the world.

Then Miss Lolita shared something else that she had learned early in her life while reading the Bible with her uncle and her minister. It was the Parable of the Talents from Matthew 25.

Lolita quoted the parable to Felicia and me by heart: "It is as if a man, going on a journey, summoned his servants and entrusted his property to them; to one he gave five talents, to another two, to another one, to each according to his ability. Then he went away. The one who had received the five talents went off at once and traded with them, and made five more talents. In the same way, the one who had the two talents made two more talents. But the one who had received the one talent went off and dug a hole in the ground and hid his master's money. After a long time the master of those slaves came and settled accounts with them. Then the one who had received the five talents came forward, bringing five more talents, saying, 'Master, you handed over to me five talents; see, I have made five more talents.' His master said to him, 'Well done, good and trustworthy slave; you have been trustworthy in a few things, I will put you in charge of many things; enter into the joy of your master.' And the one with the two talents also came forward, saying, 'Master, you handed over to me two talents; see, I have made two more talents.' His master said to him, 'Well done, good and trustworthy slave; you have been trustworthy in a few things, I will put you in charge of many things; enter into the joy of your master.' Then the one who had received the one talent also came forward, saying, 'Master, I knew that you were a harsh man, reaping where you did not sow, and gathering where you did not scatter seed; so I was afraid, and I went and hid your talent in the ground. Here you have what is yours.' But his master replied, 'You wicked and lazy slave! You knew that I reaped where I did not sow and gathered where I did not scatter? Then you ought to have invested my money with the bankers, and on my return, I would have received what was my own with interest. So I will take the talent from you, and give it to the one with the ten talents. For to all those who have, more will be given, and they will have an abundance; but from those who have nothing, even what they have will be taken away."

Miss Lolita explained that a talent was a unit of money, but the parable works well nowadays to teach us that our gifts and talents must never be wasted and hidden away, but maximized. And she said she believed that in the hereafter, we will be given a chance to review our lives in minute detail, second by second, over and over. We will be pleased with a life that was well spent and productive, or we will regret a life that was wasted and not maximized, and we will ponder the results for eternity.

While Miss Lolita spoke, I didn't interrupt. Rather, I jotted notes and added material for my future news story. Actually, I had enough to run at least ten stories, but I knew I'd have to edit it down to one thorough and insightful story. The Hagerstown murders would surely be included in Miss Lolita's story. They had to be. They were as much a part of who she grew up to be as was her uncle's influence.

Like a nagging splinter that keeps a finger throbbing in pain, the 1923 murders kept haunting me. I was sure someone in the hereafter was communicating something important to me through my dreams. Someone was pushing me onward to uncover the long-forgotten murderers. The questions I had about the murders kept banging around in my head, clamoring to be presented to anyone who would listen. I was sure it was one of the three girls haunting me, but I also thought it could be Lolita's Uncle Walter, the doctor. Someone was trying to give me clues. Every so often, the cross, the brick, and the lion ring would pop into my mind: the cross in front of the set of chipped red bricks, and the lion ring on a person's finger. But it would end abruptly with no further clues. I knew from reading Lolita's diary that she had had similar visions. How was I going to broach the subject she had once told me was off limits? The last thing I wanted to do was get a 110-year-old woman upset. She'd probably take a swing at me! I couldn't risk raising her blood pressure.

Just then, Sergeant Pawler entered the room. He looked around at first, studying each person in the room carefully. Then he walked real close to Miss Lolita and said, "Ma'am, how are you doing on this fine day?" He was as sweet as an altar boy, and his eyes were friendlier than ever.

"Oh, hi, Sergeant. I'm just grand! I've got my angel Felicia here with me. She's a doll. And for laughs, I have Louis here, who is in training for how to handle life and all its beauty."

As Lolita said "beauty," she turned and winked at Felicia, who smiled a shy grin.

She was indeed a wise old woman. She knew my heart had been broken before, and that life for me had been very empty. Miss Lolita could sense so much from my eyes, my posture, and the inflections of the words I spoke. She knew I needed an angel, someone who could give me a reason to exist. She knew I needed a pep talk about life, our purpose on earth, and, most of all, how we each are born as the greatest living miracle in the world. I needed that lesson more than anything else.

Felicia smiled at me, and once again, my heart skipped a beat. I wanted her so badly—not in any kind of sexual way, at least not at this time, but just to hold her close. I wanted to gaze into her eyes and enter another world. I wanted to escape, for even a short time, and tell her how much I cared for her. I needed her to tell me how much she cared for me. A man, as well as a woman, needs to know that someone they care for needs them very much.

That question kept coming back to me: where do we go from here? I would move heaven and earth to be with Felicia. I knew I had to tell her how I felt. I quickly returned Felicia's smile and held it for a full two seconds. I felt like a kid in love for the first time. Her eyes sparkled and smiled back at me. Just then, Pawler stared at my stupid-looking smile. His eyes narrowed as he sized me up. I glanced down at my shoes.

Sergeant Pawler looked back at Miss Lolita and smiled. "You are the rare treasure of Hagerstown, Miss Lolita. Don't let this clown here annoy you. I will be right down the hall. If he bothers you at all, just send for me and I will pistol whip him into the ground!" He giggled like a child.

"Oh, that won't be necessary, Officer. I'll just spray mace into his eyes. I always keep it handy!" She laughed.

"Oh, thanks, Miss Lolita!" I laughed. I always seem to get people pissed. "Just don't give the mace to my boss; he'll spray me blind for sure!"

"You?" she asked. "You look like a little angel."

"Don't let my pretty face fool you."

"With that load of crap, I'm out of here," said Pawler. "I'll be at the entrance. Good day, ladies." He smiled, still studying Felicia as he moved away. He knew she was beautiful. And he also realized I was crazy about her. What he couldn't figure out was what the hell she saw in me, and it clearly irked him. It was all over his face.

As he walked out of the room, he kept looking back and forth between Felicia and me and shaking his head.

"Again, I'll be at the front entrance if you need me, Lou."

"Okay, Sarge," I said.

"So, Louis, do you have enough background for your news story?" Lolita asked.

"Miss Lolita, I am getting there. But I must say, I have never met anyone as interesting as you."

"Listen, Sonny, I am just trying to be myself, and help people along the way. We all are great and special. No one is ever better than anyone else; they are just different. Anything else in the diary you want to talk about?"

"Well, there are a few things, but one thing comes to mind: the various visions you have had."

"Oh, my, I have had so many visions. You see, when I was a young girl, I had very intense dreams. At least, I thought they were dreams, until Uncle Walter taught me how to distinguish the difference between a dream and an actual vision. You see, dreams stem from the subconscious mind; they are played out while you're asleep. A vision is something more real."

"You mention early on in the diary seeing a beautiful woman in a white gown."

"Yes. When I was around fifteen, I had a few visions of a beautiful woman I later learned was the Virgin Mary."

"That's wild!" I exclaimed.

"Well, at the time, I didn't realize how very special it was, but years later it sank in."

"What was it like—the vision?"

"Oh, my—she was the most beautiful woman I had ever seen. She was enveloped in the brightest light ever. She kept telling me that I would have a long life on earth. And she told me that I would change a great many lives of the people I met along the way. And this was my purpose in life: to touch, change, and help as many people as I could."

"Amazing! Did she say anything about heaven?"

"The Virgin Mary actually showed me heaven through one of my visions. And, oh, my, I had never seen anything so pristine, so bright, so perfect in my entire life. It was only for a few seconds, but it was the most exhilarating and intense feeling ever. When I asked her if I would be going to heaven, the Virgin Mary explained that not everyone goes to heaven immediately. Many go into somewhat of a waiting area for what is sometimes a long period of time, and they graduate to heaven only through prayers said for them by people on earth.

"When I asked if I would go to heaven, the Virgin Mary said that I would, but only after many years of good deeds on earth. She said that I had to earn my way to heaven, and that I must pray for all non-believers and sinners, and for all the clergy of the world, because they, too, sin like us."

"Do you still get visions?" I asked, my mouth hanging open a bit in anticipation.

"No, not of the Virgin. Those visions started and stopped in the same year. But every few years I receive strong messages that I feel are from her, and I do receive very strong visions of other things. My uncle taught me how to calm my body to open myself to receiving visions."

"You must feel very special."

"Listen, Sonny, I will tell you that I am truly blessed. To have a life as great as mine, I can only be blessed. Every second is a blessing, and we must thank God through prayer and fasting for all that we have been given."

"Miss Lolita, don't take this the wrong way, but are you scared of dying?" As soon as the words were out of my mouth, I was almost sorry I had asked such a stupid question to a woman who was 110 years old.

Felicia looked at me with a puzzled look on her face, as if to say, "Not a good question."

Without hesitation, Miss Lolita smiled a big wide smile, looked up, and said, "Am I scared of dying? No! You see, Sonny, heaven is the ultimate reward for a life well lived. When a person believes very strongly in God, they know that passing on means graduating to a higher level. Though the body no longer exists, the spirit goes on for eternity in a place where all their loved ones have been lovingly waiting to reunite with them. It is the ultimate reward that the universe can offer. So, no, I will live my life until my number is called. And when it is, I will be ecstatic that my task on earth has been sufficiently completed. I will finally get to graduate!" She smiled a big smile.

I was speechless as I looked at this woman whose face showed the character of a life well lived, well used, well earned. I looked at Felicia, whose face showed the tracks of two sets of tears. As I observed them both, I felt my eyes tear up, too, and for the first time in my life, I didn't try to hide my tears.

I felt honored to know Miss Lolita, the Wise One. For the first time in many months, I felt truly blessed to be alive. Hagerstown had been a wake-up call for me in so many ways. Maybe having a target on my back added to my appreciation of life and the future.

Felicia also was a blessing, like an angel from heaven, an unexpected surprise. I had been at the end of my rope in so many respects, and then she magically appeared right before my eyes. And it was the eyes that met mine that did the trick.

My real concern, though, was not fear for my life, but fear for the lives of the innocent people around me. There was Sergeant Pawler, who was only following the captain's orders to protect me. He had his life on the line protecting my ass. There was Felicia, the angel from above, sent to save me from myself, but I knew that I couldn't risk anyone else knowing about our interest in one another—not until Billy Blaine and anyone else involved were apprehended. The target on my back must not include others, especially not Felicia. I could never live with myself if something dangerous happened to her. After all, I had seen a couple of suspicious-looking cars following me. But when in fear, everything can look suspicious.

And Miss Lolita—there was no way I would allow any harm to come to her, certainly not because of anything that someone was blaming me for. I would rather quit my job at the newspaper and throw all my notes in the garbage than continue putting her at risk.

My cell phone had been vibrating repeatedly over the last few minutes, showing me three people trying to reach me. I made up my mind not to answer for anyone, not until I finished my Miss

Lolita interview. I also wanted to pursue the Hagerstown murders angle of the story, because I knew that if I returned my boss's calls from the *Gazette*, he very likely would shut my assignment down. In fact, I was sure that he had had his fill of me and my antics in Hagerstown already.

My buddies Fred and Graham wanted constant updates, but I realized that I needed to cut them off for the time being because if they knew of all the violence that had transpired thus far, they might be spooked and contact the Hagerstown authorities or Glavin. I was already walking on very thin ice. I once again pictured myself flipping hamburgers at Wendy's, and flipping them on the floor. But then again I don't think I'd fare well in that job either. I don't take orders very well, or so I've been told.

"Hello there, Mary. Good to see you, too!"

"Thanks so much for bringing in Miss Lolita's all-time favorite homemade ice cream!" Mary said to me with a smile. "Miss Lolita, would you like some now?" she asked.

"Thank you so much, Mary," Miss Lolita said. "But wait about twenty minutes. We should be finishing up soon. I think I've reviewed all a hundred and ten years of my life. At least that's what it feels like!" She laughed a hearty laugh. "This young whippersnapper must be writing a novel instead of a news story! Mr. Lou, you trying to write another *War and Peace*?" Miss Lolita laughed.

"No, actually, you have enough of a past that I could do a movie documentary," I said brightly.

"Oh, my!" she responded.

"Okay, Miss Lolita, I'll be back in a short while. Don't you go anywhere on me!" Mary joked.

"Yeah, sure, like I'm going hang-gliding or something. Get a load of her, will you, Lou?"

"You probably have more energy than I do, Miss Lolita."

"Well, you're lucky I like you so much. I'm counting on you writing an award winning story there, Sonny."

"Don't you worry; it will be a gem. Just gotta make it back safely!" I looked into Felicia's magnificent gray eyes.

"Mr. Louis, I keep reminding you to come close. Are you scared I have some disease? Now come closer so I can see the whites of those eyes."

"You going to hypnotize me again, Miss Lolita? You know, I may fall madly in love with you if I get too close."

"Fat chance, Sonny! You'd have to get in line behind all those old perverts that are staying at this home. It don't matter how old a man gets, he's still a horn dog 'til the day he drops. They're all after me here!" She laughed hysterically.

"They are!" Felicia chimed in.

"They're all horn dogs?" I asked.

"That too!" Felicia smiled.

"Bunch of perverts if you ask me!" Miss Lolita said again.

We spoke about Lolita's childhood again, her mom and pop, the farm, the good times, and the early years of her marriage to D. K., who was a mechanic. We spoke about the town back then, the theater she frequented, and the movie stars of the day that she had idolized. We spoke about the very first cars she remembered, which needed to be crank-started and frequently broke down, stranding carloads of people. But she loved those peaceful days when you sipped fresh lemonade and sat on the family swing in the yard and listened to nature and the songbirds; days when women would bake fresh pies and cakes and make large meals for men who worked hard—men who could actually eat a side of beef for dinner.

She remembered days gone by when the girls would dance all evening long, innocently, and boys would not get fresh for fear of the likes of the girls' fathers. As Miss Lolita stated, "Everyone had shotguns in those days, and not many people acted up."

"That would make me behave!" I chimed in, and glanced at Felicia in time to see her blush.

"Yes," Lolita said wistfully, her thoughts many years in the past. "Those were the golden days when the family, friends, and aunts and uncles would gather 'round the piano for hours just to sing the songs they loved." she reminisced, with a faraway look on her face.

"Why, there were many a night that we went to bed with a couple of hearth-warmed bricks, just to keep us warm 'til we fell off to sleep. Then there were nasty, cold nights, some of them. And the summers we had to sometimes soak our sheets in water and wring them out and sleep on them damp, all just to keep somewhat cool in the boiling heat. No such contraption as air conditioners in those days, you know? Today's society is a little too spoiled for my liking. But I'm an old lady with too much to say . . . ."

"No, you're not!" I argued. "You are a real treasure. You are a valuable doorway to a past we all want so much to live in, but can't. Through your eyes, we are able to experience, to see, to taste, and to yearn for the times you were so fortunate to have lived through. So don't ever apologize for reminiscing about better days."

After a slight pause, I changed the subject. "Miss Lolita, now I have to ask you a tough question: What would you like the world to remember you for? And give me a powerful quote I can use, please."

"Okay, Sonny. Words to live by: God gave you a gift of eighty-six thousand four hundred seconds today. Have you used one to say thank you?"

"Awesome!" I said. "That's a keeper!" I wrote the quote down on my crammed notepad. "And how would you like the world to remember you?"

"Someone over a hundred years ago asked Andrew Carnegie, the steel empire multimillionaire, how it was possible that so many of his employees became millionaires—forty-three, in fact—while working for him. A reporter wanted to know what Andrew Carnegie's secret was. Carnegie answered this way: 'You develop millionaires the way you mine gold. You expect to move tons of dirt to find an ounce of gold. But when you go digging, you don't go looking for the dirt; you go looking for the gold.' So, Sonny, you can write this down: My whole life, I always went looking for the gold in every person, never the dirt, and everyone—I don't care who they are—has some gold in them, though it may take patience and moving mountains of dirt to find it. You see, too many people pre-judge one another, jump to conclusions too quickly, and they give up on someone too soon."

I was writing like a madman as fast as Miss Lolita was speaking. I'm the only one who can read my chicken scratch in the first place, and sometimes I need a few drinks just to figure it out. Well, also an Italian woman at the newspaper, Nancy—but only the two of us can read my handwriting. As fast as I was scribbling Miss Lolita's words, this would be even harder than usual to decipher.

There was silence for a few seconds after I finished writing. I looked at Felicia who had an "I told you she was awesome!" look on her face. Miss Lolita just stared into my eyes, saying nothing. I studied her in return, because I knew I would never come across another person so deep, so insightful, and so worldly as Lolita, ever again. This was my once-in-a-lifetime moment with her, and I tried to etch it deep into my brain. I wanted to remember Miss Lolita, her messages of inspiration, and her awesome attitude forever.

Here was a woman unafraid to pass from this world and, as she had said, "graduate" to that better place, but only after she had more than earned her place in the hereafter. No one had ever explained it like that to me before. Life is not a right, but a blessing we should be thankful for.

We should not squander our moments on earth. And, yes, we must earn our right to "graduate" to that better place above, where we just might have an eternity to review and relive every second of our lives over and over again. That was a scary thought if a life was selfishly misused.

Felicia looked at me with sadness in her eyes. I wondered if it was because she realized that Miss Lolita was ready to go to her Maker at any moment, and Felicia would lose her. Maybe Felicia had just recognized her own mortality, which can be an earthshaking experience. We are all young in our hearts. But here we were, staring at a very weathered person, reminding us that we, too, would become weathered and old-looking—nothing like we are in our prime.

The silence was deafening as I heard the humming of the overhead fluorescents, which sounded as loud as a Mack truck at that moment. My mind was working in overdrive, ruminating on the philosophy of an expert with 110 years to her credit.

CHAPTER FOURTEEN

T hen it happened. All hell suddenly broke loose! The loudspeaker blurted out the dreaded announcement to staff doctors: "Code Blue! Code Blue in kitchen! All medical personnel, Code Blue, kitchen! Please report!"

Felicia looked at me and her face changed to a very serious expression as she blurted out, "I have to leave! Please stay with her!" She left abruptly.

Nothing like this had ever happened to me before, though I had heard about it and seen it on television. A Code Blue usually meant cardiac arrest. Granted, it was a nursing home of mostly elderly residents. Still, I had a very uncomfortable feeling in my stomach. You don't expect to see anyone carried out on a stretcher when you are visiting a nursing home, simply trying to cheer up a lonely resident. And how about all the other people in the home hearing the Code Blue announcement? What was going through their minds?

I looked at Miss Lolita, who now had a sad look on her face. I was sure that she had lived through many times like this before. She looked at me and said, "They are very good in this home. The medical people are top-notch. Let me say a prayer." She was silent in her prayer, as I watched her. I also asked God silently to help whoever needed help at that moment, knowing that it was all in His hands. All we can do is ask for the best for everyone.

There was silence. Then a black woman dressed in a nurse's uniform rushed into the room and exclaimed, "It was Mary, the food care worker. Mary, in the kitchen." She ran over to Miss Lolita as if she could help the situation somehow. "Mary's heart stopped; she collapsed and cracked her head open. Miss Lolita . . . ."

"Clara!" Miss Lolita commanded the woman's attention. "Mary is in the best hands possible. Please, now. The doctors are there, and they will do whatever they can. Please stay calm. Come, hold my hand," she said, as she reached out in the direction of Clara's voice.

Clara held her hand, saying, "It was so sudden-like in the kitchen."

I looked back at the doorway and saw another woman dressed in green, no doubt an orderly. She, too, rushed into the large room. "Clara," she screamed, "it was poison. They say they believe Mary was poisoned. There was a bowl of ice cream next to where she'd been standing. She was poisoned, Clara! She may be dead!"

"Poisoned? Ice cream? But how? Who would do such . . . ?" Miss Lolita said.

"Holy crap!" I shouted. "It was Billy Blaine. Somehow he got to the ice cream I brought here today!"

"You?" Clara demanded. "What ice cream?"

"You mean someone . . . ?" Miss Lolita asked.

"Yes, the same person tried to poison me last night with something called thallium," I explained. "It is quite deadly, and it almost killed me, but I had such a diluted amount that I was able to recover."

"Mr. Lou, they wanted to kill me?" Miss Lolita asked in shock, her mouth open.

I looked at her carefully. "I'm not sure, Miss Lolita. Maybe they wanted to kill many people. Mary must have been tasting the pistachio ice cream right before bringing you some. I hope she had very little, and maybe she will be okay. They won't know for some time, though. It is a very potent poison and can kill fast. I pray she didn't serve it to anyone else. I am so glad you didn't have any!" I shook my head.

"But who could have . . . ?" Lolita snapped.

"Millie's!" I remembered suddenly. "It must have happened at Millie's. I had it stored in their freezer while the sarge and I ate lunch. Anyone could have . . . ."

Suddenly my heart dropped as if I had seen a ghost. There, standing right in the doorway of the large room, was Billy Blaine. He was sweaty and dirty, with long, stringy hair. He had a sadistic smile on his face and held a large steak knife in his right hand.

"Yeah, it was poison," he said. "Thallium is a great way to kill somebody. By the time you realize you've been poisoned, it's too late. Listen, hump-head, you should be dead. So I had to come back for you—you and the old bat."

"Mr. Lou, what's happening?" Miss Lolita spoke urgently into my ear.

"Please, Miss Lolita, don't say anything, and stay calm," I whispered back.

"Oh, so you're going to protect her, now? The inquiring reporter. Good! I'll kill her first then!" He smiled a wicked grin.

"Billy, why do you want to do that?" I asked calmly.

"Why, he asks!" He laughed loudly. "I only kill people who don't know how to mind their own business. Your mouth is as big as your ass! Asshole!"

"But . . ." I tried to reason.

"But you're going to die. Say your goodbyes. She's as old as hell anyway. She's probably happy, right, Momma?" He roared with laughter.

Then it dawned on me that the poison in the kitchen had been a diversion. Everyone had run to the emergency in the kitchen. This left Billy a few minutes undisturbed to rain his terror down on us. I would try to buy some time. Where was Sergeant Pawler? He must have gone to the kitchen when he heard that Mary was poisoned. She had been used in an attack just to get to me. I needed more time.

"Billy, you don't want to do this."

"Shut up, hard-on!" he screamed. "Don't even think of screaming or trying anything, or I'll kill some innocent people over here, just for fun. They're old farts anyway."

"Billy, this isn't you." I hoped I could reason with him and talk him down from his rage.

"You piss me off. You just don't die easy! I've got to get it over with."

"You ain't got any guts, Sonny!" Miss Lolita shouted. "No-balls Billy!" she screamed at him.

"You old bag of bones!" he screamed, and he raised the knife and ran for us. "Die!"

Suddenly the knife went straight up in the air and he grunted loudly. I protected Miss Lolita with my body.

Billy suddenly folded backwards as his knees buckled. I stared at him while preparing to die. But he fell backwards fast and someone jumped on top of him. He screamed in pain as the knife fell out of his hand and his arm made a cracking sound.

Of all possible people—it was my buddy Graham! He was wrestling on top of Billy and pinning Billy's arm way back behind his back.

"Son of a bitch!" I yelled, as I scrambled to the floor to grab the knife.

"Hit that son of a bitch a shot for me!" Miss Lolita shouted, shocking me with her words and making me smile at the same time, even as my hands shook uncontrollably.

"Kick his balls off!" she added.

Just then, Sergeant Pawler suddenly jumped on Billy with his cuffs, screaming, "You dirty piece of crap! I should kill you on the spot," he shouted.

My heart was racing faster than I ever remembered it doing. I didn't think anyone's heart could beat that fast. Pawler read Billy his rights while I tried to slow my heart.

"You all right, buddy?" Graham asked as he hugged me hard.

"Oh, I'm fine. I think I pissed myself, but I'm fine!" I tried to smile.

I went over to Miss Lolita and said, "It's all over, Miss Lolita. Everyone's fine."

"Hey, Sonny, I'm blind, not deaf! I know Billy no-balls is going to jail!"

"Miss Lolita, you really did piss him off with that comment."

"Oh, my, did I?"

"He was lunging for you."

"Yes, but you would have kicked his balls off."

"Me?" I asked.

"Yes, Sonny, you!" She smiled. "Don't ever underestimate yourself. I know your heart. It's big!" She added softly, "Real big."

"Thanks." I smiled.

"Bigger than your ass!" she laughed loudly. "I knew you would have stopped Billy cold. You never would have allowed him to harm me."

I thought about what Miss Lolita said. I was never a tough guy or a great fighter as a youngster. But I do think that if Billy had gotten any closer, I might have lunged at him to protect Lolita. Would it have been suicide? Yes. But there comes a time in one's life when you do the seemingly impossible. It may only take a few seconds, but those seconds could save a life, even if it means losing one's own life in a miscalculated move.

I hoped I would never be faced with that kind of life-threatening decision ever again. Graham did make that life-or-death decision to lunge at Billy Blaine. It could have ended very badly for Graham. If Billy had suddenly heard Graham and quickly turned, Graham very possibly would have been stabbed to death.

It was a pisser, though, how Miss Lolita got all nervy with Billy Blaine, mouthing off at him and berating him while he held a large knife! I find that many older people speak their minds. And if I were 110 years old, I might have done the same thing. In reality, it's usually not smart to piss off someone who is prepared to kill you.

But then again, Miss Lolita was very wise, and maybe she knew something about Billy's personality. Maybe he didn't have the balls to slice someone up, especially a little old lady who could have been his grandmother. Billy clearly wasn't working alone. We needed to know more about him, particularly where he was from and who he was working with.

Was it all about the Hagerstown murders of ninety years back? Could someone actually still care about something that happened so long ago? What was the motive, the gain? Why even take such a risk? And more importantly, was Billy going to talk? Or would he try to protect whoever else was involved?

"Graham!" I finally voiced my surprise. "What the hell? How did you ever . . . ?"

"Louie, Louie, Louie. You know I love you, man!" He smiled then gave me the bear hug of a mountain man. "That Harold Glavin is the boss from hell, Lou. You know that. Well, when you were being evasive and not returning his and Gloria's calls, he flipped out. He called me into his office every two hours to interrogate me about you and what I knew from our conversations. Of course, I knew very little about your

Hagerstown troubles. So he kept getting updates from the Hagerstown police captain, Joel Krolm. That's when he sent me this morning to trail you and report to him. He, of course, used the new camera as an excuse."

"Camera . . . ?"

"Yeah, the newspaper just purchased a mega-camera, very high-definition. He wants me to take some good shots of Lolita and the nursing home."

"But . . . you attacked a killer! Are you insane, buddy?" I exclaimed.

"Dude, you know I have training."

"Yeah, in making babies?"

"Knucklehead, I am trained in Tae Kwon Do. I'm a black belt. You knew that, didn't you?"

"Man, I don't remember. But you sure do know how to take someone down!"

"Damn straight, buddy. It has to do more with discipline than anything else. But if threatened, I can be deadly within a split second."

"Damn! I gotta remember that, man!"

"Well, I've got to run right now. I have to give the boss a full report or he'll fire my black ass!"

We said we would catch up on everything later that night over dinner, and he took off.

Shortly thereafter, Sergeant Pawler's backup arrived, and they took Billy Blaine, handcuffed and shackled, straight to jail.

A few officers stood guard at the nursing home, and one watched over Miss Lolita, who was in her glory. She wanted to know all about the young officer and his family, and, amazingly, she was already giving words of inspiration to the impressionable officer.

Twenty minutes elapsed while I tried to settle down. Jeremy Roberts and I spoke about the attack and poisoning incident. Mary was responding well to the medication at the hospital. It seems Sergeant Pawler had deduced immediately that it was the same thallium poison used on me, so the hospital had been ready for her as soon as she arrived by ambulance.

Roberts was stunned at the terror that one person could perform in a couple days' time.

"This town never has this much action. Someone clearly was very scared," he said. "Your boss called me about ten minutes ago for an update. He was very agitated."

"Harold's always agitated. He can't act any other way. He is always pissed off at me in particular."

"Yes, he had some choice words when your name came up." He chuckled at the memory and shook his head.

"It's a job, you know?" I said.

"Yes. Well, Lou, do you have enough for a story so far?"

"Mr. Roberts, I have enough for a couple of books. There is so much depth to Miss Lolita alone. Then there are the 1923 murders and the history of it all. And then we have the violent outbreak from Billy Blaine and whoever hired him, because we all know Billy wasn't acting alone in his reign of terror."

"Do you think we will ever have closure to those terrible murders? Though it was so long ago, those girls' deaths still hang over this town like a heavy storm cloud."

"Yes, Mr. Roberts, I do believe that we will have some answers to this investigation now that Billy Blaine has finally been apprehended. Blaine could lead us to the ringleader who hired him. Blaine is no doubt a two-bit criminal who isn't capable of masterminding and inflicting all this terror by himself. Blaine is the key, though. The authorities will wear him down and get to his connections."

Mr. Roberts excused himself for some official business.

A couple of minutes later, Felicia came back into the large room. Her face was ashen and she was clearly shaking. We hugged quickly but tightly.

"She almost died!" Felicia said about Mary. "That creep poisoned an innocent person."

"It was a brilliant diversion," I said. "He put the emphasis on the fallen victim in the kitchen, a real emergency situation. This gave Billy Blaine free rein, without Sergeant Pawler on the scene, to try to kill us. Thank God for Graham."

"I know," she agreed. "I was introduced to your friend as he was talking with the authorities in the kitchen. He's a great friend!"

"Graham is one of a kind. But I was shocked, I will admit, that he was capable of swooping in and taking down Blaine. We are taking Graham out for a fancy dinner tonight, Felicia."

"I'm right there with you!" she said with a warm smiled. "He saved you and Miss Lolita. He really is a special hero."

Miss Lolita called me over and asked me to come real close. I could see the hues of her old, brown eyes. I was used to the routine now. Miss Lolita needed to see me close up. She wanted to tell me something important—very important.

"You know, Sonny, I feel even closer to you now. We both were the target of an elaborate murder plan. We very well could have be dead if that Billy Blaine had succeeded. I'm an old woman, I will admit it, and I am not afraid to meet my Maker. I have some ideas I'd like to share with God about earth and some improvements I'd like to see here, mostly about global warming and that thallium poison, which is one doozy of a killer." She smiled a big smile. "When I get up there, though, I will surely put in a good word for you two," she said, gesturing between Felicia and me. "Now, you know that from time to time I have these strange visions. Well, Sonny, I will admit that right before I met you that very first time, I had a vision of Felicia and you walking hand in hand on a white, sandy beach and happier than ever. I also envisioned you both with a long, healthy life and blessed with children."

"So you knew that I'd fall for this beautiful woman?"

"Of course! Besides beauty, she's an angel, unmatched by anyone."

Felicia smiled shyly as she said, "I love you, Miss Lolita. You are my guardian angel."

"Now, Sonny, get real close, and put your ears up high for what I'm about to tell you," she said with a serious tone. "I'm going to only speak about this once. Got those ears up high?" She laughed.

"They're sticking straight up for you!" I said. "Shoot."

"Well, I didn't want to talk about the 1923 murders. And honestly, I thought they would go unsolved forever. But Billy may help in the investigation. So, here goes: My visions throughout the past ninety years have been consistent: the lion's head, which is actually a ring; the dead girls, all bringing me to a cross. But, after many years, the visions changed to a cemetery where the cross was located. And then there were those bricks, old chipped bricks. And, oh, yes, a serrated type of butcher's knife used in the murders. Sonny, if you follow all the leads I see, you will be able to get to the bottom of what happened ninety years ago. Now, I told you that I didn't want to go back to those days again, so I will just leave it there. Now, don't you go messing around with me and ask me any questions, or I'll chase you down the hallways here with my killer wheelchair. I'll run your ass right out of town if you don't behave yourself!" She laughed, but then she started to cough.

"You tell him, Miss Lolita," Felicia said with a happy laugh. She enjoyed toying with me.

Miss Lolita was clearly troubled about her recollection of the visions about the murders. So I didn't bother to tell her about the visions I'd had. I didn't want to tell her that mine were very similar to hers. I didn't want to tell anyone, really. I wasn't sure why, but maybe I was scared that people would think I was half a nut if I started to recount the details of my visions to everyone.

Miss Lolita could give me no additional help at the moment, so why disturb her any further? After all, we had had enough excitement for the day.

Later, Graham shared with me how he was able to take Billy Blaine down so easily. He said it's called a roundhouse kick—meaning that he snuck up behind Billy, spun around, and kicked a martial arts kick to the back of both of Billy's legs. This move basically caves in the legs, and automatically, the arms go up in the air as the body collapses. Once the arm with the knife was straight up in the air, Graham grabbed it, twisted the hand, and pulled the arm quickly behind Billy's back. The knife fell out of Billy's hand as Graham broke or dislocated Billy's shoulder, causing a great deal of pain. It was brilliant.

As Graham explained it—and as I had witnessed—it all goes down in a split second. It takes a great deal of practice and conditioning of body and mind. But you basically go on automatic pilot as a result of years of practice. The average person has no defense against the moves of a black-belt martial arts student. The only thing that would scare me, I thought, was if the assailant had a gun. There is no guarantee when a gun is in the mix.

Officer Robert Cianci, whom I had met during my first hospital stay, came up to me in the recreation room. Quietly, he said, "Captain Krolm needs you to pick Billy out of a lineup at the precinct. I have been instructed to bring you in. You ready to go, buddy?"

The officer was young and tall, good-looking in his uniform and so much nicer in demeanor than Sergeant Pawler. Maybe it was because the young officer was so new and Pawler had been in the street for years. Maybe the years harden an officer.

"Okay, I guess I can go. I'm finished here for the time being."

I reminded Felicia that we would head to the Italian restaurant at around eight, and I would call Graham's cell phone.

The precinct was quiet at 3:30 p.m., when Officer Cianci and I walked into Captain Krolm's office.

The captain motioned for me to sit and for Officer Cianci to give us some privacy and close the door behind him.

"Well, I told you this wouldn't turn out good, my young Washington reporter."

"Captain, will Mary okay?"

"She will be fine. Sergeant Pawler was quick on the scene and recognized the symptoms of the thallium poison. We called ahead and prepared the hospital for her arrival. She'll be there a few days. She's not as strong as you are, but she is fortunate to be alive.

"This whole thing could have been quite deadly," Captain Krolm continued. "This Blaine character had it planned quite well, with the attention going to the kitchen. You realize you should be dead, don't you?"

"I don't feel all that alive right now, Captain." I smiled weakly.

"Yeah, well, I did warn you it was not going to turn out well. But I need you to pick Blaine out of a lineup. Just routine, you know. Then I can fill you in a little about the case."

The lineup contained six men, mostly young, some unshaven and unkempt. Billy was easy to pick out: he was the long-haired, straggly, dirty-looking person with a nasty smirk on his face. He knew that he was dead in the water and would probably do ten years in prison. What a waste of a life, I thought. Add ten wasted years to his current age, then release Blaine after all that time locked up, and hope that he will find a real job and become a good citizen. He would most likely wind up in jail again.

Out of all the men in the lineup, Billy Blaine looked like a real thug, a hardened criminal. The others were probably undercover and off-duty officers. So even if I had forgotten that ugly mug of a face, I still would have picked Billy for the sinister look he in his eyes.

Even though I was behind protective glass, I quickly chose Billy. I felt as if he could see right through the glass and was looking me in the eyes and saying to me, "I'll be outta here soon, and I'm coming to get you." It is quite scary to look at someone who wants you dead so badly that he will risk everything and everyone around you just to kill you. I was glad to be escorted back into Captain Krolm's private office. I felt safe there. But I also remembered what Billy Blaine had done the previous time I had been here, when he shot up the precinct and an officer to boot.

Life is strange. You can walk down a street and pass a thousand people, and no one even notices you. Then one day, out of the blue, a stranger wants to kill you and won't stop trying until he succeeds. You never think of your life ending that way. You always envision becoming old and decrepit, dying slowly after many years. It really does shed new light on how valuable a life is.

The captain was happy that I had picked Billy out of the lineup. Some people get nervous and choose the wrong person. Others choose incorrectly seemingly on purpose, possibly out of fear of retribution one day.

"Now that Billy is going to jail," the captain began, "we can discuss the investigation with you."

"I knew he was no good when I first saw him at the gas station."

"Well, let's set the record straight." He glared at me. "You were always the target right from the beginning. The gas station shooting was a warning that you never recognized. Someone hired Billy to kill you for sure."

"Did Billy talk?"

"He clammed up so tight it's a wonder he still could breathe. He is a tough cookie; very hard to crack. He knows that no matter what he tells us, he will have to do at least ten to twenty years' hard time. So he isn't going to sing for anyone."

"What can we do?"

"Well, we did discover evidence of his staying in the basement of Millie's Diner. We confiscated phone numbers, receipts, and a set of keys we will try to match up to the diner's basement door."

"That son of a bitch, Sy!" I exclaimed.

"This job surprises and shocks me every so often. Sy is the last person we ever would have suspected. He is a pillar of the community, the son and grandson of preachers from the oldest church in Maryland. So, you see my disbelief that he could possibly be involved."

"Something about him bugs me."

"Well, we will be getting a search warrant for Sy's home and his business in a few hours. You are welcome to come with us tonight. We also will be picking up Sy for questioning, but I've pushed that off too, until right after midnight. I am assigning officers to protect you and Lolita, as well as guarding all entrances of the hotel you are staying at and the perimeter of the nursing home."

"Captain, I'm exhausted, and I will be meeting my friend Graham for a celebration dinner tonight. Can I meet with you first thing in the morning to go over any new evidence?"

"Okay, that will be fine," he said.

"I do have a couple of ideas I want to run by you in the morning, based on what your detectives discover tonight," I added.

"Sure, we'll meet here in the morning. By the way, I had an interesting conversation with your boss. He's madder than a wounded bull. You ignored his phone calls?"

"I didn't want him to shut me down. I felt like I was getting closer to some answers to some questions I had, and he . . . ."

"Yeah? Well, you were getting real close to the unemployment lines, buddy. He said that he had every intention of firing you and squashing the assignment tonight. That was until the old lady, Lolita placed a call to him. Whatever that old lady said to him completely changed his mind. I heard she doesn't hold anything back."

"Miss Lolita? She'll tell you to go crap in your hat if she wants to. And who could blame her at a hundred and ten years old? She even told Billy Blaine that he had no balls, and this was while he was pointing the knife at us. She is a real special person, and smart as a whip."

"Well, whatever she said to that hothead, it must have worked. I didn't add any wood to that fire. I told him that you were diligent in your job and kept your nose clean. He wanted to know if you were drinking too much."

"Drinking? Who has time for a drink? I've forgotten what alcohol tastes like, though I feel I could finish off a bottle or two right now."

"Don't make a liar out of me, or I'll lock you up with Billy in the same cell!"

"Okay, Captain." I smiled.

"You just can't let go of those 1923 murders, can you? You realize that everyone who could have anything to do with those murders is dead, don't you?"

"No, I can't let go. And, yes, I realize that the killers are dead. But someone is spooked by my interest in those murders is very much alive, and is kicking hard."

Back at the hotel, I wanted to freshen up before meeting Felicia and Graham for dinner. This time, though, I purchased a Snapple diet iced tea and drank it straight from the bottle. Ever since I had arrived at Hagerstown and the gas station the first day, I'd been a basket case. Someone wanted me dead, and that wasn't going to change for a while.

My head throbbed as I endured a call from the insane asylum boss Glavin. Harold was growling at me through the cell phone. I couldn't even make out everything he was rambling on about, but he really was pissed. Something about disrupting an entire town all by myself. And he wanted to know if I had asked Miss Lolita to call him on my behalf. He was cursing at a fast pace.

"If you died, I'd have a much better story!" he screamed. I changed the cell phone to my other ear.

"You'd miss me, boss! If someone shot me dead, you'd be sad."

"I'd miss nothing, hump-head! And maybe my ulcers would ease up."

"Well, I'll be back real soon, so you can scream at me in person." I laughed.

"I swear that I will throw your ass out in the street if you don't have an award-winning story."

"Don't worry, boss. I've got something very special. And I think there will be a second story, even bigger."

"Just remember, you are so close to being in the street. One more bonehead blunder and you'll be eating out of garbage cans."

We said our goodbyes. I still had a job, and a knucklehead as a boss. I guess many people love their jobs but hate their bosses. Some of it was my fault, I agree. After the breakup, nothing in life meant anything to me. People could read between the lines. They knew I was slowly self-destructing. Some people are so thrown by the blows life tosses their way. Life can be hell at times.

I felt grimy, as if I'd been sweating in the desert for a week. I needed a hot shower and a clean shave. But as I turned on the water of the shower, I was hesitant to enter. I remembered the scene from the movie *Psycho*. I double-locked the bathroom door and fought through my sudden sense of panic. The intense fear of the past few days had caught up to me. Knowing someone could knife me when I closed my eyes just freaked me out. I had never before taken such a quick shower and shampoo. It must have been two minutes flat. "I need a drink," I said out loud, but knew that was a road I didn't really want to continue down. I did have a problem, of course, but I had been in denial about it. Many people have a drinking problem but discount it because they feel they can function during the work day. But they fail to recognize that they are operating at a diminished capacity. Nor do they even care, while everyone around them is fully aware of their decline.

Time was moving quickly, but I still had a couple of hours before my eight o'clock dinner appointment. I lay on the bed, fixing my eyes firmly on the bubble stucco ceiling and studying it carefully as I thought and thought and thought, so much that my head ached.

I thought about Billy Blaine and how he had just self-destructed. I thought about Lolita and how very wise we seem to become just before we pass away. It's like we make all the mistakes early in life. We keep reinventing ourselves, and then, if we are lucky and very old, our mind is the only thing that still works.

I thought about Felicia, and how one person who was so perfect, an angel, could be here just for me. Was she really that perfect for everyone else too, or had I hypnotized myself through her astonishingly gorgeous gray eyes to fall madly in love with her? Was my mind grasping onto someone who could finally save me from myself? I knew I had been self-destructing; in that way, I was similar to Billy Blaine. I hated to admit it, but I knew that it was true. Even I had been in my own hellhole of a cesspool. Felicia, though, was my angel, my real answer. This was my one chance at life, and I would not ruin it, not even with alcohol or attitude. Miss Lolita's wisdom had convinced me to become a new man—a better man.

My eyes suddenly opened, and for a split second, I had no idea where I was. But I soon realized that sheer exhaustion had forced my eyes shut. The ceiling was staring back at me, and it took a full second for me to jump out of bed. It was 6:55. Then suddenly I heard it, the jiggling of my hotel room door. That must have been what woke me up. It scared the crap out of me as I shouted, "Who is it? Who's there? Hello, who is it?"

There was no answer. Then I heard the sound of running feet. *Holy crap, not again!*

When I looked out my window a few floors above street level, I saw police officers. *Great, at least my dead body will have a nice escort on its way to the morgue!*

I dressed quickly, making sure to put on a pair of pants first in case I had to make a run for it down the hallway and stairs. I listened some more, then quickly exited my room and ran for the stairs and out to where the officers were. I found Officer Cianci out front and told him of my concern. The officer smiled and said very nicely, "You know, Lou, sometimes when we are worried, our minds play funny tricks on us."

"Yeah, funny tricks, like someone axing me to death! Then we'll all agree: 'Well, I guess that wasn't his imagination.'"

He laughed. "Hey, that's a good one!"

As I chatted with Officer Cianci and another officer, who was short and pudgy, we spoke about Billy Blaine. They agreed that Graham was lucky he didn't get hurt because Billy was a dangerous character, capable of mass murder. They could tell he was not your run-of-the-mill criminal, the way he shot up the gas station and police station. But they assured me that there was nothing to be concerned about any longer.

"Yeah, that's what I thought when I was in the nursing home visiting, and look what happened."

They all agreed that someone out there in Hagerstown had put Blaine up to the violence. But they were convinced that the person behind it all wasn't capable of the violence himself, and that they would quickly apprehend that person, as well.

"Well, I'll be glad to get out of this town," I laughed nervously.

"We won't be missing you either," Cianci said, but he was laughing with me. "You stirred up a real hornets' nest, you did. We ain't seen anything quite that exciting in these parts in many a year."

"Normally we only arrest drunks at the town bar for excitement around here," the pudgy officer said. "You really got the old captain's knickers in a twist!"

"Yeah, I'm not one of his favorites, either," I agreed.

"No, you ain't!" Cianci agreed. "The captain ain't sleeping too well these days."

"Tell me about it. Anyway, you guys hear anything new on the case?"

"Nothing we can readily share," Pudgy smiled.

I left and returned shortly with some Dunkin' Donuts coffees and donuts for the officers, and joined them in some coffee as we chatted about how bad the Yankees had become in the last year, and how overpaid they all were. We agreed that money has ruined the game and taken the joy out of going to see a major league game at a stadium.

"Eight dollars and fifty cents for a plastic bottle of beer? You know how many beers I need at a game?" Pudgy asked.

"Twenty?" I asked sarcastically.

"Wise ass!" he shouted, and we all laughed.

Officer Cianci said, "What time are you meeting everyone for dinner?"

"I want to be there at about a quarter to eight."

"Good. We'll leave about five minutes before that time. It's only a couple blocks from here. I'll take you in the squad car, and I'll be watching from outside."

"I can't just walk there, Officer?"

"No. My ass is on the line, and I don't want to have to answer to my captain if you get taken out."

"I just hate feeling helpless," I complained. "So the restaurant is good?"

"That's this town's finest Italian restaurant. I eat there often," the pudgy officer said.

"Now I know it's good!" I smiled.

CHAPTER FIFTEEN

We had just left the hotel. I was riding, for a change, in the front seat with Cianci, at my request. When we were about a block away from the restaurant, suddenly Cianci said, "There's a motorcycle tailing us. Slide down in your seat, and don't even think of getting out of the car until you hear from me. Understand?" A note of firm authority accompanied his words.

"Okay, Officer."

Cianci quickly called for backup, and we pulled right in front of the restaurant, Maurino's Italian.

"Stay low, Lou," he said loudly.

He didn't need to tell me twice; my legs were folded into the floorboard.

"He's a half block back," he said, just as I heard the blaring of police sirens.

"There he goes!" Cianci said excitedly.

I heard the screeching of tires, and the chase was on. We stayed put. I stayed scrunched low.

"There he goes; he's running down sidewalks now, with the motorcycle. We have to try to corner him before he runs down people's backyards and escapes!" He yelled as if everyone outside could hear him. I stayed down, and my legs cramped up something fierce.

"You all right?" he asked.

"Fine!" I said, sucking it up a bit.

After a few minutes, Officer Cianci said, "Stay here; remain down low. I just want to look inside the restaurant to make sure it's all clear." As he stepped outside the car, he yelled a final "Don't move!"

"Don't worry. I think I'm now frozen in this position. You may need a crane to get me out again," I joked in a pained voice.

"You're doing real good, Lou," he said, and he walked to the restaurant.

He returned thirty seconds later and told me all was clear. He then came to the passenger side and helped me from my folded position. My legs were dead asleep and couldn't hold my weight. It took a minute before the blood flow returned and I could stand on my own.

Graham was already seated at a booth in the restaurant waiting for me. We hugged as if we hadn't seen each other for years. The ordeal from earlier in the day had fully sunken in with both of us. We both realized just how fortunate we were, as well as the others at the nursing home. Billy Blaine easily could have killed many people. The diversion, we agreed, was perfectly planned, buying just the right amount of time he needed to carry out a masterful and deadly act.

We spoke about Harold Glavin and how he wanted to fire me and strip me of the assignment and story I had been writing. He didn't even care where I was with the assignment, Miss Lolita, her story, or the investigation of the 1923 murders.

Graham wanted to know all about the murders. I told him everything I knew about the three young women, and how the killer had butchered the bodies. We spoke about how brazen the murders were, how no one could even come close to capturing the murderer, and how traumatic it was for everyone in Hagerstown and all of Maryland.

I explained to Graham how Blaine was key to the investigation, but neither of us could guess the identity of the mastermind behind the latest havoc, or whether there was more than one.

"Why would anyone in 2013 even care about a killer from ninety years ago? Who would try to protect them? What's the motive? There's always a motive," Graham pondered aloud.

Just then, I caught a glimpse of Felicia at the restaurant entrance. I looked carefully around the dining area, studying the room and the other diners. There was nothing suspicious. I was finally at ease for a change.

As I introduced Felicia to Graham, and she hugged him and thanked him for his unselfish act of kindness, I saw a big smile on his face and a twinkle in his eye. As he looked at me, his eyes told me, "Boy, you've got a real winner here!"

Felicia wanted to know about Graham, and he wanted to know about her, and they both ragged on me a little just for fun. We shared a lot of laughs.

As I looked into Felicia's eyes, I knew that I wanted to hug her long and hard. But I also knew that we couldn't look like we were a couple. I fought the temptation, knowing that I could be putting Felicia's life at risk if the mastermind of the recent terror knew we cared so much about each other. I was on cloud nine just being with Felicia and looking at her.

We feasted on flatbread pizza, Caesar salads, and pasta in a special homemade meat sauce that was different from any sauce I had ever had before. By the end of the meal, we were stuffed. No one had any alcohol.

I didn't want to go back to drinking, and I really couldn't explain why. I knew I had earned the right to have some wine or an imported beer. Still, I couldn't bring myself to order any drinks. Rather, I had sparkling bottled water along with Felicia and Graham. Felicia hated alcohol after her bad marriage to her alcoholic husband.

"So, Lou," Graham said, "do you have any worthwhile data for a good story yet?"

"I have enough for a ten-week documentary. There are so many angles and characters to talk about. I have to cover the 1923 murders, the town, and the great people in this town. I also have to cover what Lolita's life was like in 1923, and for Hagerstown in general."

"You know, Lou, I was sent here to report back to boss-man Glavin. But he also wanted me to tail you and, of course, take some photos with that fancy new camera. So tomorrow, I'll be taking photos at the nursing home. Felicia, I also want you there with Miss Lolita. I want shots of you attending to her as you usually do."

"All right, I guess," Felicia said happily.

"That would be good. Also, in the recreation room, we could get a good wide-angle shot including the other residents, and also Jeremy Roberts, the director," I added.

We finished up after about two hours and prepared to leave. I looked deeply into Felicia's eyes, and once again, my heart felt like it skipped a beat. How I longed to kiss her right there and then. But I knew that was a terrible idea. Our romance must be kept very low-key. The torture was killing me. There was no telling who or how many people were involved in the violence that had surrounded me since my arrival in town. Someone could do harm to Felicia just to get back at me or to use me in a bad way. That weighed on my mind continually.

Graham could tell I was crazy about Felicia, and he was genuinely happy for me. He knew firsthand how far down the road of destruction I had traveled. There was nothing anyone could do. I had to help myself. If Harold Glavin had fired me a month ago, I probably wouldn't have cared. I probably would have continued drinking and making excuses. My heart was cold to life after my breakup; nothing mattered to me then—not the job, not women beyond one-night stands, not food, not even world destruction, or if the world stopped turning altogether. I guess that happens to people suffering from depression.

So I arranged for Graham to exit the restaurant first, saying I'd send Felicia in five minutes. When it was just the two of us, we looked deeply into each other's eyes and said goodbye. I told her I would call her when I got back to the room sometime later. No kiss, no holding hands, no hug, as others in the restaurant were well aware of our actions.

After Felicia went out, I stayed a while longer and then paid the bill. I looked around carefully for any strange characters and started for the door. I would be extra-careful as I exited the restaurant, just as a precaution, and because my guard had been raised for some time now. I would look for Sergeant Pawler as soon as I hit the street, as he was due to relieve Cianci.

The cruiser was parked across the street. I could see he was sitting in the front, observing the immediate area with the engine on. I wondered how these officers on stakeouts and guard duty, sitting for hours in their cruisers, managed to stay awake.

But there he was, watching everything. Pawler was tough as nails and clearly very rough around the edges, but no one could ever say he was not a good and dedicated officer, and a good protector.

As soon as I exited the restaurant and set my feet on the front sidewalk, I heard a loud motorcycle from a distance. My eyes turned quickly in the direction of the blaring engine and muffler. The sounds of the motorcycle hurt my ears, though enthusiasts love the noisiest cycles the most.

I saw the motorcycle racing toward the restaurant and then heard a blast and then another. Before I knew it, Sergeant Pawler was out of his car waving me to get down and shouting, "Hit the deck, Lou!"

The sergeant ran into the street in the direct line of oncoming fire and the racing motorcycle, and started firing his gun at the rider on the motorcycle. I was in shock as I looked on.

I was flat on my stomach, watching the scene play out in front of me. The blasts were numerous, like loud firecrackers next to my ears.

There was no mistaking the sounds of gunfire so close. I cringed at each shot. The motorcycle raced directly toward the entranceway of the Italian restaurant, closer and closer to Pawler and me. The sergeant stood firm, aiming and shooting at the assailant. The cyclist's shots ricocheted off the façade and sidewalk of the restaurant. I remained on my stomach, motionless, but now with my hands covering my head. My body shook.

Time moves in ultra-slow motion when you're in life-or-death danger. In reality, it was only ten seconds, but it felt like minutes. And all I could think was, *I'm going to die! This is it—my ass is grass now!* I thought about Felicia, and how much I wanted to live so that I could be with her for the rest of my life.

The shots continued, too numerous to count or to figure out which guns were doing the shooting. Then, just as the motorcyclist got real close and the shots got louder, I saw the motorcycle swerve away from Sergeant Pawler and closer to my side of the street as it sped up.

The motorcycle's tires smoked and burned a line of rubber, swerving slightly out of control, and suddenly slammed into a telephone pole. It then veered off to the right, the rider bouncing off it to the left of the pole.

The motorcycle's wheels were spinning and the loud engine rumbled as the rider lay motionless.

"Stay down! Stay down!" Pawler yelled at me as he ran straight up the street to the scene of the dead-still shooter. Pawler's gun was aimed at the cyclist's head as he approached the body. He screamed something at the shooter. Then he screamed again. No movement, no sound from the rider; seconds ticked by very slowly. Then, abruptly, Pawler kicked at the body, turning it. Then he kicked at the gun lying a few feet away on the sidewalk. The gun went spinning; the body lay perfectly still. The motorcycle still roared loudly—the only noise in an otherwise dead-silent street—as its wheels slowed down. I lay motionless, looking, waiting, dreading another attack, and praying it was all over.

Pawler was on his radio calling for backup and an ambulance.

Another solid minute must have elapsed, though it seemed like forever. And not until Sergeant Pawler backed away from the motionless and heavily bleeding body did I slowly rise to a kneeling position on the sidewalk.

From there, I watched and waited. There was no movement from the body. Pawler didn't move from the scene but kept his gun drawn and remained staring at the body of the yet-unknown assailant. People crowded into the street, looking, wondering, staring somberly as the blaring sirens grew louder and closer.

Within minutes four police cruisers, two ambulances, and a fire engine had pulled up. I rose to my feet in time to see Captain Krolm get out of the trailing police car and walk up to the scene. The paramedics worked on the body to no avail. The helmet was removed and the captain bent down to look closer. He stood up straight and shook his head in disbelief. Then he turned around and shot me a long, stern look as if to say, "See what you are responsible for?"

I kept my distance, not wanting a confrontation. I didn't want to see the bloody, dead body of someone who had been trying to take my life. My hands were shaking uncontrollably, and I was sweating profusely. It wasn't until that precise moment that I felt the intense shaking. I kept my distance, mostly for my own state of mind.

People were asking questions of me as they passed by to get a closer look. All I could say was a polite "I don't know." I wanted no conversation, no looks, and no sympathy from anyone.

Louis Gerhani was not the bad guy here. I didn't ask someone to shoot at me and set the town on edge. All I had sought were answers or leads to an investigation that had been ongoing for ninety years. This was not new, but clearly, I had hit a very sensitive nerve somewhere, and someone felt he had to silence me at all costs. And now someone was dead. No doubt that "someone" was key to the Billy Blaine connection and had some direct connection to the girls murdered all those years ago.

Out of the corner of my eye, I saw Graham running up the street toward me. He had come back after hearing all the commotion.

"What the hell is going on?" he screamed, trying to decipher the scene some fifty yards away from us.

"Someone on a motorcycle tried to kill me as soon as I came out of the restaurant," I said as calmly as I could.

"Damn! You've got this whole town really pissed, my man!" He slapped me on the back. "You okay?"

"Oh, I'm fine now, but I think I just chapped my lips from kissing the concrete." I gave him a shaky smile.

"I'm sure you did!" Graham smiled. "The motorcycle guy got into an accident?"

"He hit the pole straight on after Sergeant Pawler shot out one of his tires. He's dead as a doorknob," I said, and I suddenly felt nauseous.

"Holy crap! One dude in prison, and one going to the morgue. How many more are there?" Graham asked.

"Don't know. But my nerves are totally shot," I said, shaking my head. "Is Felicia okay?"

"I saw her get into her car and head home before that maniac came barreling down the road. I'm sure she's safe," Graham said.

"That's a relief," I said, and exhaled a long breath I hadn't realized I'd been holding. "Hey man, it would be great if you could stick around tonight," I added.

"Don't you worry about that, buddy. I'm staying with you all night."

"Thanks. I don't think I'll be able to sleep anyway. I just don't want to be alone right now."

We watched the crime scene, the police, the onlookers, and the paramedics for about fifteen minutes longer. Finally, Captain Krolm looked my way and slowly walked toward Graham and me.

"Here comes trouble, buddy," Graham said when he saw the look in my eyes.

"I'll be all right," I smiled, knowing I didn't really want to face the captain, who had originally tried to get me to leave town before sunrise, to use his exact words.

The captain was looking me up and down carefully as he slowly approached. Maybe he was looking for bullet holes or blood. Or maybe he was just giving me a chance to calm down.

He looked at Graham, then at me, and said, "Graham, Louis, I see you boys are all right."

"We're fine, Captain," I said. "Graham just came on the scene when he heard the commotion."

The captain shook his head once, then narrowed his eyes and said, "You know the assailant is dead, don't you?"

"I figured as much, Captain. Was this the same guy that was following Sergeant Pawler and me earlier in the day?"

"Yes. Do you know who he is?" He looked at me, then at Graham.

"No, Captain, but I bet he's related to Billy Blaine somehow."

"It's Sy. Sy Trylan."

"Ah, so it was Sy . . . ." I said.

"Who is Sy?" Graham asked.

"Sy has been one of the most respected businessmen of Hagerstown for many years," I answered. "His brother is the pastor of the oldest church in Hagerstown. His family goes back for centuries. His father and grandfather also were pastors in the same church."

The captain shook his head in disbelief. "I knew him personally, and went to many town functions and meetings with him. I'm shocked and honestly baffled. I can't figure out why he would be involved in this mess."

"It makes a little sense to me," I said.

"How so?" he asked, somewhat annoyed. "You know, none of this would have happened if you had minded your business. I warned you."

"You know, Captain, cut the bull. . . ."

"Hey, Lou!" Graham warned.

"No!" I said. "I'm the guy that everyone tried to kill here, and I'm the bad guy? Holy crap! I'm sorry Sy is dead, but he was giving me dirty looks in the diner the first time he laid eyes on me. Sy is the one behind it all. Billy's just a pawn. He has no brains. Captain, you may have been chummy with Sy, but there's a connection to the 1923 murders here. I feel it in my bones—"

"You are very fortunate that you don't feel bullets in your bones," the captain snapped. "And if my sergeant had gotten hit, I'd shoot you myself! That being said, I will see you in my precinct, both of you, at seven a.m. sharp." As he walked away, he added huffily, "And be prepared to get out of town real soon."

"It's amazing. Really, Lou, someone always seems to be ultra-pissed at you," Graham said as we watched the captain leave.

"I just manage to bring the poison out of everyone. I'm like a glorified punching bag; people just can't keep from punching the crap out of me."

Graham stayed in the second bedroom of my hotel suite that night. I was actually quite happy that he insisted on staying with me. My nerves were really shot, and I was constantly looking over my shoulder.

As soon as we arrived at my room, I called Felicia. She wanted to know why I hadn't called earlier, so I told her about the accident and the gunman who was a local businessman.

"Sy? Are you kidding me?" she exclaimed. "I've known him for years! He's always so sweet to me. He jokes with me whenever I see him in the diner. I'm shocked!"

"Other people were shocked, too, but it was he who was orchestrating the terror against me all along. He hired Billy Blaine, and he is somehow connected to the 1923 murders, or else he wouldn't care. The investigation had been ice cold. No one even cared or remembered much any longer. And not until I started knocking on doors and questioning everyone did the hornet's nest explode."

"Sy is going to be missed. His brother . . . ."

"I know, his brother is the most well-loved pastor in this town. And, yes, Captain Krolm is somewhat pissed at me, like it was all my fault."

"Why you? This whole fiasco is not your fault. You were only doing your job, investigative reporting. It's not your fault that people got spooked because you were getting too close. I'm scared for you, Louis!"

We spoke some more. I told her that I liked her very much, and that I wanted us to go out together, meaning, I wanted us to only date each other. She told me that I was very special and smart, and that she liked me more than she had liked anyone in quite some time. I felt so happy I could have giggled. I controlled myself, but I knew I had a big, stupid smile on my face for a very long time. *Life is good. But life also can be very unpredictable and dangerous. So I'll just try to live each day to the fullest.*

Graham went to bed early. I stayed up thinking and reading. I analyzed my time thus far in Hagerstown. I thought carefully about the various characters I had met: the ones from the precinct, the library,

Millie's Diner, the gas station, the nursing home, and the restaurant. I reviewed every person as a possible link to Sy. But I couldn't come up with anyone else who could be a threat to Miss Lolita, me, Felicia, Graham, or anyone else I'd encountered along the way. I couldn't bear the thought of anyone else getting hurt.

I picked up Miss Lolita's diary from 1923. I would be giving it back shortly. But I wanted to read it carefully, just in case I might pick up any additional clues about the murders. There had to be some damning evidence somewhere, something powerful that could tempt a successful and respected businessman to attempt murder by hiring a potential killer. What could be so important? Why would Sy or anyone risk everything—his business, his family, and his standing in the community, and the embarrassment to his brother the pastor and his church?

The diary once again was delightful, an escape from the hustle-and-bustle stress of 2013. The year 1923 was an amazing time in an amazing town, where most people were as close as family members—a special time and place that could never happen again, anywhere. I reread the diary and refreshed my memory.

Miss Lolita was very young, age twenty, and a teacher's aide, teaching young teens. I read again how Lolita danced often, baked cakes, breads, and muffins, and sat around the piano with her family. She met her future husband that year, and the relationship flourished. Her beau and she spent many a night on the swinging love seat in the yard.

D. K. would drive her to town for occasional romantic dinners and weekly movies. They frequently went swimming and canoeing often, and he would have to repair the coupe car very often. That year would change Lolita's life forever—not only because of falling in love and knowing that D. K. Croome was the one she would marry, but also because of the murders, which changed her philosophy on life. Lolita became more spiritual, and the townsfolk became even closer because of the horrific murders.

These types of killings were very unusual for the early 1920s. The churches were all packed each week, and new parishioners flocked to the church in an effort to understand how God could allow such killings to happen.

Then something new jumped out at me from the diary. It was on December 31 of that year, New Year's Eve, when Miss Lolita was reminiscing about the year that was ending. She was so happy about her love, D. K., her family, and in particular, her Uncle Walter, the doctor.

But it was on the evening of December 31 that she described her disturbing dreams of the dead girls, the lion's head, the cross, and the chipped red bricks. As she recollected the dreams, she stated that the cross was on top of a large headstone that was old and very tall, and that it was by looking over the top of the cross that the chipped bricks could be seen. This was a new lead!

It was three o'clock in the morning when I read that passage after downing four Diet Cokes to stay awake. I reread the date over and over again, knowing it was a key to the killer and the investigation. My eyes were closing as I fought to keep reading. I knew one thing: a search warrant would have to be issued for Millie's—and for the Lord's Reformed Church.

Later that morning, I would be sure to tell Captain Krolm my suspicions and ask him to allow me in on the investigation scene at both locations. The captain didn't like me, and I understood that this was his town, not mine. But he had a job to do, and I would make sure that he followed through in clearing up the latest terror that threatened Lolita, me, and the town he protected.

CHAPTER SIXTEEN

A t six thirty a.m., Hagerstown is quiet, just before the rushing of residents frantic to get to work and school. For a smaller town, Hagerstown is like any other place during rush hour, with lots of traffic, horns, and vehicles rushing to and fro.

The air was crisp and cool, and the skies were a picture-perfect blue with tufts of pure white clouds passing slowly by—a perfect day to enjoy on the porch of an old home in 1923, rocking on a rocking chair and sipping fresh-made lemonade like Miss Lolita used to make.

But that was not to be. We were being driven to the precinct in the back of a police cruiser, compliments of Captain Krolm, for our seven o'clock command performance in his office.

This morning's officers gave Graham and me coffee and muffins after they made a stopover at a local deli. I was starving. My stomach had been rumbling since the night before. It was clearly my nerves, and I was surprised I even had a stomach left with all the stress I had been through.

I trusted the new young officers but instinctively kept looking out the rear window for anything even the slightest bit suspicious. At this point, I trusted no one else. I knew I was not like a cat with nine lives. I had but one life to give, and I was holding on to it for dear life.

Graham, on the other hand, was as cool as a cucumber. If I were as well trained in deadly defensive maneuvers as he was, I would be calm too. But I was never a fighter. I was one of those rare breeds who could talk his way out of almost anything.

There was a time, a while back, when I was in a bar and this big, ugly, drunk man had clearly stolen the money I had placed on the bar in front of me. I think it was merely to pick a fight. Some drunks will use any excuse to fight someone. Some drunks get abusive, and some get very depressed and quiet. Well, this big palooka wanted to fight as soon as I accused him of taking the few dollars. He got real loud and stood up quickly, knocking the barstool right over. I knew I'd better talk quick or I'd be bleeding all over the floor.

By the time I was done talking, we had become new best friends, at least long enough for me to make it out the door safely. I even bought him another drink, which could have been a mistake, but this time it worked.

Talking for me has always been better than trying to punch my way out of trouble.

The captain was sitting quietly at his desk when Graham and I were ushered in. He appeared to be deep in thought—no doubt, what with all the action his town had experienced in the past few days. I couldn't blame him for being annoyed that I had visited Hagerstown, but he must have realized deep down that I hadn't really started the trouble here. It was already in Hagerstown. It had lain dormant for many years, but it was like a sleeping giant with a huge toothache, similar to the nasty drunk who was itching for any reason to fight someone. I had set off something here, and it had mushroomed out of control.

The captain looked up from his papers and said, "Gentlemen, good morning. Have a seat, please." His tone was non-combative. He seemed resigned to the fact that there were bad people in his community, even the ones he had least expected.

"We have done a search of Millie's Diner," he began. "We shut it down and informed all the workers last night and this morning that this was an ongoing investigation. We suspected Sy, the owner, to be connected somehow to Billy Blaine, and we were right. Billy was staying in the basement of the diner. He would enter after midnight and sleep on the basement floor. So, yes, Sy Trylan was paying off Billy to cause all kinds of havoc, mostly as a scare tactic. He wanted to scare you away, and when you wouldn't take a hint, he wanted you dead. And when Billy failed to get it done, Sy tried to do it himself, although, obviously, he failed too. So, we wanted to search his office for any clues that would shed light on the investigation. We questioned Billy again, but he refused to speak, even when we hit him with the Sy Trylan tie-in."

"Captain, why did Sy choose Billy Blaine?" I asked.

"Billy is a three-time loser. He's done all kinds of things in his past, but he has never killed anyone. He was clearly out of his league. Why Billy? We don't know yet, but there has to be some connection. We'll figure it out sooner or later." He let out a heavy sigh and took a swig of coffee. He had the worried look of a man under pressure. "The mayor is all over our asses on this one. He wants answers yesterday."

That explained the captain's change of attitude.

"Captain Krolm," Graham began, "how do we know there aren't others involved?"

"We don't, son. We believe this is the end of the reign of terror in Hagerstown from this clan. But there are always sympathizers, relatives, others who want revenge because we locked up their pals. You can't be too safe. That is why we are keeping up our guard on this one. We are providing ongoing protection at the nursing home, the hotel, and wherever you boys go. The workers at the diner are also all under investigation, as is Sy's wife and his teenage son."

"Did Sy give us any new information?" I asked.

"Well, I was about to tell you what we found at Millie's," the captain said. "Besides the stash of items Billy Blaine had been using in the basement, Sy's office revealed a little more. He had notes about where you work at the Washington newspaper. He had you tracked and had a detailed list of your comings and goings. He knew your hotel room number, and he knew you were keen on Felicia from the nursing home."

"No! Is she in danger?"

"No," he said, with a tone of authority. "We have an officer covering her every move, and of course the nursing home is secure."

"If anything happens to her—"

"Lou, allow me to continue, please!" the captain snapped.

He spoke, but I didn't register any of his next words. It was just noise, background rumble. My only concern was Felicia. I tried to figure out why they hadn't attempted to harm her up to this point, or worse, kidnap her. What was their angle? Why just Miss Lolita and me? They would have more leverage if they used Felicia against me. But then again, it dawned on me that Felicia knew nothing about my investigation. But Sy and Billy were so paranoid they must have been convinced that I had the entire case figured out. Otherwise, why would they want me dead so badly? Then again, if they had kidnapped Felicia to smoke me out, they could just as easily have killed me.

Suddenly, I was shocked back to reality when the captain picked up some items that had been confiscated from Sy's office in Millie's Diner: pictures of his father, the pastor; newspaper clippings about the 1923 Hagerstown murders, with the victims' names underlined in pen; newspaper stories about investigations that had gone nowhere, suspects accused and released, and a suspect who had committed suicide but who was later cleared of all wrongdoing.

Then the captain floored me. He picked up a large lion's head ring, protected in a zip-lock bag, from a pile on his desk; it glistened under the bright fluorescent lights.

"And finally there is this large ring—a very unique gold ring that no doubt belongs to someone in Sy's family. All of these items were carefully locked away in a strongbox in Sy's office downstairs from the diner," the captain said matter-of-factly.

"That's it, Captain! That's the ring!" I yelled excitedly. "I know that ring!"

"You?" he asked. "This ring?"

"Uh, yes." And then I caught myself. I thought carefully how to proceed and not sound like half a nut.

"How could you know this ring?"

"Well, you see, Captain, Miss Lolita let me read a diary she kept during the year of the murders. In the diary, Miss Lolita described numerous dreams she had about the killer, who was wearing that same exact ring," I said.

"Not this ring, I'm sure. There are probably lots of rings that look like this. It can't be the same one."

"Captain, I need you to get a special search warrant for the church, the Lord's Reformed Church of Hagerstown."

"Lou," he began, "that is Sy's brother's church. Pastor Cornelius Trylan has been the pastor for many years. And before him, his father Seymour was the pastor. And before Seymour, his father Harvey was the pastor. All the prominent citizens from our town's past are buried at the church. Do you realize what you are asking me to do?" His ears were beet red as he clearly grew more than annoyed.

Graham studied me with a worried look, as if I had some sort of out-of-control fever.

"Yes, Captain, I realize what I am asking, but we need to search the church. I have my reasons. I just can't get into all of it now."

"Oh, so now you think you're like the hotshot TV investigators, don't you? And based on a hunch, you want me to invade the oldest and most prominent church in all of Maryland."

"We know that Sy was protecting someone!"

"Lou, stop and think about it for a minute. The murders were performed ninety years ago. The killer or killers are in the ground somewhere themselves. What are we trying to do here?"

"Captain, we are trying to help the remaining family members of those girls get final closure."

"Closure? What closure? The parents themselves are dead. It's been ninety years, boy!" The captain's face was now turning really red, and Graham's eyes were telling me to back off a little.

Out of desperation, I yelled, "Just do it! Do it for Miss Lolita!"

The captain looked at me, studied my face, my eyes, trying to figure out if I had finally lost my mind. After all, he was the one with the loaded gun, and all I had was a loaded mouth.

There was silence except for the overhead fluorescents singing their special song, a sound one could only hear in total silence.

Finally, he said, "Okay. I don't know why I'm doing this, but okay, I'll try it."

"Thanks, Captain," I said. "You won't be sorry, I promise."

"I'm already sorry. I'm sorry I ever met you. You are bad karma or something."

"Oh, come on, you don't believe that."

"Oh, no?" He gave me a crooked smile. "You're a little wacky!"

"Okay, you'll see," I promised again. "Just one more favor. I want to be at the church for your search. It's important."

"You are out of your mind, for sure! Where did you ever dig this banana-head up from?" He looked at Graham. "Some farm?"

"He is very odd, I'll agree," Graham stated, "but he has a solid-gold heart."

"Yeah, and a coconut for a head!" the captain snapped. "Okay, but listen to me, both of you: If you two get in the way during our investigation, I will personally tie you both together and stow you in the police car's trunk. Understand?" He yelled so hard that his veins were popping.

"Yes, sir," I snapped right back.

"Now get the hell out of here, and don't come back until three p.m. No wonder your boss has lost his mind . . . ." The captain mumbled this last bit under his breath as he turned his attention to the forms on his desk.

"Later, Captain," I said, as Graham and I exited his office quickly.

"You've got balls of steel, bro!" Graham shook his head at me.

Later that morning, Graham and I entered a Dunkin' Donuts shop. I had never drunk so much coffee as I'd downed in the past few days. I think the caffeine was adding to the twitching and the shaking of my hands. But I wasn't sure; I had no way of separating the fear of an attack from the effects of caffeine.

I inspected every patron in the coffee shop as well as each person behind the counter. These days everyone looked suspicious to me, like they were capable of pulling out a gun and shooting up the place. Even my right eye was twitching; that had never happened before. It is amazing how the brain can scare the hell out of the rest of your body.

"How you holding up, buddy?" Graham asked, as we stood on line.

"Me? Solid as a rock!" I bragged.

"Yeah, right!" He laughed. "You know what you told me before you started working on this assignment? You said, 'You know the most important thing that happens in Hagerstown? When Dunkin' Donuts puts out the new donuts at seven a.m.'"

"Oh, yeah, I remember that one, back in the good old days." I smiled. "Who knew there were a bunch of madmen here? Imagine—a quiet little town like Hagerstown has crazy-ass maniacs, too."

"Yeah, but you would have never met Felicia if you hadn't traveled to Hagerstown."

"Ah, Felicia. She is a special angel sent from heaven. You know, Gra, there's nowhere else I could have found someone as good-hearted and sensitive as Felicia. The girls back home are tough, and it shows through. Felicia is genuine, the real deal. I'm going to marry that woman one day. And you will be my best man." I smiled a big smile at Graham while I felt myself start to twitch to the music the coffee shop was playing. *I need a vacation,* I told myself.

By noontime, Graham and I had once again signed in at the nursing home to visit Miss Lolita. We spoke briefly with Jeremy Roberts about Sy's death and Billy Blaine's arrest.

At the home, the police officers must have numbered twelve. They were inside and outside. The captain was taking no chances, especially now that the mayor of Hagerstown was all over his ass.

The nursing home was jumping with activity—visitors and happy residents. You would never have known that an attempted killing had taken place there just a day earlier. Mr. Roberts told us that Mary, the kitchen worker, was going to be released in a few days from the hospital, and that she was doing well after a very bad time of it. The hospital finally was able to reverse the poison in her body.

I liked Mary, and was so thankful that she would be back to normal soon. These people in the nursing home work very hard and don't earn a lot of pay. By the time taxes and other withholdings come out of their checks, they go home with little to survive on in this expensive world. Still, you could never tell that from their attitudes in helping the residents. And from what I had seen, it was a tough, gut-wrenching job. I couldn't work there day in and day out.

I ran into Ken, the paralyzed forty-something man who had been in a wheelchair, like a prisoner, for more than twenty years since his car accident. It broke my heart to see him, but it made his day for him to see me and give me a smile. I guess any attention the residents got was more than welcomed. The wheelchair-bound older residents were in their usual positions in the lobby, enjoying the comings and goings. *What a life,* I thought, *waiting for nothing, and watching time slip slowly by.* I took it all in. I stored the picture in my memory so that I would learn to be a better person.

My visits to the home revealed that the women, who outnumbered the men, apparently adjusted better and participated more regularly in social activities. Many of the men seemed like fish out of water— surviving but having little fun. Miss Lolita was different. She had a purpose. She felt that she had to give back to society. It seemed like she was accumulating credits of a sort for each person she helped with a problem or gave a word of encouragement to. Miss Lolita had life figured out—something most people take for granted.

We met Miss Lolita in the large dining room. It appeared that most residents had finished lunch. Miss Lolita was just finishing up what looked like a fruit cocktail cup. She looked cute, as she had on a little bib to protect her sweater.

Someone told her that I was there to see her. As I got a little closer, her eyes lit up and a big smile came across her face.

"You know the drill, Sonny. Get up real close so I can see that baby face your mama graced you with."

"Baby face!" I said, pretending to be shocked. "That's a good one— Baby Face Lou. It's got a nice ring to it!"

Graham just laughed.

"Well, it's definitely better than that mug of a face you got stuck with!" I bumped Graham a friendly push and laughed.

"That must be the hero, Graham," Miss Lolita said. "You better get up here real close so I can see you. Don't you two boys rile me up now and force me to get out of this wheelchair and whip you both."

"She probably could smack the crap out of you, Lou!"

"The way I feel now, she'd kick my ass," I agreed.

I got real close and kissed her on the cheek, as did Graham in turn.

Suddenly, her eyes turned sad and her smile disappeared. "I heard about Sy. I felt so bad for that boy. I knew his papa and granddaddy real well. This town is going to hell in a hand basket. I am only thankful you boys are unharmed. I've been worried sick that some madman like that banana-boat, Billy Blaine, would do you boys harm or even harm other innocent people."

"It was a surprise," I said, "Sy being involved in the terror and destruction. No one suspected him."

"That's the preacher's son. Can you believe that?" she asked.

"Miss Lolita, Captain Krolm is investigating Sy and the diner, and even Sy's brother's church."

"I used to go to church there as a child. Why would Sy do such a thing? Pastor Cornelius will drop dead from the embarrassment of it all!"

"Miss Lolita, I know it brings back bad memories about the 1923 murders and all, but I saw in your diary here"—I held it up in front of her—"parts about the chipped bricks and the cross . . . ."

"You know it's from the church now, don't you, Louis?" She looked long and hard into my eyes.

"I had my suspicions."

"The father was involved. Sy's father, Pastor Seymour Trylan, was involved. I know it deep inside. God forgive me, I never took to that boy. I was a young girl, and he taught Sunday school after church. He was just plain weird. I knew it all these years. Seymour was an ugly, shy boy that none of the girls ever took to. God forgive me, I never understood why that young girl would marry that oddball boy. But she did, and they had the two boys." She shook her head in disgust. "Weird, I tell you! Wacky weird!"

I told her that they had found the lion's-head gold ring from both of our visions locked up in Sy's things. Her memory was perfect. She recalled that it was listed in her diary as a vision.

"God forgive me again, but I never could bring myself to tell anyone about my visions about the ring, the cross, the bricks, and the cemetery stone. Who would have believed me? After all, going after the clergy like that? It just wasn't done. They would have locked me up and given me shock treatments every day!"

Miss Lolita was right. Who in 1923 would ever believe a young woman who said she had visions and suspected the pastor's son of murder? She had no clear-cut evidence, and the entire town's residents would surely have had her locked up as insane.

Now I was on a special mission. I would act as the arms and legs of Miss Lolita, who was not mobile or in a position to run around town doing an investigation.

I had this burning desire to right a wrong. These days, it seems, so many individuals get away with murder, cheating, and stealing. I was tired of the guilty going unpunished. The year 1923 was different. But in the visions I had experienced, I felt the presence of the spirits of those three girls, however briefly. I felt I owed it to the Hagerstown citizens and the surviving heirs of the three dead girls. I told this to Miss Lolita, and she agreed.

"You can be my angel from heaven. You can do what I can no longer do. But if I were a couple of years younger, I tell you, I would hunt those skunks down and cut their legs out from under them, I would!" Her voice rose as she spoke until she was yelling out loud for all the dining room residents to hear.

I believed Miss Lolita. She was one tough cookie if you got on the wrong side of her. I could picture her, at her age, swinging her cane at Sy and Billy's heads, and probably connecting for a good smack too.

Maybe it was her upbringing on the family farm, or maybe that she was born in 1902. Maybe it was from growing up in Hagerstown. But whatever it was, it had turned Miss Lolita tough as nails, yet God-loving.

"You protect my boy here!" she warned Graham. "I don't want any harm to come to him! You hear me? I don't want one hair on his head to be harmed. You look me in the eyes, there, macho man. I want you to promise me." She had a stern look on her face as she waited.

"I promise, Miss Lolita. He is one of my best friends. Nothing bad will happen while I am with him. I can take care of myself, ma'am."

"Yes, I heard you with Billy Blaine. I heard you took him down good. Couldn't see a damn thing, you know. Gotta be real close, but I can hear! Don't let that white hair fool you, Sonny! Been white for quite some time you know."

"He's right. He can take on five guys at once. I'm not worried, so don't you," I lied. I was worried. The best defense is never a match for a gunshot. That was my biggest fear. In fact, I was downright scared that this reign of terror wasn't over. Maybe I was just overreacting. Maybe it had all caught up with me—the terror, the looking over my shoulder, the echoing of gunshots that kept going off, playing back like a recording deep in my brain. But overreacting or not, I was worried.

It was one o'clock when Felicia came and grabbed me. It was her lunch hour. She took me outside around the side of the nursing home where it was empty. We were like two high school kids in love. We kissed like we would never see each other again. I had never felt like that before. They say it's a chemical reaction when you fall in love, but all I know is that I tingled all over.

People hold things back in a relationship. Not me. I told Felicia that I loved her and wanted to spend the rest of my life with her. She wanted to know if I was sure. I didn't blame her. I opened my heart up 100% to her. I just knew it was right. I knew all about opening my heart entirely, only to have it torn to pieces. For months, my heart was hardened, like a brick. Nothing could soften it or penetrate it. I was like a dead man.

The heart and mind close when they've been hurt that badly. It's a protective reflex. I cared about no one for the longest time. Then Felicia just floored me. I didn't stand a chance of ignoring her. It was just meant to be. My heart of ice had melted.

I told Felicia that I was never as sure of anything else as I was that I wanted her forever and ever.

Felicia's eyes welled with tears, and I suddenly couldn't swallow past the huge lump in my throat. I knew I was too tough to cry, but I felt moisture on my face. *Who cares? Men have feelings, too.*

We saw a couple of workers in the general area, so we decided to escape to the Dunkin' Donuts down the street. I sneaked past the officers stationed at the entrance of the home and left Graham alone with Miss Lolita. It was good for him to get to know her and her philosophy. It was good for anyone to get a good dose of Miss Lolita. It would do anyone's heart good. It wakes a person up to realize the fabulous gift of life we are all blessed with each day.

Felicia and I spoke for ten minutes at the donut shop. We planned how we could spend every weekend together. We planned how I would bring out some items and a lot of clothes, and stay at her place. We would be together from late Friday through Monday morning each weekend, when I would leave early to return to work in Washington.

That was when Officer Robert Cianci entered the shop and walked up to our table.

"Officer, we were just going to come back to the home . . . ." I lied.

"Well, now you don't have to, because I'm going to be sitting in the car right outside the window here."

"That's okay—we'll be fine," I said, and Felicia's ears turned bright red.

"I'm sure you will be," he said with a smirk. "Doesn't matter; I'll still be out there. Do you think I want to explain to the captain how you two lovebirds gave us all the slip? He can be meaner than a riled-up rattlesnake!"

"Shit!" I said.

"Worse than that!" He laughed, as he quickly walked out the door.

The officer sat in the police cruiser and stared at Felicia and me. The romantic moment was ruined as we kept noticing Officer Cianci.

"So how is the investigation going?" she asked.

"We are closing in on answers. Sy was connected to Billy, and now we are going to search the church where Sy's father and his grandfather served as pastors, and where his brother now serves. I feel it in my gut that the church is a key factor here."

"That's the oldest church in town. All the prominent people, politicians, and even the founding father of Hagerstown, Jonathan Hager, are buried there. That church is hundreds of years old, and still in good condition."

"I know. The captain was reluctant about getting a search warrant for the church. He really has had his fill of me. If I am wrong, and we find no further clues at the church, my ass will be grass. And if word gets back to my boss from hell, I may get fired."

"You could always clean tables at Millie's Diner," she teased, her smile wide as she laughed. "Just kidding, Lou. Don't let it get to you. Look how much you've already accomplished here!" she added brightly.

"I know. But I can't help feeling guilty for the death of Sy. Here was a successful businessman with everything going for him. Why would someone like Sy even get involved in the terror spree that just disrupted Hagerstown and almost killed Miss Lolita, me, the officer in the police station, the gas station attendant, and Sergeant Pawler?"

"Maybe the shooter in the gas station was after you all along, and maybe shooting at the attendant was just to throw you off guard, and the shooter could have picked you off, but he failed."

"I don't think—"

"It's a possibility, though!"

I thought carefully about it for a while. "It is possible. Anything is possible in this town." The more I thought about it, the more confused I was about the entire investigation. Would I be chased out of Hagerstown, Maryland, by citizens waving bats at me? Would they hold me responsible for Sy Trylan's death? Would the 1923 murders be too old for the residents to be concerned about? All these thoughts bounced around in my head. Was my whole trip to Hagerstown just a big waste? I would find out real soon. I knew my time here was almost over. I would have to leave with or without any more answers. And my story on Miss Lolita would have to be put to paper real soon, as the newspaper and Glavin would not allow me to go much further. Glavin already wanted to fire me. He probably figured I had a story that was almost finished, so why kill it off now? Graham had even taken a bunch of photos in the past two days.

Felicia tried to take my mind off the investigation and the danger that might still exist for me. She tried to make me laugh, even telling me how cute I looked in the hospital gown that gave everyone a peek at my cute ass. Nothing was working. Death and fear of dying have a sobering effect on people. Normally, the thought of dying didn't really bother me too much. I figured that if God wanted me bad enough, well, He could have me. I wasn't in all that much of a demand on earth. But now, with Felicia in my life, I would be kicking and screaming to stay alive. I had finally found something that made this crazy world worthwhile. Love does that. Love changes everything. Even a crappy, selfish, terror-filled world is much more tolerable, even pleasant, when you have a fantastic woman in your life—a woman who cares as much about you as you care about her. No, I was suddenly very scared of dying or of losing Felicia, and closing the chapter of my life without accomplishing something extraordinary. For once in my life, I knew that facing the Lord now would be like insulting Him to His face. Lolita's words of inspiration convinced me that I had to accomplish so much more and make the Lord proud of me. After all, He had blessed me with the gift of life; didn't I owe it to Him to present Him with the gift of a life well lived?

CHAPTER SEVENTEEN

W e were accompanied back to the nursing home by Officer Cianci. It was getting very frustrating always having someone following me, protecting me, and reporting my every move to the police captain. Maybe if I were able to move about freely I would forget about the possibility of an attack. But with police presence, I had no chance to forget. In fact, it made me more nervous. I kept looking around like a nut job, but I just dealt with it. Maybe Captain Krolm was correct in his thinking that with Sy dead now, the threat to Lolita and me had finally passed.

I had given Lolita's diary back to her earlier in the day, and I was so relieved that I had. It made me nervous as hell holding on to such a piece of history as that—all 365 pages of the year 1923, handwritten in perfect penmanship. If I had lost that diary, I would have left the country. But Lolita wasn't worried. It amazed me how she had entrusted such a personal treasure to me.

I wondered if, in her infinite wisdom, Lolita had known that I would be pulled deeper into the 1923 murder investigation, and that I would pick up on certain clues she had hidden away in the diary ninety years earlier. Could it also be possible that she had somehow channeled the visions I had experienced, or was it also possible that they had come through her deceased uncle to me?

I was giving myself a huge migraine with all the wondering and worrying. The human brain is an amazing organ, but it can't be forever overworked while being deprived of down time and sleep. How long would I have to wait until I could chill out, kick back, and not worry about anything?

And what about alcohol? Without a drop of alcohol, I wondered how I was still alive. Then I caught a glimpse of Felicia smiling lovingly at me. Her gray eyes, so alive with life, told me that I was important and that we'd have each other forever. Alcohol really meant nothing, not after that smile. Oh, sure, one day I might have a glass of wine, but never again would I allow myself to get plastered, trying to deaden some old memory or current problem. Those days were over for good.

Miss Lolita asked me to come closer again as she always did.

"Listen here, Sonny, I want to talk with you before I take my nap."

"You want me to tell you a cute bedtime story?" I joked.

"Listen, you! I'll give you a bedtime story that will make your head spin!"

"A dirty one—oh, good!"

"Listen here, wise guy! There will be no bedtime stories. Get serious for me, if you still have any brain cells left in that head. I know you are in love."

"Love? Me?"

"Yes, Sonny, love! It's written all over your face! And you better take care of my little angel. And you better come visit me often. Otherwise, I'm a-coming after you!"

"I'll come visit you every week, Miss Lolita. I would be honored to see you every week. You have my word on that."

Lolita handed me a small piece of paper and said, "Many years ago I started reading books by a very special writer of inspirational works. His name is Og Mandino. I would like you to look at some of his books. One quotation of his has stayed with me for over forty years now. Please, will you read it out loud for me?" She smiled.

Felicia and Graham moved very close to me, as if they were trying to read what I was about to read aloud.

I looked closely at the typewritten piece of paper and began. "I will persist until I succeed. I was not delivered unto this world in defeat, nor does failure course in my veins. I am not a sheep waiting to be prodded by my shepherd. I am a lion, and I refuse to talk, to walk, to sleep with the sheep. I will hear not those who weep and complain, for their disease is contagious. Let them join the sheep. The slaughterhouse of failure is not my destiny. I will persist until I succeed."

I looked into Miss Lolita's eyes. They were alive with excitement. Her eyes suddenly were the eyes of a twenty-one-year-old girl with her whole life ahead of her. I got a lump in my throat, and my eyes were moist as I stared at her.

The slaughterhouse of failure is not my destiny. The words bounced around in my head, and I felt sad for a moment. I was sad for Miss Lolita, who had all the drive and energy of a young woman in her mind, but her body had been used up and could not accommodate the drive her amazing mind projected.

She smiled at me, and I noticed that the room was totally silent, as if everyone was waiting for her to speak. "If you live by the words of Og Mandino, Louis, you will never allow the world, or anyone, to beat you down ever again."

I kissed her on the cheek and thought, *Everyone needs someone as wise as Miss Lolita. May she live another hundred and ten years!* But, of course, I knew her time on earth was limited. Everyone's time on earth is limited, and we know not the total number of days with which we will be blessed. Then it dawned on me: *Miss Lolita has touched many thousands of lives in her 110 years, or more than 40,150 days. What a worthwhile and amazing accomplishment, a life truly well lived!*

Officer Cianci interrupted the moment, just before any tears could run down my face. All eyes focused on him as we waited for him to come closer.

"Lou and Graham, Captain Krolm asked me to escort you to the Lord's Reformed Church. We will be meeting the captain and detectives at the church in thirty minutes. So, please, if you will, wrap it up here, and I'll meet you in the front of the nursing home."

Felicia and I moved off into a corner of the large room. I kissed her cheek lightly, and she told me to be careful and very aware of my surroundings at all times, and also not to trust anyone.

I assured her that with Graham by my side, I would be very well protected, and I would always be escorted by an officer as long as I remained here in town. Captain Krolm didn't want my death on his conscience, as he had said to me earlier.

Graham was as excited as I was at being involved in an actual search warrant investigation. We didn't know what we would find in the centuries-old church. According to Miss Lolita, the Lord's Reformed Church was built in 1792. It was the first church in Hagerstown, and most of the important businessmen and politicians had been buried there since 1799, including the founding father of Hagerstown.

I hadn't been to the church and looked forward to visiting. I was never very religious, and usually just spoke my mind with God whenever I needed to. But there was a certain mystique about the very old church and the history of all the souls, now gone, that worshipped there.

The fact that Lolita, as a little girl, worshipped there, went to Sunday school, and then was married there really intrigued me. The fact that Sy's brother, his father, and his grandfather were all pastors at the church made it that more interesting.

As soon as we exited the nursing home, Graham and I were met at the entranceway by Sergeant Pawler.

"Where's Officer Cianci?" I asked.

"What, aren't you happy to see me?" Pawler smiled at me. Smirked would be more like the word, actually.

"Of course! You are my favorite sergeant in all of Hagerstown," I said sarcastically.

"You're a real wise ass, aren't you?"

"No, really! Cianci was going to—"

"Well, things changed, lover boy. You're stuck with me. Captain wants me to be solely responsible for your sorry ass, and your sidekick there, Robin!" His laugh sounded sinister.

As I looked him over with his military style crew cut and muscle-packed five-foot-seven build, I tried to figure out if he was the type of guy who has a couple of drinks, then looks to pick a fight just for the hell of it. I couldn't figure him out as hard as I tried. Was Pawler the kind of officer who would lay down his life for a stranger like me? Because many would not. He might just be that dedicated under that hard shell of an exterior.

My faith had to be in him, as he had the firearm, just in case there was another attack from a crazed gunman. He *had* stood his ground, after all, when the motorcycle gunman was coming right at him and me the night before. But Pawler was still a tough guy to read, and as much a loose cannon as they come.

"Now, you guys were invited special by the captain to look over the church. But I want you to stay real close to me. Don't you two go off exploring and trying to be the Hardy Boys detectives!"

We assured him that we would both be staying right behind him every step of the way since he was holding our protection, the loaded gun.

CHAPTER EIGHTEEN

T he sun was shining brightly as we slowly made our way through the heavy traffic in town. Hagerstown is busy every day from three o'clock through six o'clock. What is normally a fifteen-minute trip takes twenty-five minutes in traffic. There were no clouds, and the sun made the eighty-degree air feel like one hundred.

I was talking with Graham in the back seat of the cruiser. It's strange to be riding in the back seat of a police car with another man. I hope I am never arrested for anything and wind up in the back of a cruiser again!

Graham was asking more questions about Miss Lolita's early days, as described in the diary. I was telling him how life was spent in 1923 when my cell phone rang loudly, startling me.

Who could be calling me now? Harold Glavin had already spoken with me, and, for a change, he had not been minutes away from firing me. Felicia and I had just spoken, and Graham was with me.

The phone number of the caller was unknown to me as I answered the phone.

"Lou? Is this Mr. Louis Gerhani, the reporter?" the shaky voice asked.

"Yes, who's calling?"

"Hi, it's Brian, Lou."

"Brian?" I asked.

"Brian, from Wally's gas station, in town."

"Oh, yeah. How are—"

"Listen, I think you're in grave danger!" he said loudly.

"What?"

"Don't go to that church. I think it's booby-trapped. It's gonna blow up big time!"

"Holy crap! Why?"

"I think someone is on their way over to blow up the church when you get there."

"Brian, hold on for me. I want you to tell someone what you just told me."

"Sergeant, stop the car! Pull over!" I shouted and I held up the phone and pointed to it.

He didn't respond. Rather, he looked in the rearview mirror, somewhat annoyed, and said, "What is it now? You're getting as bad as a whiny little girl."

"Pull over! Stop everyone from going to the church! It's Brian from the gas station, and he believes someone is about to blow up the church. Pull over!" I shouted.

He abruptly pulled over and slammed on the brakes. He picked up the cruiser's radio and called in to headquarters.

He yelled into the cruiser's microphone, "It's Sergeant Pawler. Patch me in to Captain Krolm ASAP, and send the bomb squad and the fire department to Lord's Reformed Church!"

As soon as the captain came on, Pawler relayed Brian's urgent warning and convinced the captain to draw everyone back from the church until further notice.

The radio was blaring with all kinds of orders, half of which I couldn't hear or understand. The sergeant then spoke with Brian, and I could hear his normally calm tone get very excited and agitated.

"What? Are you sure you heard him correctly? Why would he want to . . . oh, really? How long ago did he leave? How many containers of gasoline? Do you know if he owns any type of firearm, hunting rifles, any other weapons? What was he driving? Now you listen to me!" he screamed. "Go directly to the station house right now, and wait for us to get back there! . . . I don't give a damn! Lock the door if you want to, but get out of there and get over to the police station. Don't speak to anyone except Captain Krolm or me! Understand? And keep the line clear for me to call you back!"

The captain and the sergeant were speaking again as we sat in the police car, still idling on the side of the road. The sergeant's voice, normally calm, was now impatient and edgy, even with Captain Krolm.

"I told you! Wally, from Wally's service station. I don't know what set him off, but he has numerous large containers of gasoline, five or ten gallons each. The kid overheard him discussing the investigation moving to the church. I don't know who the leak is! Okay! Yes, the tow truck with the station's name on the side. Okay, we'll meet you there in a few. Yes, Brian will be waiting."

Pawler turned his attention to us. "Well, we will soon find out if your buddy Brian was full of crap or very helpful in saving your asses and maybe ours too!" He was pissed. Not really at anyone in particular; just fed up with the terror spree like nothing Hagerstown had seen in many years. Maybe he blamed me, but I didn't care, because there was something going on much bigger than Louis Gerhani, something much more sinister and ugly—a major cover-up of some kind. This thing was out of hand now.

And now we had Wally, another business owner, caught up in the stream of terror. What the hell was going on? How many people did Wally want to blow up? And what the hell was his motive? There is always a motive. No one risks their world, their kingdom of riches, for a prison cell without having a solid motive.

Graham looked long and hard at me then said, "There's some heavy shit going on in this boring little town, bro!"

Suddenly, Sergeant Pawler slapped the cruiser into gear and left rubber behind as he peeled away from the curb.

"Where to?" I asked, not really expecting him to acknowledge me.

"There's an all-points bulletin out on Wally's head. I figure we're blocks away from the church, and what the hell—"

"What the hell?" I snapped, now more worried.

"Listen, Mary, don't go crapping your pants just yet. We're only cruising the perimeter of the blocks leading to the church. He can't hide. Not with that large tow truck," Pawler scoffed.

He drove very fast and erratically while I held on to the door handle for dear life. What if Wally had a gun? Or worse yet, what if he had some sort of bomb? Sergeant Pawler seemed to thrive on this sort of action. I didn't know whether Pawler was just crazy, like a real-life Rambo, or if he had a death wish. In any event, Graham and I were bouncing from side to side during the rough ride. The sergeant didn't use the siren. Maybe he didn't want to give Wally any warning, and hoped to catch him off guard.

But then again, Wally would be on the outlook for the authorities, since he knew we were on our way to investigate the church.

I don't think the captain told Pawler to go out and look for Wally. He was probably waiting at the station house for us. But here was Pawler, screeching and speeding all over.

"Let me know if you catch sight of that hump in the tow truck!" he snapped.

We went around several blocks, circling large areas. Around ten minutes later, I was getting dizzy from the wild driving.

Graham was talking fast and nervous-like, but I didn't listen to the words. Then, suddenly, Pawler slowed and pulled over. He grabbed the two-way radio and phoned in for backup at Sullivan and West End Street. Graham and I strained to see what Pawler saw. And there in the distance was the tow truck on the side street by a bar. According to Sergeant Pawler, the suspect was inside the bar called "Get 'Em Cold Bar and Grill."

The sergeant waited exactly two minutes and exited the car. "I'm going to apprehend the suspect. Stay in the car, and stay low, just in case there's any gunplay!"

"Are you sure you—"

"I got this, not to worry," he said with a fierce look of determination on his face.

"Be careful, buddy," Graham said.

My stomach was in knots as I played out all the possible scenarios that could unfold in the next few minutes. Had Wally been drinking? Could he be armed and waiting to ambush anyone entering the bar? Or could he have high-powered explosives at the ready, just waiting for the right time to set them off? I thought Pawler was insane to walk down the street. He was in the open, an easy shot for anyone with the luxury of having a window or door to hide behind while shooting at him.

As Sergeant Pawler slowly walked closer to the bar, he looked around carefully, assessing any movement in the general area. He was now twenty feet from the entrance.

"Here we go again, buddy," Graham murmured.

Suddenly, we heard the sounds of multiple sirens from oncoming patrol cars. Just then, Pawler put his hand on the doorknob of the bar.

He turned the knob and entered just as the cruisers pulled up on either side of the front entrance and stopped short.

"What balls that Pawler has!" I exclaimed.

"He's half a nut! A loose cannon, but you really gotta love the guy!" Graham said.

He was in the bar a split second ahead of the backup officers who came rushing in. A few seconds passed before we heard a single ear-shattering gunshot that made me jump in my seat, then nothing but silence. Dead silence.

Our eyes were glued on the front entrance of the mostly empty bar for that time of day.

"Holy crap! Lou, it never ends around here! You think they shot Wally?"

"I don't know. But I don't like the way the sergeant went rushing in there. That is definitely a dangerous move. Wally could be sitting there waiting for the first officer to rush through the front door so that he can open fire on him."

"Yeah, but Pawler could have caught Wally off guard and surprised him by rushing in. We'll just have to sit tight. But his backup went right in too . . . not too much lag time there."

"Let's just stay in the car, buddy. Don't look for trouble with this character."

"I'm cool. Not moving, man."

There was total silence. I could swear I could hear the ticking coming from my watch. I didn't even want to blink, thinking I might have to make a run for it. Wally was known to have some kind of explosive device.

Then it happened. The door of the bar swung open and an officer emerged. Then Wally appeared too, handcuffs securing his hands tightly behind his back. He was followed by Sergeant Pawler, who had his hand gripped tightly around Wally's upper arm. And trailing everyone was the additional officer with his gun drawn as a precaution.

They stuffed Wally into the closest police car, and then each of the officers got behind the wheel of his respective car and waited. Sergeant Pawler slowly made his way to the car. He was limping, favoring his left leg a little.

"Pawler's hurt," I said. Then I suggested to Graham, "Listen, don't say anything about it."

The sergeant got in the car, saying, "We got him, boys. Wally can't hurt anyone now."

"Are you okay?" I asked.

"Nothing a few beers can't fix, my friend."

"Sergeant, did Wally put up a fight?" Graham asked. "Did he have an explosive?"

"He was kind of surprised, I guess. He was at a pay phone waiting to make a phone call, so there was an element of surprise. It all happened quickly. He ignored my request to put his hands in the air, and he tried to kick my legs out from under me and make a run for it. I didn't go down, though. That's when I fired a shot at the ceiling, and Wally stopped short and gave up. After he saw the backup I had, Wally knew it was all over. We were very concerned, though, that Wally had some kind of device or weapon. He said he had nothing, and that all he wanted to do was make a phone call. We didn't fall for that because he had a cell phone right on his belt."

We pulled up third in line behind the first two police cars. The middle car was the one that held Wally, secure in the back seat. No one was taking any chances, even though it turned out Wally didn't have any explosives or weapons on him. He was a dangerous man nonetheless. Billy Blaine had done damage right in the police precinct by wrestling an officer's gun away, shooting him, and then escaping in a squad car. Anything is possible when it comes to capturing and bringing in a suspect. Some suspects get very desperate to escape a prison stretch that could last many years.

We got back to the precinct prior to the other officers, who requested backup to escort the prisoner to the station house. Graham and I stood with Captain Krolm waiting for Wally to be brought in. Three additional officers had joined Pawler and the other two officers. Captain Krolm wisely added the additional officers, as Wally could possibly be violent. Wally was unpredictable because he was a seemingly respected businessman who had suddenly become deadly. If Brian was correct, Wally wanted to blow up the church, and it was rumored that he had intended to kill the officers and other personnel who would have been inside doing their investigation.

Captain Krolm told us, "Wally has already been read his Miranda rights. His legal name is Wallace. F. Kaufman. And he is not talking. Our report from the bomb squad and fire department should be in any minute. As of right now, there have been no explosions at the church or anywhere else in town. We take these threats very seriously these days. If you ignore one threat, dozens of lives could be lost."

A few minutes later, we heard screaming from outside the station house. It was Wally yelling, "You killed my best friend! You're all scum! You had no right to hurt Sy! Get your hands off me! Don't touch me! I should have blown you all up earlier when I wanted to! I'm innocent! You've got nothing on . . . get your hands off . . . I want my lawyer! I have rights! Where's my lawyer?"

As Wally was led into the station house, no one stood in his way. The officers had to push against him to get him to move. He kept trying to stop, and they kept pushing him farther into the station house. His shoulders lunged from side to side in rebellion.

Wally was a huge hulk of a man, maybe age forty-eight. I estimated him to stand six feet tall and weigh around three hundred pounds. He was big-boned, a big ol' country man who looked like he could take down a couple of the officers with one swipe if his arms hadn't been secured behind him, but the biggest threat he posed now was his screaming and yelling. He was cursing up a storm.

Wally got more violent, using his body to knock down one officer. That's when more officers roughly held him and pushed him hard into the fingerprinting room.

"You'll never make anything stick. All I have to do is make one phone call. There will be no evidence left. In fact, you can call the number for me! You're all scum! My friend is dead! I want to call. Let me make one call!"

The door closed, muffling the sounds of Wally's screams and curses. It sounded like they hit him on the head.

I asked the captain what was up with Wally—did he snap? The captain explained that Sy and Wally were distant cousins, and best friends. They used to fish and hunt together. Sy might have kept Wally out of the terror until the very end. But Sy's death apparently had indeed caused Wally to snap.

"We've also established that one Wallace F. Kaufman, and our own Loretta Mistel, were an item. We believe that Loretta could have been feeding inside police information to Wally, who in turn could have fed it to Sy."

"No!" I said in disbelief. "Not cute Loretta with the beautiful long red hair. We scurried under the table when all hell broke loose and Billy shot the place up. She acted so innocent!"

"That's her," the captain said. "Love is strange, my friend. You can never tell what people in love will do."

"She's too good for that creep," I said, shaking my head.

"What do we know about love, Louis?" "Yeah, buddy," Graham chimed in. "Your track record is a little shaky. . ."

"Shaky ain't the word. Dear Abby I am not!" I laughed. "Love is blind."

"You talking about Felicia again?" Graham asked.

"Wise ass!"

The captain took a phone call while Graham and I speculated about Billy, Sy, Wally, and now Loretta. I wondered if there were any others who would be coming out of the woodwork. The notion of Wally and Loretta had caught me completely off guard. Then again, ever since arriving in town, I had been stunned by one thing after another.

Within five minutes, Captain Krolm finished his call and moved back over toward Graham and me. His face had suddenly turned pale, and he looked troubled, as if he had lost his best friend.

"Well," he began, "Wally was all set to destroy that church. But he was patiently waiting for us all to enter it first with our search warrant in hand. You see, Wally wanted you dead, Lou. But more than that, he needed to burn down that church in the worst way." He had a distant look on his face.

"But why? And why Wally?" I asked.

"Wally was there. We lifted fingerprints off two cell phones he had placed at the church. His best friend was his distant cousin, Sy. But the best part of Wally's plan of destruction was this: Wally was going to set off the explosion in the church using a remote device from some distance away from the church."

"He had a bomb?" Graham asked.

"Not exactly, but it was an ingenious plan that I have never witnessed before. Sergeant Pawler arrested Wally inside the bar. He was at a phone booth, patiently waiting to make a phone call."

"He was calling someone to set off the bomb?" I asked.

"Better than that. No, this plan was almost foolproof. The phone call from the bar would have set off the incendiary device, which would have engulfed the entire church with all of us trapped inside. We all would have died for sure, if not from the flames, then surely from smoke inhalation." The captain's eyes were more distant; he was deep in thought.

"It sounds too good to be able to work," I pondered aloud. "He was only one person acting alone."

"The only way you can understand the true plan Wally had is for me to show you the layout. Now, visualize two huge containers of gasoline strategically placed in the church with flammable items placed near them. Now watch this closely."

The captain took out his cell phone and pressed the volume button until the vibrate mode was set. He then took a pile of papers and made an incline under them using a large book. He then placed the cell phone face down on the slight incline of the papers. He then used his landline to call his cell phone. The silent/vibrate mode shook the phone, sending it down the incline until it fell off his desk. As he caught the falling phone, he said, "See the remote-device concept in action? Now, visualize the phone falling off my desk and landing in a vat of gasoline."

"But that couldn't ignite the gas," I pointed out.

"Right. But Wally was smart. There was a lit votive candle resting on the back of the cell phone. The candle was ready to ignite the vat of gas once the cell phone slid off the incline. The vibration from the call on the cell phone was intended to be the magic."

The captain once again set the cell phone on the slightly inclined mountain of papers on his desk, called the cell phone from his desk phone again, and waited until it vibrated, which started its slide off the papers and off his desk.

"I see it now. The candle and cell phone both wind up in the container of gasoline, thus setting off a firebomb. And if you have flammable items close by, you have an uncontrollable fire."

"Precisely. Now, with two containers placed apart, and the age of the church, you have an inferno that will trap all the people inside the church, but more importantly, it will destroy all traces of evidence."

"That's wild! A terrorist act for sure," Graham said. "A one-man execution machine, and all from a pay phone."

"Yes," the captain agreed. "You see, any evidence would be destroyed, including the two cell phones we learned were the disposable kind that you fill by purchasing prepaid minutes. We also traced calls from those phones to Sy and our own Loretta. Again, it was all planned to destroy the evidence."

My mind raced as I visualized the entire scene playing out had Wally placed the call with all of us in the church. Wally knew, from where he was situated in that bar by the window payphone, when we would be passing on our way to the church. He would wait for precisely the right moment and then place the call.

Wally wanted us to get inside the entrance before he set the cell phones on their slide into the gasoline with the lit candles piggybacking on the phones. If he waited too long, we might catch on to his plan and grab the candles off the waiting cellphones, putting out the flame. And without flames dropping into the gas containers, there would be no out-of-control inferno.

If Loretta, the police department employee, was Wally's girlfriend, was she also helping Sy with inside information about the investigators' next moves? Was she telling Sy when I would be somewhere? It was all quite scary how one insignificant person in an important setting could be instrumental in possible mass murders.

Billy had not cooperated in answering any questions in his interrogation interviews, but the others were cooperating more. Wally was telling interrogators that he had nothing to do with anything except the church deathtrap plan. He admitted that Sy had been the mastermind behind all of the planning and all of Billy's actions. He also said that Loretta fed him all police investigation information and future plans, and he in turn fed everything to Sy.

Wally claimed that he had nothing to do with the poison, the attempted run-down with Billy's car, the nursing home attack, or the cutting of my car's brake lines. He blamed Sy for everything.

Of course, Sy was dead, and dead men can't defend themselves. But then again, Wally might have figured what the hell, Sy is dead and can't do any hard time anyway. So, what could they pin on Wally anyway? Maybe he would get a year or two behind bars. Or maybe, just possibly, he would get off for lack of evidence. Good lawyers are much better than fair prosecutors every time.

Loretta, we were told, was being interrogated at the same time as her boyfriend. They both claimed that there were absolutely no additional members of the Sy Trylan terrorist group. No more threats. No more danger.

"The worst is over," said the police captain. Still, I couldn't stand down mentally. I needed a good long night's sleep—at least twelve hours. But I knew that wouldn't happen anytime soon. First off, there was no way I could sleep restfully without some sleep aid. And even if I were drugged like a zombie, how could I possibly sleep now? There was still so much more to do. I needed to see how Sy fit into the 1923 murder cover-up, and why. I had my strong suspicions, but without actual proof, no one would ever believe me. There needed to be final closure on this case.

The police captain told us that we had the all clear to go into the church and onto the large surrounding grounds as long as we were accompanied by police. The bomb squad with their bomb-sniffing dog, along with the fire department, had scoured the church and nearby areas. The gasoline containers had also been carted away. The church was being guarded, and no one was allowed on the grounds without police clearance.

"There should be no more incidents in my town now. At least not from this group," the captain said with a sigh of relief. I had my doubts.

After all, I had let my guard down in the very beginning when Billy Blaine was first taken into custody. Then all hell had broken loose in the station house.

Ever since I had come to town, I had had a nervous twitching in my cheek. If the stress got any worse, I was afraid they might admit me to the nursing home's funny-farm room, where I heard they serve chocolate pudding every day at three.

First Billy, then Sy and Wally, then Loretta—and for what purpose? So many ruined lives over murders that took place ninety years ago. Then I thought about the pimply-faced string bean of a guy from the gas station, Brian Fawlta. He had gotten a concussion from Billy that first day. The kid had been so in awe of me and the fact that I was a reporter from Washington, but if it hadn't been for him, we all could have died. He had gone out of his way to warn me about the church. I made a mental note to drop by and thank him personally, and to ask the captain to recognize him in some way—maybe give him an award of some kind.

CHAPTER NINETEEN

Once again, we were on our way to the church. At five p.m., we were a convoy of four police cars. Graham and I were once again in the rear of Sergeant Pawler's patrol car, making small talk. He was telling me about his wife and three children, and how family life had saved him from a life of crime, drugs, and gangs. He admitted to me that early in his life, he was a street thug, and then he met Joan and married at the age of eighteen. It was his wife who saved him. And when they were blessed with three children, he realized that he was put on earth to raise his children to be good people and productive citizens. The martial arts also taught him discipline of the highest degree. Although he could kill a man twice his size with one quick and massive blow, for seven years now, he had never had to use force on a person except for that one tangle with Billy.

Pawler was his usual self; by now I'd gotten used to his stiff military-style personality. I could swear you'd get better conversation out of one of those crash dummies. But he was good protection, and that was what we needed. I could imagine him blowing someone away and going back to work the next day as if nothing had happened. "Tough as nails" was my best description for old "Iron-Heart" Pawler.

I had never seen this church before, but I'd read a little about it—the oldest church in Maryland and in many surrounding states too, for that matter. I had always been intrigued by history, and this church and cemetery screamed of history. As we pulled up closer to the sprawling grounds, I could see the oldest monuments and cemetery stones I'd ever laid eyes on. Many of the names and dates chiseled into the stones were worn smooth and no longer legible.

The oldest graves were the closest to the church and the entranceways on each side of the ancient red brick church. We drove right up to the front of the church, and I stared at massive double wooden doors trimmed with heavy iron ornamentation that appeared to be original. The doors had to be around twelve feet high, and I couldn't help but wonder how much they weighed.

My mind wandered as I studied the tall, ancient, red brick structure with large bells hanging in the bell tower of its steeple. I wondered how many men it took to build the church, how long it took, and how difficult it must have been without modern equipment.

Sergeant Pawler took the lead into the church, even though several officers were standing inside and outside guarding against any additional intrusion.

The church was magnificent inside, with very high ceilings of hand-painted religious pictures, high stained-glass windows, and pews that were aged and appeared to be of hardwood oak. I had no idea what was original and what was refurbished, but it gave me the feeling that God was inside the very structure I was walking around in.

The captain motioned for me to join him near a wall to the right center of the church.

"You see here, Lou, this is precisely where Wally placed his remote fire-bomb device. As simplistic in design as it was, the entire church would have been engulfed in minutes. Wally had two locations set to go off simultaneously in the church. Once he made a call to his two cell phones with the lit candle resting on top of them, that would have set off a chain reaction leading to the firebomb and the ultimate explosion once the gas lines were compromised. And depending on our exact location in the church, we all would have been trapped by smoke and fire."

"How did Wally figure all this out?" I said.

"Wally was a master mechanic with a keen knowledge of mechanics, mathematics, and construction in general."

I looked all around the walls for any recent structural changes and saw none. I walked behind the main part of the church, hoping I could find some well-hidden box or anything that would shed some light on the nearly century-old murders.

The captain looked at me and said, "Lou, I will warn you that my men and the bomb squad have been all through this structure with a fine-toothed comb. I don't know what you think you will find here. I think you're going to hit a dead end."

We spoke some more, and I asked if I could have a few moments alone to say a prayer. He agreed immediately, and I moved to the very first pew in the front of the church. No one else was in the pew near me. Graham stayed with Pawler and the captain, talking about the attempt to fire-bomb the church.

I sat in the first pew and looked out onto the altar, the large hanging cross, and the fresco painting across the entire wall behind the altar. I am not a very religious man, but I do say my prayers and talk to God on my own time schedule and when I'm in the mood. I have nothing against any kind of religion, as long as it is helpful to those who participate.

But today was different. Today I needed to pray. I needed to thank God for my life, for protecting me like a cat with nine lives. I needed to acknowledge that I was a changed man after meeting and talking with Lolita, and after falling for Felicia. How very special I felt to be alive after all that I had been through. God could have let me die after finally finding the only woman who was truly meant for me. But He didn't.

I sat and I spoke from my heart to God, and acknowledged everything good I had in my life. I didn't kneel, because I didn't want God to see me being phony, but rather as myself.

A strange thing happened, though, as I gazed at the large painting behind the altar. All kinds of images were depicted in the painting—objects, men, children, trees—but as I stared, I could swear that I could make out the full form of the Virgin Mary in a flowing gown holding a string of rosary beads across her two hands. Now, I knew that the Virgin Mary was not a part of the painting. Everything that was meant to be recognized in the painting was clear as day and visible to the eye.

I looked away, knowing that my mind was playing tricks on me, as could well be expected in my exhausted state. I focused on a crucifix for a few long moments then I looked at the mural again, staring at various objects. Then, once again, I focused on the spot where the Virgin had suddenly come out to me from among the objects in the painting, and once again, there she was, in all of her glory, dressed in the same flowing gown.

"There, you've really done it now!" I said to myself in a low voice, thinking that she had appeared to me as a sort of warning because I had made her angry. "I must be in trouble now." *Maybe I should have knelt. Oh, well, too late now.* So I spoke from the heart to the Virgin Mary, Mother of God, for about ten minutes straight. And every so often, I would try to fool myself into thinking that the picture of the Virgin wouldn't pop out at me from the background of the painting. But I was wrong. She was there every time.

"Are you studying to be a priest?" The voice from behind me startled me, making me jump up.

It was Graham.

Somewhat spooked, I answered, "Just thanking God for Felicia and still being alive, bro."

"You know, you can pray anywhere, and they hear you," he said.

"Yes, but the last time I fell off the bar stool and said a prayer, I don't think it got through!" I laughed.

"Ah, but you're wrong. Perhaps that is the only real prayer that made it straight through," he said with a smile, and clasped his arm around my shoulders.

I sat in silence for a moment and thought. That time in the bar when I was cockeyed drunk probably was the lowest point of my life. And I did plead for help, though it was only a five-second request until someone helped me off the barroom floor. Graham must be right.

"Come on," he said, "the captain wants to go down below and investigate the other areas."

We went down some old steps that had become concave with wear from all the years of service. It appeared that no one had upgraded the downstairs area of the church. The walls were some old form of mortar, rough and rustic. Large areas of the downstairs weren't being used and could be used as a bomb shelter if needed. I took it all in carefully.

The pastor used one big area as an office, and it was decorated with the oldest gray steel office furniture I had ever seen. No wasting the congregation's donations here. The captain, with Graham and me looking on, went through the file cabinets and desk drawers, but he found nothing unusual—just plenty of dust and cobwebs.

According to the contents of his office, the pastor was as pure as could be. Not one bad thing could be found to discredit him. It was so hard to comprehend that the vicious Sy Trylan was the pastor's brother and had come from a long line of religious leaders.

"Captain, we have to check the walls of this basement. I feel there is something . . . ."

"Lou, stop looking for something that isn't there. You're looking for evidence from ninety years ago. Face the facts, you can't just wish to find something and then make it suddenly appear."

"But I know it's here somewhere."

"Okay, we'll amuse you a little more, but I'm warning you. When I say it's over, it will be over!"

Sergeant Pawler stared at me long and hard. Although he didn't say a word, his eyes said it loud and clear: "Asshole!" But I still loved the man who looked after me so well.

This entire trip to Hagerstown was doing me in. The more I tried to calm down, the worse I stressed out. Now I felt my forearm muscle spasm uncontrollably. I wondered if my newfound nervous condition was reflected in my face. I felt like an idiot.

I was sure those many visions of Lolita's visions and mine were a definite sign. There was something on the grounds of this church. But would I be closed down far too soon before finding anything useful?

Graham looked at me and then at the others. He didn't have faith in me at that moment, and I couldn't blame him. And quite honestly, at that very moment, I had the urge to go back upstairs, sit in the first pew again, and see if I could still locate the Virgin Mary, who seemed to appear from nothing in the wall-to-wall mural behind the altar.

But I knew full-well that the very moment I stopped forging ahead in pursuit of the ninety-year-old evidence, that would be the moment the captain would call it quits and shut the whole operation down.

"Captain, can we please investigate the grounds around the church?" I asked, while Pawler shot me a glance that said, "I'd rather grab a few brews at the corner bar." I paid him no mind. He was a real hammerhead.

"Sure, sure, you go right ahead, help yourself," the captain said, rather sarcastically.

As we all walked up the stairs and out of the church, Graham asked me, "Any gut feelings, Lou?"

"Not a clue," I replied in a low voice.

He glanced at me with what looked like pity.

We walked all around the exterior of the church. Pawler and Captain Krolm were speaking about certain tombstones of their ancestors and other prominent Hagerstown citizens.

Whenever I've walked around a cemetery—there have only actually been a few times—I have been amazed at the tombstones, especially the ones over two hundred years old. Many still declare the name, birth date, and death date of an individual clearly and plainly, as if the stone had been erected only yesterday. Still, it made me sad as I calculated the ages of some of the deceased. Many children had only lived months or a few years. They were from the 1800s, but it still made me sad to think of how many children had died so young, and the grief their parents must have experienced.

As I walked on, I felt transported back in time, looking at the stones and the dates. There was not a cloud in the sky, the bluest skies reflected down onto the cemetery, as we slowly walked around. The air was warm, but the sun was now at an angle at that late time of the day.

I tried to recall the diary description, the conversations with Lolita, and the few visions I had experienced. For a while I continued walking on my own, strolling briskly among the headstones, waiting for something to strike me as familiar. Nothing. As I studied the church, I couldn't help but marvel at the brick and stone structure. *How long can bricks hold up?* I wondered. Bricks can weather, but most of the time one cannot put an exact age on a structure made of brick. This structure was no different, being over two centuries old and still standing strong.

I must have been strolling, studying, and contemplating on my own for twenty minutes while the others huddled near the entrance of the church, patiently waiting for me to get frustrated and get this whole investigation thing out of my blood. I kept glancing at the captain, who was shooting me looks. I knew I had only a few minutes before he made us return to the precinct.

I was some distance from the right side of the church when I suddenly felt dizzy and tired. Maybe I was getting dehydrated. Or maybe I was overtired from lack of sleep for days. I slowly backed up and leaned against a fairly new, upright cemetery headstone. The spinning slowed down to that of a slow-moving merry-go-round that was just about to stop.

Graham was way in the distance with the officers, but he saw me sitting and quickly rushed toward me. The others stayed, gathered and talking. As Graham made his way over, I watched his blurry form then looked at the sky again. It was then that I saw another strange blurry figure, not moving, but rather facing me and staring at me. I blinked several times to focus my eyes better. . As I stared at the strange man, Graham arrived by my side.

"Are you all right, buddy?" he asked.

"Oh, I'm fine," I said without making eye contact looking in the distance..

"So, you're just going to take a nap while Pawler and the captain are ready to chew everyone's head off?" He laughed.

"Aw, let them wet themselves!" I snapped, like I was some tough guy. Then I realized that the man I was seeing in the distance, though not completely in focus, was Walter Klug, Lolita's millionaire uncle, the doctor. I got up and slowly walked toward the form. Slowly, his body became better focused until he appeared to be a man of eighty years, with white hair and beard, tall and slim, in a dark suit.

Graham was following right behind me.

I stopped and said, "Graham, do you see anyone directly in front of us, standing by the wall of the church?" I knew what his answer would be.

"Ah, no . . . ."

"I didn't think so."

"Why? You see someone standing there?"

I didn't answer him.

"You sure you're all right? Maybe you need some water or something to eat. Let's just get out of here. This place is freaking me out anyway."

I walked closer, maybe fifty feet from the man, who was motionless; he just stood there looking at me. He stared, expressionless. I didn't even blink.

As I made my way ever closer to the side of the church, I came upon the oldest and largest monuments. One in particular was directly in line with where the old doctor stood standing idle and looking right at me.

I suddenly stopped short in my approach, looking first at the monument, then at Lolita's uncle, whom no one else could see. There, right in front of me, was a six-foot-tall granite monument, with a cross on top of it, also made out of stone. This was the cemetery stone that Lolita had visualized so many times, and the stone cross I had seen in visions sent to me. As I looked at the cross atop the monument, which faced the side of the church and had its back to me, it blocked out the doctor somewhat. And then suddenly, while I was looking at the cross against the profile of the doctor, he just disappeared completely.

I just stood there staring for what seemed like minutes but was merely seconds, waiting for the old man to magically reappear. I was hoping he could give me the answers I was so desperately searching for.

Graham came real close to me and studied my face as if I had some strange and foreign disease that could take my life.

"Buddy, you're making me very nervous now. Do you have a fever? Let me feel your forehead," he said, reaching for me.

I pulled back from him. "I'm perfectly fine, Graham!" I yelled. "I just saw something that could help us. Just work with me here!"

"Well, work quickly, bubba, 'cause the law is quickly approaching us. I think they've had their fill of this place, but especially of you. They keep going on about how they need a good strong cup of coffee."

I ignored Graham and stared in the direction of the old doctor, who was no longer visible. Then, while in somewhat of a daze, it dawned on me. The doctor had been trying to get me to walk up to where his ghost-like form had been standing. Now that he had disappeared, the cross was lined up to the side of the church. I quickened my steps with Graham tailing me, and from the corner of my eye I saw Pawler, the captain, and two other officers closing in on Graham's back.

When I reached the side of the building, I closely studied the structure from two centuries earlier. The foundation of the church came up about two feet, made up of square stone blocks. Above the two-foot mark of stone were the original red bricks that the entire church was made up of.

I looked closely at the stone.

The captain sneaked up behind me and startled me. "Let's wrap it up, my friend. We gave it a good—"

"I've got it!" I screamed.

"Holy crap, you see someone else?" Graham shouted. "I think I've got to be somewhere . . . ." He laughed nervously.

"No. I think I have a real lead here."

"Where? Now where are we going, I've about had enough of this merry-go-round," the captain said impatiently.

"No, it's right here! It was right here all along. This is what everyone was visualizing for years. It was right here in the side of the church all along."

"I don't understand you, so humor me, please," the captain said sarcastically.

Sergeant Pawler snapped, "He ain't got squat, Captain. He's just wasting—"

"Please, let him talk!" the captain commanded.

Everyone was silent after that.

"I can't tell you exactly why I know this," I said hesitantly, "but there is evidence right behind this wall here." I pointed at the square stone foundation.

"And how did you come to this conclusion, may I ask?" The captain narrowed his eyes in doubt to my response.

"Look, I don't know how to explain it, Captain. I just know that this wall is holding answers to the 1923 murders. Look right here," I said, and I pointed directly to a specific block of stone. He studied my eyes like I could be out of my mind.

Then everyone moved in real close and looked at me, and then at the stone.

"You see the bricks on top of the stone here? Look closely. You see the chips around the edges, and the uneven mortar all around this particular stone? It has clearly been removed from the wall and re-cemented in again later."

Everyone looked at the first row of red bricks lining the top of the foundation. Then they looked very closely at the one square stone that had chips around it.

"I'll be a son of a bitch!" the captain murmured. "How could you know this?"

All I did was refer back to Lolita's diary, for fear that everyone would think for sure that I was a loon. "Lolita has a diary she kept for the entire year of 1923. In it, she tells of many dreams she had about some chipped bricks and the cross of the large monument right there." I pointed to the large stone monument that was now behind us all.

"That one?" the captain pointed.

"Yes, that's the one!" I said excitedly. "See, you can tell that it was—"

"Sergeant, what do you think? We have a search warrant and reasonable suspicion here." The captain looked at Pawler.

"Absolutely, Captain," he said. "I've got a couple of tools in the trunk there." He pointed toward the patrol car.

Graham shook his head in disbelief and said, "I don't really know what is going on here, Lou, but I do know there are ghosts in the place. And you've been talking to the ghosts, and it's just freaking me out, man!" His eyes grew bigger.

"Calm down, or you'll soil your bloomers there, buddy," I told him. Everyone laughed.

Sergeant Pawler and one other officer chiseled around the stone to loosen it. As they worked, someone showed up with bottles of water and hot coffee. I think I was indeed slightly dehydrated, and that had been causing some of the lightheadedness.

Still, I was sure that I had seen Dr. Walter Klug standing next to the side of the church. He was slightly transparent in form, and he was standing right in front of the chipped brick and square stone. The only other thing he could have done to be more helpful was to hit me in the head with a rock. He had led me right to the correct spot.

All the signs Lolita and I had been given screamed out: the church, the red bricks, the stone, and the cross atop a monument. How stupid I felt for not figuring it out sooner. It all made perfect sense now.

Pawler kept chipping away directly under the first line of bricks. We could clearly tell that the stone had been removed at some time, and then re-cemented back in place. The rest of the bricks and stones looked untouched.

My cell phone was vibrating uncontrollably. I had set it to vibrate as we made our way to the church. I couldn't have any distractions. I needed to focus one hundred percent on the church and grounds.

Felicia had called three times. And the maniac boss, Glavin had called twice. He really was a pisser. I had never been fired from a job over the phone before. This clown always told me I was fired, but he never followed up on it. I think he was on a power trip. He always screamed loudly, but he always allowed me "one last chance" to keep my job. He reminded me of a loud fog horn that hurts the ears.

All the calls had gone to voice mail. I knew I would have to answer a lot of questions, but I had nothing concrete to tell anyone yet. Funny thing, though—concrete had been the missing link for so many years.

Graham was clearly excited, like we were digging up a lost treasure chest of gold coins worth millions. Of course, what we might find could be very valuable, or damning, to the reputation of one or more individuals. Or just possibly, we would hit a dead end and come up empty.

If we came up empty, I knew I would be finished in many respects. I would surely be the laughingstock of Hagerstown. I would be hated by more people than I could ever count. Imagine someone shutting down a church and ordering a search warrant to rummage through the oldest church in the state. Imagine drawing attention to the most respected pastor in town. And now, tearing into the side of a landmark church, all on the whim of a snot-nosed reporter on the balls of his ass, someone so close to being fired that the smell of McDonald's hamburgers was already in the air. Because that's the only place I'd be able to work after blowing this gig.

I was very nervous.

The chiseling slowly continued for what seemed like hours but in reality was only minutes. Each tap of the screwdriver sounded like an explosion in my ears against the silence of anticipation that filled the air.

In between hammering, the sergeant and the captain shot me glances that said, "You'd better be right, knucklehead, or you can start running!"

Even Graham's expression was not too encouraging. My stomach was rumbling up a storm as the acid burned. Every tap of the hammer seemed like another nail in my coffin. I scanned my eyes around the grounds and down each row of grave markers to see if the good doctor was around to give me moral support. But, no, I was on my own, flying by the seat of my pants. The seconds ticked away.

Then, finally, something good happened. A sharp young officer who was watching from a distance came over with a crowbar, the kind that has a tool on one end for prying off hubcaps and a tool on the other for loosening lug nuts. He suggested that Pawler dig on the sides of the square stone, just enough to fit the crowbar in to pry it out. It appeared that the stone was a foot square.

The sergeant was working up a real sweat, so I wanted to bust his chops, being that he had no sense of humor about him. I said, "Watch out, Sergeant, let a real man get in there!" I rolled my sleeves up and moved up to the stone foundation. If looks could kill, I would have died right there. Everyone laughed, and that was what we all needed at that moment. Pawler just got more pissed and slammed the hammer that much harder.

After another five minutes, the captain yelled, "Yeah, now we're talking!"

The stone moved about an inch. Then, with a few more slams, it moved a little more.

"I should have just backed the squad car into this damn wall!" Pawler yelled after slipping with the hammer and slamming his hand hard. I backed a few more feet away from him, as the captain encouraged him on. "No, you've got it now, Sarge!"

I could just see Pawler trying to knock the wall down with his patrol car. His temper was on the wild side, for sure.

"There damn well better be a body in this wall, Mr. Reporter," Pawler yelled out, as his finger bled out a little more.

I backed away even further until I heard Graham yell, "It's coming out now, Lou!"

We all crept in closer and gathered around Pawler as he wiggled the crowbar from side to side and loosened the stone inching it from its resting place inside the foundation wall.

Two officers helped Pawler lift the stone out of its setting by wiggling it from side to side. Slowly, the stone pulled away. The captain had his face up close to the hole, and the rest of us were within a foot of it ourselves.

Slowly, the captain stuck his right gloved hand into the square hole. We all held our breath as he exclaimed, "Well, I'll be dipped!"

His hand came out with a bag of some sort, a dark and old-looking type of burlap sack.

"Holy shit!" Graham said.

I suddenly got very lightheaded as I realized that this could be it. This could be exactly what Lolita and I had had visions of. Could this be evidence from ninety years ago? Why here? Who would ever think of murder evidence being hidden in a house of God? Brilliant? I guess it was, because for ninety years, no one had been the wiser. All these thoughts rushed through my mind in a split second as I looked on.

"Captain, what's in the bag?" Pawler asked impatiently. He always was a rambunctious individual. We waited and watched the captain.

"No. We will analyze the contents in the precinct lab. We do not want to contaminate any of the evidence. But I will tell you, it feels like a weapon of some kind."

We knew that we could not open the bag or even handle the bag without gloves. The bag and its contents could contain fingerprints and DNA.

We closed up the square hole as best we could so no one would be able to realize what evidence we were able to secure from the site. The captain instructed each of us not to discuss our search, or the find, with anyone. He would inform us when we could speak about the church and our findings.

We all headed back to the precinct to patiently await the careful opening and analysis of the bag and all of its contents.

I had to call Felicia and tell her that everything was all right, but that I could not discuss anything else until I was informed by Captain Krolm.

Felicia only cared that I was unharmed, and that there was no more violence after Wally's fiasco and the involvement of Loretta from the station house. I assured her that everything was fine.

Harold Glavin was altogether different. He sounded like he was disappointed that I was still alive and well. I think he secretly wanted me shot up or dead, because he'd have a front-page story for his newspaper. Reporters, I had learned, were a dime a dozen with Glavin. He would merely assign a young, up-and-coming reporter to continue the news story.

But what he didn't know, and I couldn't tell him then, was that I had the most exciting news story going all the way back to those girls' murders in 1923. I had an award-winning blockbuster story, and he'd probably pee his pants if he knew how good the story was.

All I could tell him was, "I promise you, Harold, that when I can tell what I already know, and will know shortly, you will be blown away!"

"Bullshit! That's all you ever talk all day is bullshit! I should have fired your sorry ass last week. Don't bullshit me, son—"

There was no winning with Glavin, so I just cut him off. I could imagine the cursing tirade that went on in his office as he screamed into the dead phone. "Hello! Hello! You there, you little sonofabitch!"

I turned the cell phone off, though I felt like stomping on it as if it were Glavin's beet-red head.

Tensions were at an all-time high at the police precinct. Wally's lawyers were demanding his immediate release, blaming everything on Billy Blaine. There were lawyers representing the present pastor, Sy's brother, Cornelius Trylan. The pastor was incensed that the captain had been granted a search warrant, shutting the church and the cemetery down to the public, including him. They threatened a large lawsuit. And the mayor was all over Captain Krolm's ass for the flack he was receiving from the citizens of Hagerstown over the arrests of Wally, Loretta, and Billy. And it seemed like everyone but Felicia and Graham despised me. I needed to wrap things up and disappear from Hagerstown, fast.

We all were seated in the conference room—Graham, Pawler, Officer Robert Cianci, and the captain—eating take-out hamburgers and coffee while we waited for forensics to come back with something concrete on the latest bag of evidence.

We waited for what seemed like an eternity for any word. It seemed like the entire town had stopped cold, and I felt like I was responsible for the closing of the diner, the church, and the cemetery, as well as for the poisoning of Mary, the food aide at the nursing home. If Billy had succeeded in poisoning Miss Lolita as originally planned, I wouldn't be able to live with myself or ever face Felicia again.

My appetite was nonexistent as the pit of my stomach burned from overactive stress acid. I downed some coffee for whatever energy I could derive from it, but that only produced more acid, and then more pain. I wondered how much more I could endure.

The captain kept getting called out of the room during the two-hour wait, and each time he returned, he looked more and more pissed off. Sergeant Pawler gave me looks like he wanted to pistol-whip me, but I just smiled at him like I was gay and had a crush on him. That always made him look away and hate me even more. I always knew how to bring out the pissy part of a person. *Maybe he's a distant relative of my boss*, I joked with myself. I was burned out mentally. I no longer cared.

Graham was making small talk, but none of it was even registering in my overloaded brain, which was about to shut down any minute, if my excruciating headaches were any indication.

The last time Captain Krolm left the room, Sergeant Pawler went with him. I was glad to get rid of Pawler, even for a few minutes, although my mind kept reminding me that Pawler had saved my life in the street when Sy tried to run me down and shoot me up. *Heroes don't always have the most pleasant ways about them, but they do know how to get the job done,* I mused.

Graham used the phone in the corner of the room to speak with his wife and children, and I chatted with Officer Robert Cianci. He was the nicest person I had met at the station house. He was very respectful and didn't act like a man eaten up with power, as some officers do. I was sure he would have a long and successful career with the force.

When the captain finally came back into the conference room, followed by the sergeant, he had a few pieces of paper and a folder.

"Well, gentlemen," he began, "we have some real findings here." His face was ashen, and he looked as though he had lost his best friend.

"It troubles me terribly, these findings." He shook his head. "And I just had to disclose them to the mayor. It is a sad day in Hagerstown history, for sure. But be that as it may, we must stand for what is right and just, no matter whom it brings down or affects."

Pawler just stood at attention, looking at the captain and not making eye contact with anyone else.

I knew the news was going to be huge, something that would make headlines around the country.

"Here's what was inside the old burlap bag that was inside the foundation of the church." He looked at his typewritten papers. "There was a large butcher knife that had remnants of blood on it. We are doing DNA testing, which will take at least a week, but we believe the DNA of the blood samples will match at least one of the Hagerstown girls murdered in 1923. Furthermore," he said in a lower tone, "we have lifted fingerprints off items inside the garbage bag that match one Sy Trylan, the owner of Millie's Diner."

Graham's look was one of total confusion, although it was all falling in place in my mind. My worst suspicions were now playing out in real life. I gave Graham a smile and a little nod, as if to say, "Wait for more to come out."

The captain continued. "We believe that it was Sy Trylan who was hiding the damning evidence that would ultimately have implicated his father, the pastor's son from 1923, Seymour Trylan, who was a twenty-three-year old back then in 1923 when his father, Harvey Trylan, was the minister.

"Seymour is our suspect in all three girls' murders, as well as those of some missing girls after that time. We have a bloody fingerprint from Seymour that, unbelievably, ended up on his personal Bible, which was also in the bag of tricks. It sickens me to report that one of our most respected members of the clergy committed such heinous acts and went on years later to lead a church for many years.

"In a letter found inside the bag, Sy admitted to hiding away the evidence right after his father's passing some forty years ago. We believe that the present pastor, Sy's brother Cornelius, was not part of, and did not contribute to, any of the cover-up of his father, the killer from 1923.

"We also lifted fingerprints from the ten-inch knife, which we believe was used in all the murders and possibly more. We do believe, and Sy has disclosed in his letter, that years after the murders, his father repented, changed his ways, and went on to become a well-respected pastor of the church. Sy also disclosed that he unexpectedly came across the hidden evidence, linking his father to the crimes, when his father was elderly. Sy agreed to keep the evidence under wraps for all these years to protect his family name and the reputation of his father. This bag was intended to remain hidden forever or at least until after Sy and all of his family had passed on.

"Sy's letter from the bag also stated that no one knew his father Seymour committed the murders but him, and that his father spoke very little about any of it. Pastor Seymour died at the age of eighty-four, some sixty years after the murders. No one ever knew that he was a murderer, but inside his Bible is a handwritten admission and confession to God. The pastor was a very sick individual as a young man, and refused to admit his wrongdoing to society." The captain looked like he was going to be sick. I felt sad, too.

"I ask that you not discuss this until tomorrow morning after our eight o'clock press conference with the mayor, governor, and FBI, which has always been in charge of the Hagerstown murder investigation."

"Captain," I spoke up, "was there anything else in the bag?"

"There were a few other items, such as women's undergarments that contained blood, pictures of various girls, and photos of his family. He had pictures of his wife and two of his sons. There were things that we will go into at the press conference. But for now, I will reiterate, do not speak to anyone at all about the investigation, please, I beg of you. That's all I am willing to disclose right now. I have to get back on the phone with the governor in five minutes."

He quickly left, and the officers and Pawler followed him, leaving Graham and me with our mouths hanging wide open.

Graham looked at me wide-eyed and said, "Buddy, we just witnessed history in the making—the solving of a ninety-year-old mass murder. You're the man!"

"Thanks . . ." I murmured, though it hadn't really sunk in yet. "It is hard to believe that someone could get away with such vicious killings, and maybe even more we are unaware of, for so long. Who would ever suspect the pastor of the largest and oldest church in town? Talk about staying under the radar."

"Hey, what's the deal with you seeing strange things lately? And why do you look so weak all the time?" Graham asked.

"I'm just exhausted," I said. "I think I'm tired of worrying who wants to kill me next. And even though it's over, the stress goes on."

"I hear you, but I'll be right by your side. I got your back."

"Graham, I did have a couple of very vivid dreams, or maybe visions, similar to what Miss Lolita described in her diary. They were of the murders and pieces of evidence. And, yes, at the cemetery I did have a brief vision of Miss Lolita's Uncle Walter, the doctor who helped her see things. I know it is hard to believe, but the vision of her uncle is what actually led me to that stone's hiding place."

"That's wild, man!" he said. "Do you think you still have the powers to see?"

"No." I smiled. "I thought long and hard about what I had seen: the faces of the dead girls, the bits of evidence, the uncle, the cross, and the brick. I am beginning to believe that Miss Lolita is an angel from God."

"An angel? You need to get some sleep, Lou!"

"Look, Miss Lolita is the sharpest senior I've ever seen. She is so philosophical, and she can read people's feelings at will. She had all those visions very early in her life. Maybe, just maybe Lolita sent me those dreams, being that she couldn't get out of the home and her sight is gone."

"Pal, I don't know." He shook his head.

"I'm just wondering out loud," I said.

"I will admit that someone wanted your help in finally getting justice for those girls' murders. It could be the uncle or even the dead girls, but someone gave you that intense desire to dig deeper. Even when you should have escaped this town to protect your own ass, you kept driving on, trying to find out more. So, yes, someone helped you. But you may never know who."

We waited around a bit longer in the conference room, just in case anything new might be shared, and we spoke about Felicia, my plans for the future, and the amazing Miss Lolita.

CHAPTER TWENTY

G raham and I spent some time that evening watching a Marx Brothers movie, *Horse Feathers,* just for a few laughs. We pigged out on chips and dip and had a good time. Anything to take our minds off the violence we had experienced.

Graham left for his own room after the movie and called his family again. I called Felicia, and we stayed on the phone for at least three hours. When people are in love, they can talk on the phone for hours, talking about nothing in particular, but they never get enough of each other. The conversation can be ridiculous in nature, but oh so important.

Felicia asked specifically about the investigation of the murders, but I explained the gag order and that the next morning I would be able to tell her everything. She didn't press me for more information, but rather was more concerned about my safety and mental state. She was worried that there were others out there looking for revenge against Miss Lolita and me, but I assured her that everyone connected to the violence was already behind bars.

Still, she was concerned, and she cautioned me to be extra careful in my comings and goings. I explained that Graham and I still had round-the-clock police protection. She felt much better when she heard that.

I explained that I had had a conversation that evening with the police captain and had gotten permission to visit Miss Lolita at eight o'clock the next morning to tell her in person what had happened in the investigation. Captain Krolm told me that Hagerstown's most celebrated citizen deserved to be informed of all the developments prior to any media coverage from a press conference. After all, he affirmed, "she lived through that time in history. That alone is truly amazing."

The early morning air was crisp and cool due to the heavy cloud cover and misty rain. Graham and I once again were being chauffeured in the back of the police cruiser. Officer Robert Cianci was driving us this morning.

The wiper blades seemed to tap out a musical rhythm as we made our way out of town to the nearest open diner since Millie's was still closed. It was rumored that Sy's family would have a grand reopening of the diner in about two weeks. They were renovating the inside to make it look entirely different and new.

It was early when we reached the nursing home. Most of the workers had yet to punch in for the day. Many of the residents were still not up and out of their rooms. No one expected any earth-shattering news or was even aware of the eight o'clock press conference. I was looking around nervously out of habit.

Miss Lolita was up and dressed early, as usual. She rose no later than six a.m. each day. In my interviews with her, she had said, "Life is for the living!" and "Time is a-wasting! We'll all be dead a long time; might as well shine now!"

Felicia was at the nursing home early that day, knowing that I would be seeing Miss Lolita before the press conference. She was waiting for me and came running over when she saw the police cruiser pulling up to the entrance. We hugged long and hard as if we hadn't seen each other in a month.

"You scared me silly yesterday!" she said in a nervous tone. "Especially when you wouldn't answer the phone or return my calls while you were at the church."

"Well, I'm fine now . . . ."

"That's not the point, Louis." She grabbed my arm.

I knew she was right, but I had felt at the time that I couldn't speak to anyone—though if things had been turned around and it had been me wondering about her well-being, I would have been nervous as hell thinking the worst.

We hugged a few moments more, not caring who saw us anymore. After all, the cat was out of the bag now. We were crazy about each other, and the threat of danger had finally passed, as far as the authorities were concerned. I would slowly accept that, too.

We walked into the dining room to visit Miss Lolita. Graham had stayed behind, talking with the officers standing watch at the home's entrance. He wanted me to have privacy when I spoke with Miss Lolita.

I was there primarily to tell Miss Lolita about the discovery at the church, and the fact that her former pastor had been the killer everyone had sought for the past ninety years.

Felicia walked over to Miss Lolita and told her I was there to see her. Miss Lolita's face lit up and a big smile emerged. Her eyes were alive with excitement.

"Well, time's a-wasting! Get over here, you big lug, and kiss me one big one!" She laughed.

"I know, I know, get close. I know the drill." I smiled as I gave her a kiss on her cheek.

"Don't you wise off on me. I'll put you over my knee! Don't let this gray hair fool you!"

We all laughed. "That's why I brought my buddy, Graham. I may need protection from you!"

"Where is that young hero?" she asked.

"Oh, he'll be here soon." I squeezed her hand.

I looked at her old eyes and suddenly felt bad for her. I thought about her possibly being an angel from above, sent here to help us all to help ourselves. I felt bad that Miss Lolita probably didn't have too many more days on earth to help others. I squeezed her hand and felt tears welling in my eyes.

"So why are you here so early? You trying to get a free breakfast?" She giggled.

"Yeah, that's it," I said as my voice cracked and the lump in my throat grew. I had come to love and admire this special treasure of a wise and loving person.

"What's wrong? Are you okay?" She sounded concerned.

"Oh, I'm fine. I just have to tell you something important."

"You're not going to propose to me, are you?" She cracked herself up.

"Damn, you ruined it!" I laughed. "No, seriously now, Miss Lolita, what I came to tell you is that we found evidence hidden at the old church—evidence from the 1923 murders. And the killer of those young girls was Seymour Trylan."

"That kid was a cornball even as a young'un!" she exclaimed. "We all had our suspicions about him. He was nothing like his father, bless his soul. Pastor Harvey Trylan was a saint, a gem of a man. Pastor Harvey is saving me a spot in heaven."

"Well, Seymour was a very sick individual who tried to change his ways, according to the evidence. And his son, Sy, came across the evidence many years later. He tried to protect his father and his family name, but he went too far."

Miss Lolita now had tears running down her face. "I remember all those girls, all the families of the girls. It was a terrible time, yes, it was, back then. The funerals were the hardest of all. Heartbreaking, it was, for everyone."

Felicia and I both put our arms around Miss Lolita and held her tightly until her sobbing stopped.

"There will be a press conference in about twenty minutes. Police Captain Krolm and the mayor will be disclosing all the evidence and suspects. The captain has a gag order on everyone, but he gave me permission to inform you before anyone else learns the details."

Miss Lolita blinked rapidly. She was utterly silent, as if she was lost in thought. Her mind was suddenly back in 1923. I was worried about her, and watched her closely.

Felicia sat quietly, held her hand and continued looking loving at her. I had zoned out. I was lost in my own thoughts, wondering what it must have been like for Miss Lolita and the citizens of Hagerstown after the three girls were murdered: the anger, the heartbreak, the frustration of being helpless in apprehending anyone connected to the murders. So many years passed without any kind of closure. No wonder Miss Lolita couldn't discuss the murders. That kind of pain remains dormant, but it is easily rekindled.

We all moved to the recreation room and spread the word about the upcoming press conference. Everyone in the general area gathered around, and the buzz of talking increased by the minute. This was a big story for Hagerstown, even for the very young. The murders of 1923 were so shocking that information about them had been passed down from generation to generation.

We listened closely as the captain and the mayor spoke for perhaps ten minutes, and then they answered only three questions. What they shared was very informative, but just a little more than what I'd known already. The people in the recreation room, though, were mostly in shock. it was hard to believe that the pastor, the father of Sy of Millie's Diner, had been the killer. And the news that Sy had been hiding evidence and trying to kill people in order to protect his father's name was an unexpected turn of events. There was a lot of silence and gasps, but the buzz turned to a loud roar after the press conference was over.

Miss Lolita now had a smile of satisfaction on her face, knowing the puzzle had finally been solved. It didn't matter that the pastor, Sy's father, was long gone. Justice was important, and the reputation of the Trylan name would never be the same again.

Miss Lolita asked me to wheel her to her semi-private room and asked Felicia to follow us. Graham had viewed the press conference, and was happy to remain in the recreation room talking with many of the residents.

Miss Lolita's room was small. She shared it with a younger, sicker woman. It was clean and neat, and had inspirational quotes hanging on the wall on Lolita's side of the room. No one was in the room as we rolled her to her dresser.

"Louis, I want to talk serious with you for a few minutes, okay?" she said with a cute smile.

"Okay," I answered hesitantly.

"First off, I want to thank you for visiting and doing a story on me. I want to thank you for solving the murders. I think you are a fine young man. If I were only two years younger, I would allow you to marry me." She laughed.

"You'd be quite a handful!" I joked.

"I know, my handsome man. I want you to remember what I say to you," she said seriously.

Reaching for my notebook and holding my pen at the ready, I waited.

"We are each a reinvented and motivated force of those who have passed, but who so positively inspired and influenced us." She smiled and waited as I scribbled. "You got that one?"

"Got it. Love it. I'll use it in the story!"

"Remember that those loved ones who have passed are the same ones who are watching you, rooting you on from the hereafter." She continued. "Always, always remember that you are the greatest living miracle in the world." She looked deeply into my eyes and continued: "Think about this carefully, tomorrow morning, bright and early: You wake up, open your sleepy eyes while still in bed. Then you notice that God is standing at the foot of your bed, studying you for minutes. He is staring, admiring the greatest miracle of his creation. No words are spoken. He smiles a loving smile at you, then suddenly disappears. Let me ask you this: How will you live that day?"

Before I could answer, she went on. "Just remember, every day, God goes through this entire routine with you and every one of us. Why? Because he is God, and God loves each one of his greatest living miracles!"

Felicia had tears rolling down her cheeks. I had a lump in my throat that stopped me from my usual quick-witted response. I had nothing I could say, so I said nothing. I blinked rapidly and just stared deep into her eyes, and I waited.

Miss Lolita was truly an angel from God. She had to be. There was no other explanation.

"And remember this, too," she said. "Every day is a precious gift that must be carefully unwrapped and thoroughly enjoyed."

"Miss Lolita, I will include all these in your news story." I tapped my pen on the notepad.

"Great! You know, Louis, enthusiasm is contagious. It will multiply and affect and infect those who most need it!" She smiled a motherly smile at me.

Miss Lolita asked Felicia to wheel her closer to the dresser. She instructed Felicia to reach inside the bottom drawer for a small strongbox. With the strongbox on her lap, Miss Lolita worked the combination lock and opened the box. She pulled out a newspaper clipping. She looked at it, showed it to me, and quickly read from it. "This," she said, "is from 1923. It pertains to the murders. You see, my Uncle Walter, the doctor, created a fund for a reward. It was for a sum of $100,000 for the identity of the murderer or murderers of the three Hagerstown girls.

"You, my fine friend, will be the recipient of this reward fund. I will see to it."

Miss Lolita handed the original, yellowed clipping to me, and I read it twice. With my mouth agape, I looked at Miss Lolita and said, "I can't . . . ."

"You can't? My tiddlywinks, you can't! You can, and you will accept the reward. I will see to it that my daughter, who is the trustee of my uncle's trust account, has it awarded to you. No doubt it will be presented to you by our esteemed mayor himself at some kind of ceremony."

Felicia looked at me and said, "Louis, you earned every dime of that reward. If not for you, no one would ever have figured out that Pastor Seymour was the killer and his son was hiding all the evidence. Besides, you need the money."

I looked at Felicia with her warm, loving eyes and her smile that melted my heart. I knew she was right.

Miss Lolita reached into her strongbox again and pulled out what looked like a handkerchief. She handed it to me and said, "This is something very special. I give it to you from my heart. Use it in good health."

I took the crumpled handkerchief and looked at it. It was very old, had a design embroidered on it, and was discolored with age. I slowly unwrapped it to find something inside. When I got it out, I discovered that it was an engagement ring. I looked at Miss Lolita. She studied me for a second and said, "That ring was my mother's engagement ring. I kept it all these years, saving it for the right moment."

"I don't understand . . . ."

"Listen to me, you young whippersnapper! I'm an old lady, and I want to be happy for my short time left on earth. You want me to be happy, don't you?"

"Yes. More than anything."

"Then, look that angel there in the eyes and do the right thing. Make me proud."

I looked at Felicia long and hard, dropped to one knee, and said, "Felicia, I love you, and I would be honored to spend my life with only you. Would you do me the honor of being my wife?"

Felicia's eyes welled up as a beautiful smile stretched across her face. She glanced at Miss Lolita then looked at me for a second or two, and said, "I will marry you, Louis Gerhani. I will spend my life happily in love with you forever."

"Well, get off your knees, knucklehead, and place the ring on her finger, before she wises up!" Miss Lolita laughed loudly.

The ring fit perfectly, and we kissed. I heard loud clapping and turned to see Graham and Sergeant Pawler in the doorway, smiling.

"Now, that's the first good thing you've done since you invaded my town," Pawler said.

Miss Lolita said, "Now, that made me happy! Thank you!" Tears were rolling down her face.

"I have one last saying for all of you," she announced.

I quickly reached for my notepad.

She waited three full seconds until we were all paying attention. Then she said softly, "There are only two ways to live your life: one, as though NOTHING is a miracle, and the other, as though EVERYTHING is a miracle."

CPSIA information can be obtained at www.ICGtesting.com
Printed in the USA
BVOW05s0254090415

395368BV00001B/10/P

9 781630 473518